If the
Shoe Fits

Sally DeFreitas

PublishAmerica
Baltimore

First printing

At the specific preference of the author, PublishAmerica allowed this work to remain exactly as the author intended, verbatim, without editorial input.

ISBN: 1-4137-8749-5
PUBLISHED BY PUBLISHAMERICA, LLLP
www.publishamerica.com
Baltimore

Printed in the United States of America

Dedicated to my daughter Susan
who showed me the way.

PROLOGUE

She paused in front of the mirror—smoothed her hair, tucked in the blouse, straightened the skirt, then frowned at her reflection. Something wasn't quite right—maybe the shoes. The brown heels came off and she pulled another pair from the closet, then sat down to buckle the tiny straps around her ankles. She had always been proud of her slender ankles. *You could have been a model,* was a comment she had heard more than once from the men in her life. Little did they know.

Shortly after midnight she parked the car and made her way down the dimly lit path to the building where they had agreed to meet. She moved quietly but she wasn't nervous. After all, this wasn't the first time—they both knew what was going to happen. She pushed the door open and stepped inside. The lights were on but she didn't see anyone, so she paused and spoke his name into the darkness.

From the unlit corner behind her, a shadowy figure materialized. An icy wave of fear rose up in her chest as she turned to see who it was. But there was no time for recognition. There was only the terrifying thought that something had gone terribly wrong – then pain, a blinding light and, finally, the welcome comfort of darkness.

CHAPTER ONE

Madeline Maxwell was already missing on the morning of the Cedar County Chamber of Commerce Breakfast. Her absence, however, had not yet raised any serious concern among her friends and coworkers. After all, Madeline was a single woman of a certain age—certainly old enough that no one had any business nosing around in her private life.

Which didn't stop some of us from giving it the occasional try.

"So where is our Madeline this morning? Are we supposed to save her a seat?"

Reporter Ivy Martin claimed the chair next to mine at the table reserved for members of the press and other minor dignitaries. Ivy almost splashed me with the cup of hot coffee she was holding while she arranged her chocolate donut, notepad and clutch purse on the table.

Before I could reply, Ivy turned to wave at someone who had just entered the room. She did this with a characteristic jerk of her head which let me know I was supposed to remember her question and be ready to answer it whenever she focused on me again.

While Ivy ignored me, I looked around and decided that the chamber of commerce breakfast meeting was proving to be one of my better assignments. The spacious dining hall boasted knotty pine walls, exposed beams, and ceilings that I put at thirty feet high. Morning light poured in through cathedral windows. Some of that light brightened an enormous painting of horses that grazing against a backdrop of snow capped mountains. Another wall displayed a collection of mounted steer horns and colorful Native American rugs. Clearly the décor was intended to make us believe that we were in Montana instead of Michigan.

"Oh damn!" Ivy said as she discovered a smear of chocolate on her mauve linen pantsuit. While she attacked the chocolate spot with a wet napkin, I wrote "Tracy Quinn, *Shagoni River News*," on my name tag and slapped it on my lapel. When I looked up, Ivy had her aristocratic nose pointed in my direction, waiting for a comment on the whereabouts of our missing friend.

"Beats me," I said, spooning sugar into my coffee. "I called her twice yesterday and got no answer, not even her machine. She must have gone somewhere for the weekend."

"But she's supposed to speak here this morning." Ivy gestured toward the room, which was fast filling up with the movers and shakers of Cedar County. "I can't believe that Madeline would miss an opportunity like this."

As though it might offer a clue, I picked up my program. Opening it, I saw that Ivy was right. Madeline Maxwell's name was there and she was to be officially recognized for her work with the tourism council. "You're right," I said, "this is her kind of show." Madeline was in real estate and worked hard at getting her name out.

"Well, she's a big girl." Ivy bit into her donut with lips peeled back in an attempt to preserve her lipstick. "She probably went off on a moonlight cruise. You know she's a sucker for any guy with a boat."

Ivy was speaking from experience. The three of us, Madeline, Ivy and myself, had been known to frequent the local watering holes, particularly the Sailors Rest. That dockside pub had a summer clientele that included Lake Michigan yachtsmen who liked to shelter in the harbor of our old logging town, Shagoni River.

On these outings, Ivy focused her considerable talents on getting men to buy us drinks, but generally kept her flirtations inside the bar. Madeline, however, was more likely to disappear with a man, leaving us unsure whether the mutual purpose was real estate promotion or lust. Possibly both. As for me, the only men I found myself attracted to were inevitably frightened off, either by my liberated views or the fact that I stand five feet ten in my Birkenstocks.

Ivy elaborated on her cruise theory. "I'll bet you that Madeline is on a sailboat this very minute, drinking some excellent champagne."

I warmed to the fantasy. "After a highly satisfying roll in the hay, no doubt."

"Maybe a threesome," she said, twirling a strand of hair.

Ivy and I were indulging a bad habit of ours—holding a private conversation in a public place. Suddenly I realized that the people around us had stopped talking. The white-haired gentleman across the table turned his good ear in our direction and began to adjust his hearing aid. I winced and kicked Ivy.

"Oh, you mean that *barn* she's showing," I said with my voice cranked up a full decibel. "The one with all the *hay* in it."

Ivy caught the ball, ran. "I hear she had an offer of *threesomething* on that place, but the seller wouldn't budge."

The man lost interest in our conversation and our voices return to normal. "I am a little worried," I said. "After all, it *is* Monday morning."

"I guess people in real estate make their own hours." Ivy affected a dramatic sigh. "Unlike humble reporters who have to go where assigned."

"And drink bad coffee at chamber breakfasts."

"At least I had the weekend off." She fingercombed some imagined knot from her long, dark hair. "Did you have to cover that horrible biker event?"

"Ivy, you should have warned me." I grimaced at the memory of my Sunday assignment. "It was forty acres of motorcycles—Hell's Angels on parade."

She laughed. "How about Easy Rider Returns ——with many friends?"

"My sinuses are still plugged—I think I may have permanent hearing damage."

"Bet you got some great pictures, though."

"Oh sure. Tough looking guys and tougher girls. All in black leather, covered with tattoos and chains."

"Big butts, big bikes, dust and noise. A perfect Sunday afternoon."

Ivy Martin and I have a lot of conversations like this. We met last fall while covering an election and quickly bonded over the coffee and sticky baked goods that fuel those late night marathons. By the time the last vote was counted, we had shared our life stories, dissed our ex-husbands and trashed our editors. Strictly speaking, the two of us are rivals, since I write for the local weekly and she's a stringer for a daily forty miles to the north. But so far, we've managed to avoid competition. It's far more fun to freely share our news tips, gossip, and totally biased opinions.

"Hello there, and *thank you*." Ivy flashed her megawatt smile at a blushing young man as he set our plates in front of us. Since Ivy tends to ignore female servers, I thanked the plump girl dressed like Annie Oakley who brought orange juice and refilled our coffee cups. Ivy and I were still talking when the squawk of microphone feedback brought us to attention.

"Take a look at this," she said. "Here's our host."

"That's the owner?" I pulled out my notebook.

"That's him, Tom Halladay."

A tall, fortyish man was making his way to the podium. Tom Halladay wore a western-styled suit and maroon leather boots with heels that clumped when he walked. His shirt was maroon and the black string tie featured some kind of stone. When he turned to the audience, I saw a long, narrow face with a cleft in the chin, punctuated by a reddish-brown mustache that drooped at the corners. With wavy hair that curled just below his ears, the overall effect was that of a gambling man in one of those low budget westerns.

"Not bad," said Ivy, "except for those ridiculous cowboy boots."

"At least they match his shirt. Suppose he has ten colors?"

While we were dissecting his appearance, Halladay had begun to speak. His voice was surprisingly deep. "— pleased to welcome the chamber of commerce and other Cedar County officials to the newly renovated dining room of the Diamond D Ranch. Some of you have already played our new eighteen-hole golf course and there is a free pass available for anyone else who wants to try it.

"About the history here —." Halladay glanced at his notes. "This was a busy summer resort back in the thirties when people came here by boat from Chicago, but it closed during the Second World War and never reopened. The place was falling into ruin until my wife and I acquired it and decided to turn it around."

Ivy reached over and wrote on my notepad, *'this guy didn't have a cent until he married Ms moneybags over there'*.

Ivy rolled her eyes toward the woman seated next to Halladay's empty chair. The wife sported salon blonde hair, an out-of-season suntan and a blue dress that looked a little more cocktail party than breakfast meeting. Her frozen expression made me think she had sacrificed some of her facial mobility under the surgeon's knife. As Halladay spoke, she sometimes moved her lips, making me think she might have written the speech for him.

'so this is our new power couple?' I wrote on Ivy's program.

'bet she makes him toe the line '

'she didn't buy that dress in shagoni river….'

Halladay was still going on about all the work they had done. "The sauna is finished and the swimming pool is almost ready. Our restaurant is open to the public with a menu that will soon include wine and cocktails. I'm happy to report that we are already booked full for the coming holiday."

'this must have cost big bucks' I scribbled on Ivy's note pad.

'let's find out how much'

Halladay was still talking. "We currently employ eighteen people and will hire more for the summer season. The Diamond D Ranch is going to jump-start the local economy and provide jobs that will keep young people in Cedar County."

'what do you bet they're all minimum wage?'

' with no benefits ...'

Now Halladay was talking about future plans for the operation—a campground, riding stables and paraplane operation.

"What's a paraplane?" I whispered.

"No idea."

Halladay ended by saying that the Diamond D was going to bring a new vision of prosperity to Cedar County. Then he yielded the podium to a short, balding man who introduced the tourism council. The man noted Madeline Maxwell's absence, saying she had been detained by "unforeseen circumstances."

"That means he doesn't have a clue either," whispered Ivy.

I nodded and kept writing.

The last speaker was Toby Whitlow, director of the economic development council. Whitlow said he was negotiating with a light-manufacturing firm that might locate in Cedar County. Then the meeting was over and people were moving toward the doors and their Monday morning obligations. Ivy waylaid Whitlow while I approached Tom Halladay.

"I'm Tracy Quinn," I said, "with the *Shagoni River News*. Do you have time for a few questions?" Halladay looked me over and nodded gravely. Out came my notebook. "How big is the ranch?"

"Five hundred and eighty acres."

"And what have renovations cost so far?"

Halladay coughed into his hand and named a figure with an awful lot of zeroes. He craned his neck as though trying to see what I was writing. Lots of luck, I thought, I can hardly read it myself.

"And what is a paraplane?"

Ivy appeared beside me, notebook in hand. She tossed her long hair in Halladay's direction and he warmed to my last question.

"A paraplane is an ultra-light, experimental aircraft that's very easy to fly. We have three of them in our hangar and they'll be used to take guests on scenic rides over the sand dunes. An army buddy of mine will be the pilot, and possibly instructor, if anyone wants lessons."

After that, Halladay reverted to one-word answers. When he made a big deal of looking at his watch, we thanked him for his time and left the nearly empty room. We walked outside through a pair of heavy wooden doors and stood blinking for a moment in the brilliant May sunshine. A gravel walkway led to the still unpaved parking lot. Ivy stumbled and caught my arm as one of her narrow heels dug into the gravel.

"What do you think about this amateur airplane business?" she said when she had recovered her balance.

"I'm not sure. This whole place feels like a theme park."

"Well, I don't like it at all. The sand dunes won't be the same with tourists buzzing overhead in mini planes."

"Oh yeah. So much for our nude sunbathing plans."

"Frankly, I think this ranch concept is ridiculous." Ivy waved at a pole covered with signs giving directions to the Bunkhouse, Happy Trails, Horse Hollow and the Back Forty. "We're the Midwest, not the Wild West. This has nothing to do with Michigan."

"Maybe so, but my guess is, the city folks will eat it up. Halladay is playing on a myth lying deep within our collective psyche. How do you think Reagan got elected?"

"Oh, that's scary. And now this guy rides in and claims to be the economic savior of Cedar County. What's your take on him?"

"A little strange, don't you think?" We paused beside my dented Honda. "He's dying for publicity, but gets all tight lipped around the press."

"That's because we're *female* press, silly. The wife keeps him on a very short leash. Didn't you see the looks she gave us?"

"Um, not really." Near as I could recall, the lady had given us the same haughty stare she bestowed on everyone else in the room. But Ivy had this way of seeing things where I was clueless ——and sometimes she was right. "I've got to run," I said. "Marge is gunning for me."

"Marge the Sarge. Lucky you."

I opened the car door and slid behind the wheel. "Be sure to call if you hear anything about Madeline."

"I will—and you do the same." Ivy started to walk away, then turned back. "Our girlfriend may have got herself in real trouble this time."

"You think so?"

"Just a feeling."

I spun a little gravel on my way out of the parking lot. According to my watch, I had exactly ten minutes to reach Shagoni River for a meeting with my editor, Marge Enright.

I'm still getting used to calling myself a reporter. I didn't study journalism in college, but then, who did? The reporters I know mostly have degrees in English Lit. or Shakespeare, if they have any at all. In my case I had earned a useful degree—in education. But I learned too late that facing down a room full of pre-adolescents made me physically ill. In four years I had tried three grade levels at two schools but never got through a day without stomach cramps. Several doctors agreed that my symptoms were job related and promised me a bleeding ulcer if I didn't get out of the classroom.

So I gave up teaching and tried a few different things. First came technical writing, which paid well, but got so tedious that I started drinking too much. Next was a venture into advertising, which was not a good fit, to put it kindly. Eventually I landed a job doing public relations for a hospital in the suburbs of Chicago, a job that lasted for almost ten years. I might still be there, not exactly challenged, but not unhappy either, if my closest relative hadn't died.

It happened in the summer of 1999. Without warning, my grandfather's generous heart stopped beating, leaving me heir to his lovely, unkempt house in the lakeside village of Shagoni River. My first impulse had been to sell the place and get on with my life. But then my grandfather's lawyer, Les Tattersall, showed up and helped me change my mind. Tattersall pointed out that a house with flaking paint, sagging porches and mysterious plumbing problems does not add up to a quick sale. He advised me to move in and make some basic repairs before I put it on the market.

The timing was right. There had been rumors at work of cutting my hours; and my best girlfriend had just moved to California (with my ex-boyfriend), so there wasn't much holding me in Allenwood. Within weeks I made one of the bolder moves of my life. I quit my job, put my worldly goods in a U Haul and arrived in Shagoni River just in time to get caught in the only traffic jam of the year, the one that accompanies the Fourth of July parade.

Then came job hunting. I found, to my chagrin, that a West Michigan town too small to have its own stoplight offers little in the way of full time employment. I was about to give up when Tattersall rescued me again, this time directing me to the town's weekly newspaper where there was a rumor of a vacancy. As it turned out, Marge Enright was thrilled to discover someone who could write a complete sentence and would work for pathetic wages. A deal was struck and I've been with the *News* for almost a year now. Sometimes Marge gets on my nerves, but I figure the situation is temporary, so I let a lot of things go by.

Marge was waiting for me when I waltzed in at nine-thirty five.

"You're late," she said.

"Sorry," I mumbled as I slid into the plastic chair we affectionately call the hotseat.

My editor surveyed me from behind her desk. She was wearing her usual hairstyle—a gigantic mound that was probably intended to deflect attention from her enormous hips. Or at least balance them. Since this was city council day, Marge was dressed in her best outfit—a tent-shaped navy blue dress with a white sailor collar, accessorized with blue plastic earrings. The effect was that of a ship under full sail.

Marge got right to the point. "Tracy," she said, "I've got your photos from the motorcycle rally, but the captions don't make any sense."

I walked around her desk to examine the proofs – this happens a lot because I know zilch about news photography. It just happened to come with the job and I just happened to own a second hand Nikon. Together we scanned the proof sheets, squinting at the tiny pictures. They showed a stream of motorcycles going down Shagoni River's main drag, and a sea of machines and people at the Hilldale campground.

"I like this one," Marge said, indicating two leather clad couples sitting on monster Harleys. "But the caption doesn't make any sense."

She was right. The caption for number twenty-one said it was Father Radonis, blessing the bikes. Way off. I peered at the bikers in the photo she had chosen, searching for a clue. One of the women had an angel tattooed on her arm and that jolted my memory. Angel was the biker chick's real name.

Scanning my photo notes I found, "# 25. Angel and Murphy Morrison of Kalamazoo —— Angel's sister Beulah with her boyfriend (no name)." So my captions were about four numbers off. So what?

"This is it," I said.

"You sure?"

"Sure, the guy even gave me his card." I pulled the card from my wallet. "He's a stock broker with Fenner and Branville."

"Cute," she grunted. "Did you put that in the story?"

"Sure, weekend warrior, old bikers never die—that sort of thing."

"Okay. Why no name on the other guy?"

"Wouldn't give his name. But he gave me permission to use the photo."

"Okay, fine," she said. "But I thought you were a little heavy on the complaints about noise and rowdy behavior."

"Hey, not everyone is thrilled to have five thousand bikers in town. Jake said the police were called out four times Saturday night."

"Maybe next year they can find another location, farther from town."

"The Diamond D is working on a campground."

"Tom Halladay would love the business," she said with a snort, "but bikers probably don't fit his image of an upscale resort. How was the breakfast?"

I gave her a quick run down of the morning's event, avoiding any mention of Ivy.

"Okay. Give me about fifteen inches on it—by noon. Any other leads?"

I glanced at my notes. "The next EDC meeting might be worth following. And Halladay is talking about a paraplane operation."

"What's a paraplane?"

"Some newfangled amateur mini plane."

"Do a story on it. Get photos. We'll use it for next week."

Marge dismissed me and I moved to my workstation – a desk in a corner of the newsroom. The place has bilious green walls so I have taped up a travel poster to provide me with a calming view of the Pacific Ocean. I hid out there long enough to tweak the motorcycle piece and write up the breakfast meeting. After lunch, I covered the road commission, a dull affair where men in muddy boots talked about washouts and the price of gravel.

Back at the office, I was ready to leave when our news editor, Jake Billington, caught me. I like Jake and probably get along with him better than I do with anyone else at work. He looks like he just escaped from a Norman Rockwell painting, with wide blue suspenders and half glasses perched on the tip of his nose. A fringe of hair circles his head like a tonsure.

"Tracy," he said, "you'll have to do that mayor exchange story tomorrow."

"Well, sure, but Marge said you were going to cover it." I've learned to be cautious because sometimes he and Marge issue me conflicting orders.

"I was, but I've got me a problem." Jake reached around to massage his lower back. "My sacro-iliac is giving me fits, and the visiting dignitaries are going for a dune ride. We want a picture of the two mayors out by the lighthouse."

"Why me?" I sputtered. "I've never even been in a dune buggy."

"All the more reason for you to go."

Such logic. "Okay, I'll do it. What time?"

"City hall by nine thirty. They're having a little reception for the visitors and then car pooling out to Mickey's Dune Town."

I picked up some film and made it out the door. It was past five o'clock but the sun was still high and bright in a cloudless sky. Two old duffers sat on a bench in front of the post office, reading their mail and eating ice cream. See, that's the trouble with a little town like this. When spring comes, you forget how horrible the winter was, and think it's just such a cute and wonderful place to live.

Shagoni River, population 990, has its entire downtown located along three blocks of Hancock Street. Those three blocks embrace the yacht club, marina and village hall, the newspaper and post office, Lumbertown Bank, Miller's Grocery and Anderson's Drug. Interspersed among these more or less permanent fixtures are the small businesses that change their names and faces from one summer to the next. The village curves around Arrowhead Lake which offers a public beach and a channel to Lake Michigan, making it a tourist delight.

My postal box offered nothing in the way of interest and I was seriously considering an ice cream cone when I remembered the missing Madeline. So I walked over to her work place, Flagstone Real Estate, to see if they had any word of her. The place was closed up tight. So I walked across the street to Buried Treasure Antiques where I had better luck. Stepping inside, I found the proprietor, Gavin Macleod, at work

Gavin is nice to look at—just short of six feet tall, with a ready smile and unruly hair. His eyebrows are so bushy as to look a little demonic, but the effect is offset by emerald eyes that border on the angelic. His khaki pants and forest green shirt looked as though they just been ironed. Gavin was busy with customers so I found an old rocking char with soft velvet cushions and sat down to wait.

Immediately I began to relax, soothed by the scent of dried rose petals and the sad, mellow voice of Billie Holiday lamenting lost friends and lovers. Fringed and jeweled lamps cast muted light on subtle patterns of polished wood. Gavin was up front making a sale, surrounded by mirrors, stained glass and dishware that sparkled in the sunlight. A couple in matching black jackets had just selected a marble pitcher and washbasin. Gavin smiled and chatted while he wrapped their purchase and managed to look interested when the woman showed him photos of her grandchildren.

"Tracy," he said as he locked the door behind them, "I was going to call and suggest a trip to the Brown Bear."

"You must have read my mind. My lunch was an apple and a bag of corn chips."

"Just give me time to close up." He flipped a light switch and turned the sign.

"Have you seen Madeline today?" Gavin owned a duplex about a mile north of town, where he lived on one side and rented out the other. Madeline had been his renter for the past two years.

He turned and looked at me. "Odd you should ask. Phil called around noon with the same question." Phil Cutter was Madeline's boss.

"What did you tell him?"

"That I hadn't seen her since Friday." Gavin yanked the cash drawer and put it in a safe. "Phil said she didn't show up for work today, and he couldn't get her on the phone."

"I haven't seen her either. She wasn't at the chamber breakfast this morning."

"I went home at noon and her car was in the carport. So I knocked on her door." Gavin put on his jacket. "No answer."

"Did you peek in the windows?"

"Of course not. I'm her landlord, not her confessor."

"Is Phil going to call the police?"

"I wanted to. But then he reminded me of that time when Madeline took off for Las Vegas—well, that was before you knew her. But Madeline's an independent lady. We decided to wait until tomorrow."

"Okay. If you guys aren't going to worry, I won't either."

We both got our cars and Gavin followed me home. My grandfather's house, no, make that *my* house, sits on a hill with half an acre of lawn sloping down to the street. Lots of yard work. Maple and walnut trees grow in no discernible pattern, and a row of lilac bushes borders the long driveway. A big wraparound porch with missing posts makes the place look like an old lady with missing teeth. Gavin admired the oval of frosted glass in the front door.

"Don't you ever lock your house?" he said as we walked in.

"Grandpa never locked it so there isn't any key."

I left Gavin examining the fieldstone fireplace and slipped into my bedroom where I changed into jeans and a sweatshirt. Emerging, I found him on his knees with a corner of the rug folded back. "Gavin, what are you doing?"

"These are hardwood floors," he said. "If you got a sander, you could —."

"Please, stop. I've told you I'm just trying to make this place livable—then maybe salable. But sanding floors does not appear on either list."

"Sorry. I get carried away." He stood and dusted off his pants. "How are things coming?"

"Since you ask, I just spent a week's salary to replace a dead water heater. I almost hit you up for a shower."

"My condolences."

"And I'm pouring toxic chemicals down the kitchen sink, trying to dislodge whatever is living down there."

"I thought your drain was frozen."

"So did I. But spring's here and it's still plugged. The roof is patched but it's a temporary fix." I heaved a sigh. "I just don't have the money to fix this place."

"You could take out a loan."

"Then I'd be here forever. Come on, let's go."

We were almost out the door when he pointed to the flashing light on my answering machine. "You've got a message."

"We're hungry. I'll get it later."

"It could be Madeline."

"Damn, you're right." I pushed the button and we listened to the message. The caller was a female but it wasn't Madeline. It took me a few seconds to recognize the voice, which I hadn't heard for several years.

"Tracy, I hope you don't mind my calling. I got your number from my dad. Oh this is Brooke, remember me, ha ha, I guess you should. Well, I really need to talk to you about something, like, important. The thing is—my life is a pretty crazy right now. My mom got married again, did you know that? Anyway if you could call me, my number is —"

The tape ran out before she could finish the number, but it was an area code I didn't recognize.

Gavin looked at me, eyebrow raised.

"Let's go eat," I said, "and I'll reveal a chapter of my past."

CHAPTER TWO

"Who was your surprise caller tonight?" said Gavin after the waitress had taken our orders.

We were both wearing jackets, the only customers foolhardy enough to sit outside on a cool May evening. Other folks were huddled around the TV at the bar. But we preferred the sweeping view of Arrowhead Lake and the gentle cacophony of tree frogs in their mating mode. The deserted deck also provided a good spot for private conversation.

"I haven't seen Brooke in five years," I said. "Not since the divorce. I told you about Steve, didn't I?"

"Steve was the husband, right?"

"Right. Brooke is his daughter. So she's my ex-stepdaughter."

"What was she like?"

I paused, remembering Brooke as the frightened, gap toothed kid who had appeared in my life, suitcase in hand, on a Friday afternoon early in the marriage. Steve had wanted so much for us to like each other, but didn't have a clue as to how to make it happen.

"Poor little Brooke," I said. "She scared me to death at first, no fault of her own. Being around a kid probably stirred up all my bad feelings about failing as a teacher. There I was, thirty years old and childless, trying to figure out the marriage thing and the stepmother business all at once."

The waitress bumped the door open, deposited our food in front of us and disappeared back inside.

"Once we got past the awkward stage it turned out okay. We played hopscotch and Clue, and when she was older it was Monopoly and backgammon. She liked me to braid her hair, we went shopping together." I took a cautious bite of my burrito. "Sometimes I got the feeling that Steve was a little jealous, though we never tried to exclude him. It was a girl thing, I guess."

The burrito was so pungent it cleared my sinuses. I cooled my mouth with a gulp of beer. "How's the burger?" I nodded at Gavin's fare, the house special Papa Bear.

"Delicious. Juicy." He retrieved a pickle slice that had fallen loose and tucked it back in the bun. "Did Brooke spend much time with you?"

I nodded, my mouth full. "Brooke stayed with us a lot of weekends—and a couple of times for the whole summer. When Steve was working and I wasn't, I'd bring her up here to Shagoni River and we'd stay with my grandparents for a week or two."

"How old is she now?"

"She was five when we met." I started calculating. "I was married for nine years, divorced for five. She would be about nineteen."

"What's she doing?"

"She graduated from high school last year. I know because she sent me an invitation. But I didn't think it would make sense for me to actually show up."

"Why not?"

"Think about it. She's got her divorced mom and dad in the same space which is bad enough, so who needs the dad's second ex-wife? How would you even introduce someone like that?"

"As an ex-stepmother?" Gavin smiled, making those fine wrinkles around his eyes.

"So I sent her a graduation card and a check. Brooke sent a thank you note and said she was going to college somewhere in Ohio. That's the last I heard of her until tonight."

We finished our food and had a second beer. By the time we left it was after eight but still full daylight. Gavin dropped me at home and we promised to call each other if we had any news of Madeline. Once inside, I put on some old blues music and settled down with a book about Great Lakes shipwrecks. Exploring my grandparents' library makes me feel closer to them—he was big on maritime history and she favored poetry, the old fashioned kind that actually rhymes. Just as I was getting comfortable, the telephone rang. I got up and crossed the room, grumbling all the way about my need for a cordless phone.

My ex-stepdaughter was on the line.

"Tracy, it's me, Brooke. I hope it's okay that I'm calling you."

"Well, sure —." Her voice was more mature now, but still unmistakable, and it stirred up some long buried memories. I took a deep calming breath, like in yoga class. "What's up, Brooke?"

Her words tumbled over each other as Brooke told me she was busy writing finals, had almost finished the semester, could hardly believe that her freshman year was nearly over. None of this explained why she was calling me. I said the encouraging things that I thought an adult was supposed to say, and waited for the fast pitch. It didn't take long.

"Tracy, I'm calling you because I really need a place to stay."

So that was it. "For how long?" I squeaked, trying to imagine having a teen-aged visitor for a weekend—maybe even a week.

"For the summer," she said, leaving me, literally, speechless. Hearing no response she continued. "See, my mom married this guy, Walter, who just gives me the creeps, and I absolutely can't live with them any more."

I felt my mouth go dry. "What about your dad?"

"Dad's living in Miami and I just hate it there. It was too hot in the winter, can you imagine it in the summer, no way. I love Shagoni River, I know I could get a job there."

I took another deep breath, which failed to have any noticeable calming effect. "Have you talked to your mother about this?"

"She won't care. She doesn't care what I do."

I knew this wasn't true. "Brooke, absolutely, I must talk to your mother before I say yes or no about this. Have her call me, okay?"

Brooke reluctantly promised to have her mother, Jocelyn, call me so we could discuss her daughter's summer plans. Not that I was anxious to talk to my ex-husband's ex-wife. Probably I was just playing for time.

I hung up the phone and stared out the window, barely noticing the colors that were deepening over the western horizon. Brooke's phone call had me rattled. I knew that I didn't want to share my house with a nineteen-year-old, but at the same time, I couldn't think of a good reason to refuse. I needed time to think, someone to talk to, and a stiff drink—not necessarily in that order. I was staring into space, my book forgotten, when a knock on the front door interrupted my musings.

Through the oval window, I recognized Jewell Lavallen. I pulled open the door and found my best friend in her running mode, face flushed, blonde hair coming loose from the purple headband that matched her sweats. Though well past forty, Jewell looks so young she has to produce her driver's license to buy a drink. Maybe the bartenders just want an excuse to take a second look into those incredible eyes of hers.

"I hope it's not too late," she said. "I was out for a run and decided to pop in."

"You are never too late. Come on in." I gave her a hug and took her into the living room where she collapsed on the sofa. "You're the answer to a prayer," I said.

And I meant it. There was not another person in the world I would have chosen to have in my living room at that moment. Jewell had been my friend since the day I sat beside her Sociology 101 and discovered that I was a week behind in the class. Without hesitation, she had shared her notes, introduced me to her numerous friends and eventually taken me home for visits with her large, boisterous family.

After college we had stayed in touch but over the years our contact waned to the annual Christmas card. Then about three years ago, Jewell called to tell me that she and her family were moving to Cedar County. Her husband worked for an insurance company that had transferred him to Stanwood, the county seat. Jewell, with a nursing degree, had quickly found work at the hospital in Wexford, twenty miles to the north. Shagoni River was becoming something of a bedroom community.

"I'm so glad you're back." I dropped beside her on the sofa. "Here I was wishing for someone to talk to, and you appeared like magic."

"I was only gone a week, but thanks for missing me."

"How's your mom doing?"

"Her surgery went fine, and she's on her feet. Dad can handle things now."

Jewell stretched, bent down to touch her ankles. "What's happening? What did you want to talk about?"

"I just had a phone call that's got me all flustered."

"From who?"

"My ex-step daughter." I let out a sigh, wondering why this was such a big deal. "She wants to come here for the summer. I'm trying to figure out how to say no."

"How old is she?" Jewell always gathered information before giving out advice. "How long has it been since you've seen her?"

I filled her in on my history with Brooke and recapped our phone conversation.

Jewell listened carefully. When I was finished she said, "Don't let yourself get caught up in her drama. If you're not ready for this, just tell her so. I really don't see that you have any obligation here."

Jewell's advice was pretty much what I wanted to hear— that I had no obligations to Brooke at this point in our lives. I was quiet for a moment, examining the cross-stitched flowers on a pillow. Finally I looked up and said, "There's something else, though."

"Like what?"

"I guess this whole thing goes back a lot farther than just Brooke." Jewell just looked at me and waited. "You know my mother died when I was seventeen."

"You told me about that."

"It happened right here, I don't think I told you that part. Mom and I were visiting that summer. She went out for groceries and never came back. The guy who ran her off the bridge did a few years in jail and then left the state. I hope he never comes back."

"What about your dad?"

"Dad was never really in the picture. Mom didn't have much to say about him." I picked up a faded photo of my grandparents with me in the rose garden when I was about five years old. I fingered the photo, set it back down. "So here I was, seventeen years old, my mom just killed, and no real family except for Gram and Gramps. They did what they had to. They packed up all my stuff and moved me into that big bedroom upstairs. Shagoni River High got another senior, and my grandparents got a miserable teenager."

"It must have been hard," she said softly. "Hard for all of you."

"Hard doesn't begin to tell it." I stood and walked to the window. "It was culture shock for me, uprooted from Portage Heights where I had my pack of friends, shopping malls, all those teen age essentials. Shagoni River felt like the end of the world. The kids here actually went ice skating in the winter— outdoors, I mean, on the lake." I shook my head at the memories. "I went a little crazy that year. Spent a lot of time smoking pot with boys under the bleachers, drinking beer at beach parties. Wouldn't obey curfew, wouldn't listen to anyone. Poor Grandma got high blood pressure and Grandpa took up pipe smoking."

"I remember them—from the times you brought me here during college. They seemed very proud of you."

"They were. And despite all my complaints about this town, it was my home base, my refuge all through college. Somebody always had a summer job for me—waiting tables, cleaning cottages, life guarding down at the beach. Shagoni River looks after its own." I sat down. "The times when I really hated school and wanted to drop out, I just thought how everybody was rooting for me. How bad they would feel if I quit. That's what got me through in the end."

"So now it's your turn."

As usual, Jewell had gone right to the heart of the matter. "I didn't know this house came with such a price," I grumbled.

"It's not such a terrible price," she said, "and anyway, it's pay-back time. You're the adult now, and a young person is looking for safe harbor."

"But I don't want to be an adult," I protested. "Responsibility scares me. Besides what kind of role model would I be?"

"Probably as good as her mom. Maybe better in some areas." She smiled. "What's the worst that could happen?"

"Brooke might be as nasty and thoughtless as I was."

Jewell laughed. "Like I said, it's your turn now."

The room was dark except for the glow of a distant streetlight. I got up and turned on a lamp. "Let me give you a ride home," I said. "I've kept you out past dark."

Jewell stood. "I almost forgot – we're having a party this Sunday. It's a cookout on the deck with burgers and salmon, and everybody brings a dish to pass. Are you free?"

"Are you kidding? Sure I'm free."

"We'll start the grill at six, but come early if you want a boat ride. Paul has his boat in the water and he loves to show it off."

"I'll be there," I said, just as the telephone rang. I picked up, motioning for Jewell to wait.

It was Ivy. "There's still no answer at Madeline's," she said. "Have you heard anything?"

I told Ivy about my conversation with Gavin. "He and Phil agreed that if she doesn't show up by tomorrow, we'll need to do something. Jewell's right here. Let me ask her."

Jewell had nothing to add. She hadn't seen Madeline in over two weeks. Then Ivy started telling me about the time Madeline went to Las Vegas until finally I had to cut her off. I drove Jewell home. As I dropped her off, she reminded me again about the party.

"Shall I come early and help you get ready?"

"That would be great."

"Thanks for listening to my problems."

"Any time," she said. "Now get a good night's sleep and don't feel rushed into making a decision."

Great advice, but sleep was elusive. Too many things were running through my mind. I was angry at Madeline for being so inconsiderate of her friends, but mostly I was wondering what to tell Brooke. Alternately I was pleased that she had turned to me, and then irritated that she had re-opened a chapter in my life that I thought was neatly closed. The last time I looked at the clock it was almost two-thirty.

Sleep deprived, I arrived at city hall with a pounding headache and a sour disposition. The scent of percolating coffee promised relief. I followed my nose to the council room where I found half a dozen people standing around a table that held the coffee urn and a box of bakery treats. With a perfunctory good morning to our mayor, Clancy Fredericks, I grabbed a mug, filled it, and snagged a pineapple pastry. Sugar and caffeine, I mused, are the fuels that start the collective engine of this country every morning.

Clancy said some words of welcome to our guests from Welston. When my mouth was full and my fingers gooey, Clancy proceeded to introduce me to the visitors. I swallowed fast, rubbed my fingers on my jeans, and shook hands with the visiting mayor, his wife, and the Welston village manager. I mumbled some polite questions about their visit so far, and silently cursed our mayor's timing. Clancy's wife sent me a commiserating smile.

The caffeine got my adrenaline flowing and I was feeling decidedly more sociable by the time our village manager, Jim Mcneely, arrived. Jim apologized for his late arrival and explained that he had been trouble-shooting out at the wastewater plant. To be honest, it wasn't just the caffeine that improved my mood. The sight of our village manager never fails to raise my sociability quotient.

Jim is about thirty-five and utterly gorgeous. He has dimples that deepen when he smiles, sea-blue eyes, and eyelashes that most women would die for. He probably could have been a model, but he's only five feet seven so he became our village manager. The world's loss has been Shagoni River's gain. Besides being cute, Jim Mcneely manages to keep our village running efficiently without overspending its skinny budget.

A white van bearing the Diamond D logo appeared in the parking lot. The mayor looked out the window and said it was time to head for the sand dunes. I nodded toward the van and said, "Tom Halladay doesn't miss a trick, does he?"

Clancy grinned. "We're getting a free round of golf after the dune ride."

"Then I'd better take my own car," I said. "Meet you there."

Fifteen minutes later we were climbing aboard a dune buggy at the staging area of Mickey McGee Thriller Dune Rides. Our buggy was a four-seater, with no roof and no doors, but sturdy roll bars that were probably meant to look reassuring. I was not reassured.

Clancy and his wife took one seat, the mayor from Welston and his wife got another, the two village managers filled a third and that left me to ride shotgun with the driver. Since this was a high profile crowd, Mickey himself was behind the wheel. He shoved a baseball cap down onto his bristling gray hair and gripped the wheel with large knuckled, leathery hands. As we roared out of the parking lot, Mickey turned and yelled at his riders over the sound of the engine. After thirty years of dune driving, he had a practiced spiel.

"We've got two thousand acre of sand dunes out here—biggest park in the state." Our driver stole only the occasional glance at the road as he talked. "These dunes are constantly shifting, about twenty feet every year. They cover up anything that gets in their way. Once in a while they swallow a whole cottage. Hang on now."

He turned abruptly onto a bumpy two-track that led into sparsely wooded hills. "We're coming to Termite Bridge now," said Mickey. "It's in pretty bad shape so I need your help. Everybody hold your breath—it'll make us lighter." Though his instructions were patently ridiculous, I took a deep breath and held it as we traversed a narrow wooden bridge.

"We lock this up at night nowadays." He pointed to a swinging metal bar that served as a gate. "Too many high school kids was coming out here to party."

Suddenly I remembered being one of those kids who had roared across Termite Bridge in a pickup truck under a full moon. But I didn't tell Mickey.

"Remember the glaciers?" Mickey said, as we bounced over exposed tree roots. "Some of you might, you're older'n me. Ha ha. Well, the glaciers pushed a bunch of bedrock down here and ground it up in little pieces. That's where we got the sand." As a geology teacher, Mickey was not half bad. "Then the glaciers melted and that's where we got the Great Lakes. Here we go now."

We began to climb and the vegetation disappeared. As the hills got steeper, our buggy accelerated and sand began to fly. My camera threatened to go overboard so I tightened the strap over my shoulder and held the grab bar with both hands. We crested a hill and went airborne for a second, then landed with a resounding thud. The two women screamed as we hit, but I just groaned. No wonder Jake had refused this trip.

The whole world was sun, sky and sand. We crested another dune and Lake Michigan appeared below us, spread out like a blue silk scarf. Mickey raced down to the water and then swerved, sending up a silver spray that doused everybody on his side of the buggy. "There's the lighthouse," he said, pointing to a tall, cylindrical structure that looked out over the lake. Mickey drove toward it with two tires in the water.

"It's the Little Point Sable Lighthouse," he yelled through the spray "— built about 1870. They had full time tenders then, real government jobs. It was pretty lonely out here." Gradually he slowed the buggy to a crawl. "Now the whole thing's automated. Nobody lives out here except a couple of ghosts."

We choked to a stop about thirty yards from the structure which was featureless at ground level except for yellow bricks and a weathered door. We all climbed out and stood on the soft sand. I stretched and bent cautiously, checking for breaks or sprains, but everything seemed in working order. Then I remembered my assignment so I lined up the two mayors in front of the lighthouse for a photo; next I added the two wives, and finally the two village managers. I stepped back and was working the telephoto lens when the photo session screamed to a halt.

"What's that thing up there on the beach?" Clancy's wife was shading her eyes with one hand, pointing north with the other.

I moved up beside her and looked. The object that had caught her eye was pale yellow, almost blended in with the sand. It was about the size of a big log ——or a body.

"It's a swimmer!" I yelled and my lifeguard training kicked in. I dropped my camera and started running. Mickey must have seen it too, because he jumped into the dune buggy and headed down the beach.

Mickey got there first. I saw him jump out and kneel to take a pulse. When he looked up, his face was the color of ashes. The body was that of a woman, face down in the sand, with one arm and one foot in the water. The visible arm was blue and the legs were nearly black. Mickey shook his head.

I stopped suddenly, tasting bile. The sun started to spin in the sky. Panting, I fell to my knees and retched up my pineapple Danish.

The sodden clothes were familiar. One look had told me far more than I wanted to know. The body that had washed up on the Lake Michigan shoreline was clad in a yellow corduroy skirt, ivory blouse, and a peach colored vest. I had seen that ensemble several times before, on my friend Madeline. She had a way with colors.

"Keep the others away," Mickey said hoarsely. He motioned toward the group walking slowly in our direction. "They don't need to see this."

27

CHAPTER THREE

Jim Mcneely and I sat on a small dune, far enough from the water to be on dry sand, close enough to carry out our assigned task. The sun was high over head and warm on my shoulders. Lake Michigan lay in front of us, a serene cobalt surface that stretched away to meet an almost equally blue horizon.

A pair of seagulls wheeled overhead, checking perhaps to see if the humans on the beach had any food for them. 'Flying rats' is what some folks call these screeching, strutting birds because of their willingness to devour anything that people throw away. I had a really unwelcome thought right then, and wondered if seagulls ate carrion.

The village manager and I were alone on the beach, except for the body of Madeline Maxwell, which we had been assigned to watch. Shortly after our grim discovery, Mickey had radioed his office and then hustled the other passengers into the buggy and away from the scene. I'm not sure how Jim and I got the guard duty, except that our mayor didn't want to desert his guests, Mickey was driving, and that pretty much left the two of us on seagull patrol.

Mickey had told us that his dispatcher was calling 911 and we should keep watch until someone from the sheriff's department showed up. So that's what we were doing. It's not like we had our eyes glued to the corpse. In fact, I kept my eyes trained on the sky and the seagulls, except for the occasional glance down to the waterline. My thoughts were in turmoil as I struggled to understand how my lively friend Madeline had turned into this discolored body on the beach.

"She must have been washed off the pier," I said, "like that kid from Chicago last summer." Despite repeated warnings from those in authority, people did get washed off piers every summer, all up and down Lake Michigan.

"Maybe," said Jim, "but it doesn't seem likely. The weather's been mild for several days."

"I guess you're right." I searched for a logical explanation. "Maybe she was walking the pier, slipped and fell in."

"It's possible. But that would mean the body was carried pretty far north."

I shaded my eyes and looked down the beach. Nothing but sand and water. "How far are we from the channel, do you think?"

"Maybe two miles."

Jim was puncturing all my theories. "Okay, so what's your explanation?"

"She must have been on a boat."

"Madeline has a little Sunfish," I said. "She took me sailing once last summer."

"Do you think she would have taken it out on Lake Michigan?"

"Not a chance. Besides, she wasn't dressed for sailing."

"Then she must have been on someone else's boat," he said.

I recalled my conversation with Ivy, the one where she said that Madeline was a 'sucker for any guy with a boat'. I turned to Jim. "You mean she could have been out for a joy ride and fallen overboard?"

"Something like that. But it seems strange that nobody has reported it. Do you think ——?"

Jim stopped mid-sentence and we both listened. The sound of an engine reached our ears just before we spotted an all terrain vehicle coming up the beach from the south. The ATV carried two men in brown uniforms. As the vehicle came closer, I saw the Cedar County Sheriff's Department insignia on one fender.

"Guess that's the sheriff," I said.

"Looks like our vacation is over."

The four-wheeler slowed as it passed the lighthouse, then pulled to a stop by the pastel object on the beach. The two men got out and hunkered down on either side of the body. Then one of them noticed Jim and me, and motioned us down. I had been hoping they would come up the hill to talk to us, but no such luck. Jim and I got up and walked toward the two officers. Sheriff Benny Dupree was tall, broad shouldered and bald, but I didn't recognize the other officer, who was shorter and had wavy hair the color of dishwater.

"Who's the other guy?" I said to Jim.

"Curt Laman. He's a sergeant."

We stopped a few feet away. The men stood up to meet us. Jim and I had both dealt with Sheriff Dupree in the past, and he seemed to remember who we were. Now he cast us a quizzical look, as though wondering if we had arranged this death in order to have time alone on the beach.

"Has anyone touched the body?" said Dupree.

"Just Mickey," I said. "He tried to get a pulse."

Dupree snorted like that was the dumbest thing he had ever heard. I wanted to defend Mickey but decided it was irrelevant. Instead, I told the sheriff what had happened. That we were out for a dune ride with visitors from Welston, stopped at the lighthouse for photos, and spotted the body.

Jim pretty much repeated the story.

"Is this the usual route for Mickey's ride?" said Dupree.

"As far as I know. I never rode with him before." I looked at Jim.

"The mayor brought me out here when I was first hired," he said. "It seemed like pretty much the same route."

Dupree looked at the Nikon hanging around my neck. "Did you take any pictures?"

"Yes, but just people in front of the lighthouse. That was before we found the –"

"Understand," said Dupree, "we don't want no pictures in the paper of a dead body."

"I'm sure Marge doesn't either," I assured him. "Would it be okay if I took a shot of you two—with just the lake in the background?"

"Yeah, I guess so."

I stepped back, raised my camera and clicked. Dupree sucked in his belly for the photo but Laman was busy writing up the report.

There was the sound of another engine and I looked up to see a jeep approaching from the north. The vehicle ground to a halt and two people got out, one male and one female. I recognized the gray-haired man as the park manager and pegged the hefty female as his assistant. Both wore forest green shirts and pants. The four officials began a conversation that did not include Jim and me, so we backed off. I took a few shots of the uniformed group, taking care not to include the object of their discussion.

The uniforms continued to ignore us, so Jim and I retreated to our dune. I wondered if we were going to be left there to hike back to civilization. But a few minutes later, the lady ranger came over and said she would give us a lift to dune ride headquarters. Gratefully, Jim and I joined her in the jeep. Our driver, whose name was Marian, proved to be cheerful and talkative, probably relieved to have an assignment that took her away from the body. On the ride back, all of us shared the fact that we had just seen our first corpse. Outside of a coffin, that is.

Marian left Jim and me at the dune ride parking lot. A kid who looked about fifteen was hosing down one of the buggies, but other wide there was no activity. Just then Mickey came out of is office. He said the State Park was closed for the day and the sheriff had made him cancel all dune rides.

"Kind of bad for your business," said Jim.

"Yeah, but we'll probably make up for it," Mickey said brightly. "Now everybody will want to visit the spot. People are funny that way."

"Mickey, you've been on the dunes for years," I said. "Is this the first time you've found a body on found a body the beach?"

"First time I found one I wasn't looking for."

"How's that?"

"The other two were recovery efforts, I guess you'd call them. You know, swimmers who had gone missing. But today—well, this was kind of different. You guys need a ride to town?"

"Thanks, but my car's right over there." I dug into my camera case for the keys.

"Do I get to ride with you?" said Jim.

"If you don't mind a messy car."

"Not a bit."

I unlocked my car and cleaned assorted trash from the passenger seat. Jim climbed in, offering no complaints offering no complaints about the dust, the dents or the debris. Mickey waved as we pulled away.

"Guess we both missed lunch," I said.

"If you'll stop at the Brown Bear," said Jim, "I'll buy."

"Really?"

"Sure. To show my gratitude for the ride."

After all the shock and excitement, I couldn't tell if I was hungry or not. But since I had left my breakfast back there on the sand, I probably was. In any case, having lunch with Jim seemed like a good way to postpone going back to work. As the only customers at the Brown Bear we had prompt service—I had a grilled cheese sandwich, he had the corned beef, and we both had coffee.

"Village hall has probably ground to a halt without you," I said.

"And what about the newspaper?"

"I'm not the boss, so they'll carry on. But Marge may not be happy with me."

"Maybe we should write out tardy slips for each other."

I dropped Jim at village hall and by the time I got back to the office, it was almost four o'clock. The bad tidings had preceded me, so it wasn't like I had to break the news to anyone. Jake was in the newsroom.

"I guess the people from Welston won't forget Shagoni River anytime soon," he said as I walked in.

31

"Yeah, we arranged them one hell of a reception." I dropped my jacket, camera and notebook on my desk.

"Come take a look at my story."

"I've got some photos to go with it." I handed over the film, then followed Jake into his office where I sat down and scanned the story. It was pretty complete. He had quotes from the mayor and Mickey, plus a statement from the sheriff's office. I added a few details and confirmed the time and location. Working on the story made it seem like—well—just a news story and I was starting to feel fairly calm, sort of on automatic pilot.

Then Marge showed up. "And where have you been all day?" she said.

"Having a day at the beach," I said just to shut her up.

Marge wasn't amused. "Someone saw your car at the Brown Bear," she said. I didn't respond so then she started chewing me out because I had missed some stupid zoning board meeting. Jake doesn't usually intervene, but this time he did.

"Cut her some slack," he said. "She just found her friend's dead body."

Marge glared at us but didn't answer.

I sought refuge at my desk and tried to write up the mayor exchange visit which had now been reduced to the status of a sidebar. It was slow going because I had a lot of trouble just remembering how to operate the computer. As I struggled to locate some statistics about the town of Welston, my mind kept reeling back to the sight of Madeline's bloated body. As I squinted at my morning's notes, I was overwhelmed by feelings of guilt.

If only Madeline had been with me, or Ivy, or any of her friends, this could never have happened. We would have saved her. Where were we when she needed us? I couldn't think, I couldn't spell, I couldn't write. It took me two hours to complete a ten-inch story that probably still needed major editing.

Jake stopped by my desk. "I just talked with Sheriff Dupree," he said. The body has been officially identified. Madeline's boss Phil Cutter, had that honor."

"Well, good," I said, suppressing a shudder. "I mean, I'm glad no one asked me to do it."

"Your photos look good."

"I didn't have time to write any notes. Do you want me to look at the proofs?"

"Nah, don't bother. I'm using the one of Dupree and Laman."

The story and my photos took up a good chunk of the front page, so Jake said I didn't have to write anything else. That was a relief. My other pending story was about stray dogs at the landfill and I just wasn't up for it. It was past six-thirty when I packed up to leave but Marge and Jake were still working. The paper goes to press on Tuesday night and one of them would still have to deliver it to the printer.

As for me, I just wanted to get out of there. Both Ivy and Gavin had left messages, but I didn't want to call them from work. Once in my car, I realized that I didn't much want to go home either. So I headed, like a homing pigeon, like a compass pointing north, for the place where I would find food and comfort. With my thoughts in a muddle and my radio playing some very loud rock music, I headed down Arrowhead Drive to the home of Paul and Jewell Lavallen.

Lavallens' house is on Arrowhead Lake about a mile west of town, a split-level brick and glass construction nearly hidden behind a grove of cedar trees. Perfect setting, perfect couple, perfect kids, both in college. Sometimes these two make me feel like the ultimate loser. How do they do it? Is it just blind luck that leads people like them to find each other, and someone like me to pick a man who will leave me emotionally battered and none the wiser? Or is it perhaps genetic, based on my mother's obvious miscalculation with my absent father? Whatever the reason, I was happy to know at least one couple who didn't give marriage a bad name.

I found Jewell on her knees, transplanting a flat of impatiens into one of her many flower beds. She threw down her trowel and met me with a hug. "I've been trying to call you," she said. "Was it really awful?"

"Yes, it was awful. I've never found a dead body before."

"Well I have, but they were usually in a bed."

"How did you hear about it?"

"Paul heard it at the office. Come on inside." Jewell left her flowers and I followed her to the house, our feet scrunching on the white pea gravel of the driveway. Once inside, the aroma of garlic and basil enveloped us. "Paul's cooking tonight," she said with a smile.

Paul Lavallen came out of the kitchen and wrapped me in a bear hug. I love getting hugs from Paul. He's six foot two, with a football player's body, and so far none of it has gone to fat. His brown beard and steel rimmed glasses make him look like a college professor.

"Tracy," he said, "good to see you. You're staying for supper."

I didn't argue. Jewell and I went into the living room and I relaxed into their expansive sofa. Sitting there, I soaked up the tranquil scene in their backyard and let it soothe my jagged nerves. A pair of geese ruffled the surface of Arrowhead Lake and Paul's fishing boat, *Jewell of the Sea*, bobbed gently at its moorings. Jewell handed me a glass of Chablis and sat down beside me.

"How are you feeling?" she said.

"Mostly numb, I guess, and a little guilty." I looked at her. "Does everyone feel like this when a friend dies so—so unexpectedly?"

"People have a lot of different emotions, but guilt is usually one of the strongest. In a way we feel guilty just for being alive, when some one we care about is not."

As we talked I felt the knots in my stomach begin to loosen. Jewell has a way of doing that for me. "I need to make a couple of calls," I said.

Jewell handed me the phone.

Ivy wasn't home but I reached Gavin. "Tracy," he said, "you're supposed to report the news, not make it. What happened?"

I filled him in on the story of my morning. I was getting good at telling it, I'd done it so many times. "I guess you'll need to find a new renter," I said. My attempt at levity sounded hollow, even to me. Paul announced supper so I rang off, telling Gavin I would stop by the store as soon as I had a chance.

"Careful, this is extra hot," Paul warned as he set the dish of bubbling lasagna on the table. Jewell brought out a tossed salad and garlic bread. Paul refilled my wineglass. If I could remember exactly how much I ate or drank at that meal, I would probably be embarrassed. There seemed to be a big empty spot somewhere near my solar plexus that I was trying to fill.

"You did a great job on the lasagna," I said to Paul as I reached for a second helping. "Did you practice while Jewell was away?"

Paul shook his head. "I do microwave when I'm alone." He glanced at his wife. "This is Jewell's welcome home dinner and it's pretty much the limit of my cooking skills."

"At least you try," said Jewell. "My dad is completely helpless in the kitchen. I had to cook for both of them until mom got well enough to hobble out there herself."

Despite occasional detours onto other subjects, our conversation kept returning to Madeline's death. We wondered aloud how such a thing could have happened while we were going about our lives, a few miles away.

"Maddie does drink a little," said Paul, "but I can't see her getting soused enough to jump into Lake Michigan."

"She was wearing her good skirt and blouse," I said. "One of her business outfits."

"What about her car?" said Jewell.

"Gavin said it's still in the car port."

"Did she say anything about her plans for the weekend?" said Paul.

"Just that she was busy. And that could mean almost anything—going to see her parents, some kind of business deal, or a man in the picture. With Madeline we were never sure."

Our talk continued in that vein but we were pretty much going in circles. We moved on to less distressing speculation, about her family, whether there would be a funeral and where to send our condolences. Jewell brought out some chocolate ripple ice cream and served it up in red glass bowls.

"Tracy," she said, "what's happening with your stepdaughter?"

"Oh, that." Yesterday Brooke's reappearance had seemed a major crisis. Today I hadn't even had time to think about it. "Basically we're at a stand off," I said, "until Jocelyn, the mother, calls me." I filled Paul in on my stepmother status, then nodded at the family photos on the wall. "And how are your bright, wonderful children?"

The picture gallery included shots of a girl on horseback and a boy in soccer uniform, plus several of the whole family doing outdoor stuff. I had last seen their kids during the holidays, when the son presented himself with bright blue hair that stood in peaks.

"Derek's got his hair a natural color now," Jewell said, "and he's only wearing one earring. So I guess that's progress. Scholastically, well, he just squeaked through his first year at Michigan State. He'll be home in a couple of days, looking for a summer job."

"How about the girl—Sarah?"

"Second year at U of M," said Paul, "and she loves it. In fact, she loves it so much that she's not coming home this summer. She got a job in Ann Arbor and she's going to stay there."

"Must be fun for you," I said, "having one at each place." Michigan State and University of Michigan were legendary rivals, especially during football season.

Jewell smiled. "Paul played for State," she said, "so he's a diehard Spartan fan. I feel like I have to side with Sarah, just to keep things even."

"The double tuition payments, that's another kind of fun," said Paul.

"I keep telling him if he'd sell the boat, we could keep them both in school for a whole year." Jewell glanced pointedly at her husband.

"No way," said Paul. "That boat is my relaxation and it's cheap therapy. Besides, sometimes I even catch a fish."

I found their gentle bickering to be oddly reassuring. So these two were human after all. Jewell and I cleared the table and loaded the dishwasher. Paul turned on the gas log in the rec room fireplace and we settled down to watch a movie about a French jewel thief who was really a CIA agent. By the time it was over we had finished the bottle of wine.

Paul offered to drive me home but I refused, feeling that I had already imposed on them enough. So I drove cautiously, probably about thirty miles an hour, and fortunately didn't encounter any overly zealous law enforcement personnel. As I walked into my house, the clock on the mantel startled me by striking midnight. The light on the answering machine was flashing, but I didn't play the messages. I felt like I'd had enough bad news for one day.

By twelve thirty I was in bed, snuggled under my grandmother's hand-made quilt. And there, cradled in that downy warmth, I realized that I hadn't even brushed my teeth. Too bad. I slept fitfully and dreamed about screeching seagulls that flew in circles around a lighthouse while somebody, somewhere, kept calling for help.

CHAPTER FOUR

"Local Businesswoman Drowns in Lake Michigan!"

The headline was emblazoned across the front page of Wednesday's paper along with two of my photos. I grabbed the newspaper and took it to my desk. I had considered taking the day off, but decided that staying home with a hangover would not improve my mood. So I began my workday hiding behind the paper, drinking coffee and trying to pretend I was functional.

Eventually I got to work on my story about stray dogs at the landfill, but I was constantly interrupted by phone calls. One of them was from Ivy, who sounded on the verge of hysteria, so I spent the better part of an hour talking to her. Our conversation went over the same territory multiple times. We each reviewed our last meeting with Madeline, mining every word she had said for possible clues. We speculated on what her plans had been for the weekend. We agonized over what had gone wrong. There were rules against personal phone calls at work but I couldn't see any way out of this. Besides, Marge was out of town for the day.

My next call was from Sheriff Dupree. He said a crew from TV 13 was going to interview him for the evening news, and asked me if I wanted to be part of it. I declined but told the sheriff I would be watching for him. "Must be a slow news day in Grand Rapids," I said to Jake, who had just walked in.

Jake was grousing about the headline Marge had affixed to his story. "I said it was an 'assumed drowning'," he grumbled as he slid into a chair. "Nothing's sure until after the autopsy."

"Autopsy ——?" I swiveled around to face him. "Don't we already know that she drowned?"

Jake gave me a look which suggested that he couldn't believe my ignorance. "It's the law," he said. "When somebody kicks off, and they're not in a hospital, there's an autopsy. Just because she landed on the beach doesn't mean she drowned —maybe somebody didn't like her."

I was too upset to respond. So far, I had not imagined Madeline's death to be anything but a bizarre and tragic accident. Jake saw my distress.

"Hey, it's just routine," he said. "They do it with everything, car accidents, drownings, people who die in bed. Hell, maybe she had a stroke and that's why she went in." I wanted to explore this line of thought but Jake cut me off. "Aren't you supposed to be somewhere?"

"Oh right, the high school." I was scheduled to cover a Drug Education Program and it was going to start in 5 minutes.

I parked in a spot reserved for staff and entered the auditorium. Two hundred hormone driven adolescents were laughing and flirting while they paid scant attention to the police officer on stage. I took a seat and listened while the speaker enumerated the damaging physical effects of drugs and alcohol. I could have added a few vivid details of my own. The kids calmed down a little when the officer showed them slides of burning cars, twisted metal and young people sobbing in remorse after killing a number of their best friends. Afterward, I talked to the principal who told me he was concerned because funding for the Drug Education Program was in jeopardy. I promised to make that a prominent part of my story.

I went home for lunch and had a bowl of soup. By afternoon my head felt better and I whipped out three stories, which effectively cleared my desk of the dogs, the drugs and a new doughnut shop in town. After work, I stopped at the Treasure Chest and found Gavin getting ready to close. With a grateful sigh, I collapsed into my favorite chair.

"Everybody's speculating about poor Madeline," Gavin said as he turned over the sign. "Is there any real news?"

"Jake said there's going to be an autopsy. And Benny Dupree is supposed to be on Channel 13 tonight."

"If we hurry we can catch the news at the Bear – if you're willing to drive, that is." Gavin smiled apologetically "My car is over at Sam's getting a new muffler." Sam Blankenship ran the only auto repair service in town. Sam was reasonable and fairly competent, but no one had ever accused him of being fast.

"It's a deal." I said.

The parking lot at the Brown Bear was nearly full but I sneaked into a corner spot, one advantage of having a small car. We climbed the long flight of stairs to the deck and were quickly engulfed by a noisy crowd that appeared to be equal parts fishermen and summer cottage owners.

"Looks like the season is upon us," muttered Gavin.

"Don't complain. The summer crowd is your bread and butter."

"I'll try to remember that."

We went inside and found a small table by a window. Hank, the owner, came out from behind the bar to take our order. Hank looks a little like a bear himself—tall (even by my standards), barrel chested, with a bushy red beard and matching hair that reaches his collar. He was wearing the faded jeans, plaid flannel shirt and hiking boots that seemed to constitute his entire wardrobe, regardless of the season.

"Got some really good perch tonight," he said by way of a recommendation. I took his suggestion and so did Gavin. "You guys know that woman who drowned?" We acknowledged that we did, and told him the sheriff was supposed to be on Channel 13. "News just started," said Schober.

Gavin and I got up and stood in a spot that allowed a view of the TV above the bar. Minutes later we were rewarded with a picture of Sheriff Dupree standing next to a sharp-featured woman with short black hair. "We're in the tiny resort town of Shagoni River," she said, "talking to the sheriff of Cedar County. Sheriff, what can you tell us about the body found yesterday on the beach at Sable Point dunes?"

Blinking against the lights, Dupree said the body had been identified as that of local real estate agent Madeline Maxwell, who was last seen alive on Friday.

"And has the cause of death been determined?"

"The death appears to be from drowning," he said, "but an autopsy is pending. The situation is under investigation."

The woman said, "Thank you, sheriff," and the screen flashed to a car commercial.

"You didn't even get credit for the discovery," Gavin said as we returned to our table. I told him that was fine with me. We made small talk until the perch arrived and then focused on the food.

"This is great," I said, dipping a morsel into tartar sauce. "Hank does know his perch."

"And the home fries are almost worth the trip. This is Cedar County three star dining."

"You're right. But sometimes I do miss big city fare."

"Oh me too— stuff like Indian curry or German pancakes."

"Even Chinese take out. Do you ever miss the city?"

"Sure, but a weekend trip to Lansing or Ann Arbor takes care of that."

"Gavin, how on earth did you end up in Shagoni River?"

39

"Didn't I ever tell you about Jess Barnard?"

I shook my head.

"I was tending bar in Grand Rapids. Jess was a regular. One day we got to talking about antiques and I confided that old stuff had always been my secret passion. So when Jess invited me to come up here and be his partner, I said yes in a heartbeat."

"When was that?"

"About seven years ago. Jess was only in his sixties, but maybe knew his days were numbered. Three years later he died and left me the store and the duplex—both with hefty mortgages. At first I didn't think I could manage, but Jess had taught me well. Things have turned out okay."

"You seem to be doing all right."

"I'll never get rich here, but I like living here."

"Me too, now that winter's over."

"Hey, what's happening with your stepdaughter—what was her name?"

"Brooke. She called again, and this time we talked. The kid had a wild idea about coming here for the summer, but I doubt if her mother will let her."

This time we didn't linger. As soon as the food was gone we headed back to town

As we approached Gavin's duplex, the upstairs windows flashed gold reflections from the westering sun. The building was well maintained, surrounded by a neat lawn that disappeared into a forest of birch and maple. Gavin often complained that he couldn't raise tulips because of the deer in the neighborhood who regarded them as a delicacy. The place had twin entrance doors separated by a juniper hedge and a cement walk that connected to the double carport. As I pulled into the drive, Gavin let out a whistle of surprise. "Look at that," he said.

"Look at what?"

"Madeline's car is gone."

The carport was indeed empty with no Cutlass Supreme in sight. "Was it there yesterday?"

"It was there this morning when I left for work."

"Well, we know Madeline didn't take it."

"Right. So who did?"

"Maybe you should call the sheriff."

"I will. Come on in."

I followed Gavin into his living room, where a delightful mish-mash of shop overflow mixed with more functional pieces. His computer was perched on a roll top desk and the printer rested on a carved end table. I went straight to my favorite spot and peered into his aquarium, a tall glass cylinder where rainbow hued fish swam through castles and seaweed, with the whole scene doubled by a large mirror.

Gavin dialed 911 and told the dispatcher his situation. Within minutes the phone rang back. A brief exchange followed, his part being mostly "yes," "no," and "okay." When Gavin hung up he looked at me and said, "That was Sergeant Laman. He told me what happened to Madeline's car. It's been impounded and they're searching it."

"Impounded? Why? And where did they get the keys?"

"He said the keys were on the seat of the car."

"No way. Madeline would never have been so careless."

"And get this." Gavin walked to the window. "We are not to go into the other half of this building. Madeline's apartment has been sealed off."

"Sealed off?"

"You know. Like a crime scene."

For confirmation, we went outside and inspected what we still thought of as Madeline's front door. Sure enough, the door was sealed with yellow tape that read, "Police Line, Do Not Cross." We stood and stared at the door, then at each other, as the sun slipped behind a ridge of trees. Gavin sat on the brick stoop and put his head in his hands.

"What do you think this means?" I said.

He answered without looking up. "What it means is that Sheriff Dupree knows something—something he didn't tell us on the evening news."

Thursday morning I arrived at the county board meeting and found Ivy already there, looking chic in a burnt orange jumper with an apricot neck scarf. Next to her I always feel a bit drab. The board members arrived and settled themselves around the horseshoe table in upholstered chairs that tilted or turned to accommodate their sizes and shapes. Ivy and I were consigned to metal folding chairs at a table with peeling black paint.

Ron Langlois, the county administrator, came in and handed everybody some photocopied pages. Langlois has lots of dark hair and a wiry gray mustache, a combination that gives him a young/old appearance.

"Ron must have liked your story," Ivy whispered. She pointed to the handout which turned out to be a copy of my recent front page story, "Condos or Corn; Which way for Cedar County?"

This kind of attention always makes me a little nervous. "I'm not responsible for the dumb headline," I whispered. Ivy leaned over to reply, but fell silent when the chairman, Lathan Dirkse, gaveled the meeting to order.

Dirkse, a small man with lots of energy, had been on the board for as long as anyone could remember, but today he had a surprise for us. "District two will have a new commissioner next year," he said. "I've decided not to run for re-election. My wife and I want to spend the winters in Arizona, see more of the grandkids. I'm not going to endorse anyone for the upcoming election so the field is wide open." Dirkse cut short the murmurs of surprise and regret with, "Okay, let's get down to business."

The board moved briskly through the morning's agenda. They approved payment of bills and heard the county clerk's request for more help in her office. The meeting slowed when two citizens complained at length about a neighbor they claimed was running a dog kennel without a license.

'another dog story for us' Ivy scribbled on my pad.

'i just finished dogs at the landfill'

Then Langlois called the board's attention to the "Condos or Corn?" story I had written for the News. "It's a good question," he said. "Believe it or not, developers have their eyes on Cedar County. Unless we decide what kind of growth we want, just about anything can happen here."

"Such as the Diamond D Ranch?" This comment came from Grady Bunch, the district four commissioner. Subdued laughter rippled around the table.

Ann Doyle, the only female commissioner spoke up. "Lathan," she said, "that Diamond D is in your district. What do people over there think about it?"

"Well, that ranch business, that's got a few folks riled up," said Dirkse. "Some people say Tom Halladay put one over on the zoning board, that he lied about how big it was gonna be. Others say he downright bought them off."

"I've heard that their construction equipment tore up the road out there," said Doyle, "and now the road commission wants them to pay for it."

"Fat chance they'll get anything out of Halladay," said Bunch. "He's a slippery one."

"I don't imagine Halladay is very popular in the township right now," said Doyle.

"Well, it works two ways," said Dirkse. "That ranch puts tax money in the township treasury—and it provides jobs for our kids. I've got a grandson and a niece who expect to work there this summer. So I'm sort of keeping my mouth shut."

42

"What about that liquor license he's after?" said Langlois.

"That's another bone of contention," said Dirkse. "See, a lot of folks out there go to that Reformed Church. They think a liquor license would signal the end of all decency."

"How about you?" said Bunch.

"Us Catholics, well, we don't mind a drink." Dirkse smiled, looked at his watch. "Well, we got ourselves off track and it's time for lunch." Dirkse adjourned the meeting and the room gradually emptied.

Ivy and I were ready to leave when Langlois approached us. He offered a few words of condolence about Madeline's death and then complimented me on my story, saying it was timely and well written. Ivy sniffed and tossed her hair. I said something intended to sound humble, and then asked him about the process of getting a liquor license.

"It's not easy," he said. "The state liquor commission does all kinds of background checks. The applicant has to be squeaky clean, with hardly a traffic ticket."

"Don't the locals have any say about it?" asked Ivy.

"They certainly do," said Langlois. "The township board has to endorse the request—or it goes nowhere."

"Sounds like a story," Ivy said as she dropped her notepad into her sleek leather handbag. Together we exited the courthouse and paused under the portico, peering into a day that had turned from heavy fog into fine misty rain. "I'm having lunch at Schooners," she said, "if you want to join me."

"Sure. Sounds okay with me."

"You remember, of course, that you owe me a lunch."

Actually I didn't remember. Ivy's claim must have been based on some obscure wager that I had long since forgotten. But I didn't quibble, because I have never won an argument with Ivy and probably never will. I just told her I had to run an errand and would meet her there. When I groped my way into the dim interior of Schooners Bar, Ivy was already seated at a tall table sipping a frothy pink concoction.

"I think the barkeep starts mixing that thing the minute you walk in, " I nodded at her drink.

"I needed this," she said. "I've been so upset over Madeline that I hardly slept last night. And today I can't concentrate."

I ordered coffee and a Reuben sandwich but made no further comment about her choice of beverage. Since I had already used Madeline's death as an excuse to overindulge, I didn't feel in any position to criticize.

"We should send flowers," she said.

"Sure," I agreed. "As soon as we know when and where."

"Have you heard anything about a funeral?"

"Jake said the autopsy would hold things up a day or two. Somehow that surprised me. Don't we already know that she drowned?"

Ivy shook her head vehemently. "There is *always* an autopsy. Even I know that much." Our food arrived and we made room for it on the tiny table.

"I kind of hate to think about it," I said when the waitress had left. "The autopsy, I mean."

"Well, I'm *not* going to think about it, because I intend to enjoy this meal—which you are paying for."

I reminded her that the wager did not include her expensive drink. She laughed and ordered another one. Our conversation moved to Dirkse's retirement. "That news took me off guard," I said. "He's in my district and I never had a clue."

"I heard about it over a week ago. Sworn to secrecy of course."

"Damn, Ivy. You are always so far ahead of me."

"That's why you hang out with me." She poked at her seafood salad. "With Dirkse out, a lot of people will be sizing up their chances for that seat."

"I wonder who will run."

"I know someone who's planning on it."

"You have the biggest ears in Cedar County." The sauerkraut fell out of my sandwich. "Who is it?'

"Someone you know quite well."

"So tell me." She smiled, clearly enjoying my bafflement. I considered everyone I knew who had any political aspirations and came up blank. "I give up."

Ivy waved a celery stalk at me. "This is not for publication. It's utmost confidential."

"Okay, I promise. Scout's honor, blood oath, whatever you want."

"I'll kill you if you tell anyone. It's Paul Lavallen."

She had the pleasure of my totally mystified, how could I be out of the loop reaction. "But I just had supper with them, and Paul didn't say a word. What makes you so sure?"

"Let's just say a little bird told me."

We finished eating. I called for the check and calculated the cost of Ivy's lunch but not her drinks, and paid it along with my own bill. Somehow the total seemed higher than it should have been, but I didn't have time to negotiate. Marge was back in town and I was late for a staff meeting.

"I see you've been hanging out with Poison Ivy again," Marge said as I tried to slink past her office. *Did this woman have spies in every restaurant?*

"Don't worry," I said. "I didn't give away any state secrets." Maybe Marge's distaste for my friend stems from the fact that Ivy worked here for two years and then moved on to the larger newspaper. Maybe Marge thought she 'taught her everything she knew'. Maybe Marge would say that about me someday.

I followed my editor into the break room, wondering if the black stripes on her red tunic were supposed to have a slimming effect. If so, they failed miserably. Marge took her seat at the head of a long wooden table and laid out her glasses, calendar, day planner, notebook, pencils, and sticky notes. I sat next to Lorna Frazer, a motherly woman who had just finished wiping up something gooey from the table. Kyle Sprague, an admitted computer geek, came in and sat across from us.

"Jake's going to be late," said Marge, "so we'll start without him. Kyle, when are your games this week?"

Kyle is a skinny guy in his twenties with a habit of chewing on pencils. He claims a degree in journalism though I wonder what good it does him since he never seems to write about anything but sports. Kyle unfolded a schedule, provided the dates of upcoming track meets and asked if he could do a feature story about fly-fishing. Marge gave him the okay.

Marge turned her attention to Lorna, our part-time reporter. Lorna is pretty in an Old World sort of way, with a square face, wispy blonde hair and a little overbite. Speaking softly, Lorna said she wanted to do a story about some junior high boys who were trying to raise money to build a skate park. Probably one of the boys was hers. With four kids in school, Lorna was a natural to write about the innumerable school plays, band concerts, and fund-raisers, and we were happy to let her do it. Marge okayed the skate board story.

"Tracy, what happened at the county board meeting?"

I told her about Dirkse's impending retirement and the dog kennel complaints.

Marge indulged in a thin smile. "Think you can you handle another dog story?"

"I guess that's my current specialty."

"Better talk to the alleged kennel owner," she said. "Get the other side. How about the airplane business out at the Diamond D?"

"I called Tom Halladay. He set me up for an interview with their pilot— tomorrow morning."

"Good. Be sure to get pictures."

The last order of business was assigning the innumerable meetings – school board, village, county and township. I was delighted when Kyle drew the road commission, everybody's least favorite. When the meeting was over everybody left except me. I was filling out my weekly schedule when Jake walked in, emanating his personal aura of sweat, cigar smoke and Old Spice. He sat down across from me with a look on his face that made me think he had news. I was right.

"I just saw the coroner's report on Madeline," he said.

I laid down my pencil and gave him my full attention.

"She didn't drown after all. She died from a blow to the head."

Suddenly I felt short of breath. "She must have fallen on the rocks," I said. "She must have been walking on the pier."

"Sorry, Tracy, but it doesn't look that way."

"Why not?"

"The blow had a lot of force and was confined to a small area. As though she had been struck with a weapon—something like a hammer."

I stared at Jake, my mind reeling.

Actually, it was all simple enough. Madeline had not died in any tragic, unforeseen, bizarre accident.

Someone had killed her.

CHAPTER FIVE

"You really ought to let me take you up."

"I'm not feeling very brave today."

"Come on. You'll enjoy it."

"I don't think so."

I was at the Diamond D Ranch, standing outside a corrugated metal building called the hangar and talking with Marvin Crouch, the resident pilot. Crouch was a little shorter than me, with sloping shoulders and wispy blonde hair going gray. Horizontal lines creased his forehead and stubby whiskers sprouted from his narrow jaw. In his dark blue shirt and pants, he looked like a mechanic ready to work on somebody's car, and I wondered if he would soon be pressured to trade his work clothes for western attire.

Crouch really wanted me to go flying with him. He hauled one of the machines out into the sunshine for my inspection.

"You could take some pictures while you're up." He cast a hopeful glance at my camera.

"Thanks. But no thanks."

"It's the safest recreational vehicle in existence."

I had my doubts about that. In fact I had doubts about the whole venture. But the guy was so pathetically eager that I heard myself saying, "Okay, I'll give it a try."

His face lit up. "You won't be sorry."

As he prepared for our flight, Crouch gave me a visual tour of the craft. He started with the tiny wheel in front and moved back to larger wheels under the rear seat. He showed me two car-sized batteries, the engine, the gas tank, and finally a huge propeller in the back that was at least four feet in diameter. "This is the parachute," he said spreading a pile of fabric on the ground and struggling to untangle a maze of cords. So far I hadn't seen anything that looked like a steering mechanism.

"How do you steer this thing?"

"With my feet," he said, pointing to the forward seat footrest.

I was starting to have serious doubts about the venture but it seemed too late to back out. Crouch handed me a jacket and helmet and made sure I had them on right. Then he donned his own helmet and said, "Okay, let's go."

I climbed into the rear seat, muttering a prayer to the patron saint of fools. "Just relax and enjoy," Crouch said cheerfully as he strapped me in. He took the driver's seat, in front of mine and a good eighteen inches lower. *At least I'll have a good view when we crash.* We faced a runway that looked like a recently mowed hayfield. Crouch turned the key and the engine coughed to life. Seconds later I heard the soft whir of a propeller but I still didn't believe we were going to go airborne.

I was wrong. We rolled forward and I felt a backward tug as the parachute filled with air. Within seconds the chute was over my head and our wheels cleared the ground. We rose steadily as the propeller pushed a stream of air into the chute, which, according to my information, was now acting as a wing.

Eyes closed, I gripped the armrest. The wind carried away my body heat and I was grateful for the jacket Crouch had forced on me. This was not like one of those open cockpits in the old movies—it was more like a flying bicycle. Cautiously I opened my eyes and saw blue sky, white clouds and the top of a helmet. Overhead, I saw a great balloon of pink and green fabric. Looking down, I recognized the Diamond D lodge, Arrowhead Lake and the road between them fast disappearing into the trees.

The noise and the helmets precluded anything in the way of conversation. Crouch gestured toward the sand dunes, then we turned and headed toward them. As promised, he was steering with his feet. I slowly unclenched my fingers and willed my pulse to return to normal. What a sight. A great crescent of sand dunes stretched out below us, peaceful as a sleeping cat. On the lake side was the lighthouse, scene of my recent unforgettable discovery—on the land side, I saw the roof of a cottage, partially buried by the restless dunes.

Fumbling, I opened my camera and struggled with the focus. Was there a setting for dangling in the air? 'Infinity' seemed like a good guess. I made the adjustment and tried to get a picture of the buried cottage, which was receding as we moved toward the lake. Struggling to keep the frame of the aircraft out of the picture, I leaned out at a precarious angle. Marge owed me hazard pay for this one.

Soon we were over Lake Michigan. Below us, a trio of sailboats heeled before the wind, like small white birds in flight. The boats were soon dwarfed by a gigantic ore carrier that as it chugged northward, leaving a long V in its wake. Two sportsfishing boats were heading for the channel, their morning charters finished. My film was almost finished too, so I closed the camera and settled back to enjoy the ride.

That's when Crouch let me know it was time to head back. Well darn, I was just starting to have fun. On the return trip we floated over the channel to Arrowhead Lake, the Brown Bear Restaurant on a bluff overlooking the channel and then the Diamond D golf course. When the landing field came into view, Crouch throttled back and brought us down in a gentle three-point landing. He jumped out and gave me a hand down, wearing a grin that made him look about ten years old.

"Well, what do you think? Are you glad you went up?"

"I'm glad I went up." I stood and took off the helmet. "But I'm more glad to be back on solid ground." He looked a little crestfallen. "Hey, it was a great experience. My editor will be thrilled with the pictures."

"You could learn to fly one of these. It only takes a few hours."

"Are you kidding? I have enough trouble driving a car."

"But there's not so much traffic up there, no cops either. Want some coffee?"

I said yes, partly out of curiosity to see how he would make good on the offer since the hangar appeared to offer few amenities.

"Come on in," he said.

I followed him inside. The place was cluttered with piles of old stuff that looked like it had been pushed aside to make room for the shiny new aircraft. A workbench full of tools occupied one corner and the far wall was lined with bicycle wheels and chains that spilled over onto a tattered brown sofa. Surrounding the sofa was a morass of rags; newspapers and cardboard boxes, a broken chair and what looked like a woman's shoe. Did Crouch have a lady friend? Maybe just a shoe fetish.

Crouch took two mugs from a rusty tin cupboard and disappeared out the door. He returned with the mugs full of water and popped them into a dusty microwave. "Have a seat," he said.

He indicated two cracked vinyl chairs flanking a dusty Formica table and I sat in one. He pulled a cup from the microwave and stirred in coffee granules.

"Hope you don't want cream." He pushed the cup toward me.

"Black is fine," I said, eyeing the bowl of speckled sugar cubes. While he fixed his own coffee I located my notebook and pen. "So what can you tell me about these powered parachutes?"

Crouch sat down, stirred his coffee, and took a sip. Then he was off and running. "The powered parachute was developed by the US military in the eighties, but the things didn't catch on until ten years later when someone started selling them to the general public. They run on regular gasoline, same as a car. The tank holds ten gallons, enough to keep you up about four hours. The really nice part is, you don't need a license to fly one. Unless you want to carry passengers. These things are so new that the FAA hasn't had time to worry about them. I'm planning to get a dealer's license, so if you want to buy one, keep me in mind."

Did I look like I could afford a recreational airplane? Salesmen usually fold after one look at my car. But Crouch was clearly onto his favorite subject and ready to talk indefinitely about anything to do with aeronautics. After about ten minutes, I tried for some personal history.

"How long have you known Tom Halladay?"

"Long time."

"I understand you were in the service together."

"That's right."

"Have you been flying since then?"

He nodded. "Midwest Airlines."

I was trying to think of a way to ask him why he had abandoned Midwest Airlines to hang out at the Diamond D when a woman appeared in the doorway. Roxanne Halladay was dressed in tight jeans and a shiny black jacket bearing the Diamond D logo. She sported the same sleek helmet of platinum hair that I remembered from the chamber breakfast. But her feathers seemed a little ruffled.

"Marvin, where in blazes is Tom? He was supposed to be here an hour ago."

"Haven't seen him," said Crouch. "Maybe he went to town. He's got the truck."

"I know he's got the truck. I need that too."

Roxanne stepped inside and Crouch introduced me. "This is Tracy Quinn. She's doing a story about us for the paper."

Roxanne ignored me until she heard that I worked for a newspaper. Then she favored me with a weak handshake and said, "Hi Tracy, nice to meet you." The greeting was accompanied by a head-to-toe sweep which implied that I should rush out and get a complete make over. Either that or kill myself. She turned back to Crouch. "Tom needs to get down to the garage. We've got four couples coming in for the golf package and not one of the carts is working."

"How about if I take a look at them?" he said. "Can't be much harder than these things."

Roxanne looked relieved. "Great. And could you look at the Jacuzzi while you're at it?" Crouch glanced at me apologetically.

"No problem," I said. "I've got more than enough for a story. But I would like to finish this film. How about some shots of you standing by the para-thingy?"

Crouch reluctantly posed for me. I got a couple shots of him and then Roxanne joined him. They stood together, framed by the circular propeller guard with Roxanne smiling and leaning toward the center.

"Good shot," I said. "Thanks for everything."

On my way out, I met a red pick up truck and pulled aside to let it pass. The driver was Tom Halladay, complete with ten-gallon hat. He rolled down his window and yelled, "Hey Tracy, how was the interview?"

"Great," I yelled back. "Marvin took me for a ride."

"I knew he would. He's a nut about those things."

"Your wife is looking for you."

"Nothing new there." He flashed me a grin. "Hey, come out and play golf some time. Free pass for reporters."

"Not me, I don't know how."

"I'll give you a lesson."

"Rain check."

"Sure thing. Take care now. See you later." The red truck pulled away.

Did I want a free golf lesson from Tom Halladay? Not really. I drove back to town, thinking about the power structure at the ranch. According to Ivy, Roxanne's money was behind the whole operation, so she probably called most of the shots. Marvin Crouch seemed to have desperately needed practical skills. But Tom Halladay was the public face of the business, the one with the charm and the cowboy charisma. Apparently he had charmed his way into the whole scene—Roxanne, her money and the ranch.

Madeline's funeral was on Saturday. A lot of people said they were going, but in the end it was only three of us—Gavin, Ivy and me. It was a two-hour drive to the city and then we had trouble finding the church but no trouble finding seats. The place was barely half full and the service was mercifully short. Afterward, we met some of Madeline's family and spoke to her mother, a tall, thin woman wearing a black suit and a hat with a veil. She invited us to have refreshments in the church basement. We refused politely, pleading the long drive home. On the way back I went ahead and told Gavin and Ivy what I had learned from Jake about the results of the autopsy.

"So she didn't drown?" said Ivy.

"According to Jake, there was no water in her lungs. She was dead before she hit the water."

"I knew it was something like that," said Gavin, "but I didn't want to start any rumors."

"And how did you know?" said Ivy.

"Phil Cutter," he said. Phil was Madeline's boss at Flagstone Real Estate. "Phil came into my store yesterday and he was fuming. You know how he gets red in the face? Well, he looked like an overripe tomato."

"What made him so mad?" asked Ivy.

"A detective came into Phil's office during business hours. The visit got his whole staff upset."

"What did the guy do?" said Ivy.

"Phil said he went through everything in Madeline's desk. And when he left, he took about half of it with him—address book, calendar, files, correspondence."

"The guy sounds obnoxious," I said.

"Phil said he really wanted to throw him out. Apparently having a cop in the office is not conducive to business."

"You may find out," said Ivy. "You're probably next on his list."

"We're probably all on his list," said Gavin.

Back in town, we convened at my place where we wiped out a pizza and seriously damaged a gallon of ice cream. Afterward we sat in the kitchen, drinking coffee and comparing our impressions of the afternoon.

"Madeline's mother looks a lot like her," I said. "Older version, of course. Was that man the father or stepfather?"

"I'd say stepfather," said Ivy. "She told me her dad died when she was about ten."

"I thought Madeline had a sister," said Gavin. "Where was she?"

I pictured the family members we had met. "There was a brother, his wife and three kids. No one who looked like a sister."

"Gavin's right," said Ivy. "She told me about the sister. Younger, I think. Her name was Louise, and she stood up at Madeline's wedding."

"Madeline was married?"

"Not for long I guess."

"Was the ex there, do you think?"

"Maybe he was that guy in back, the one with the pony tail."

"If so, her taste has changed."

We pieced together the bits of information each of us held about Madeline's life. The picture we managed to create had a lot of missing pieces because there was so much about her that none of us knew. But we skirted the one question that none of us was ready to deal with—the question of who might have killed her.

Gavin stood to leave. "I have to go. I'm opening up shop tomorrow."

"You'll be at the party, won't you?" said Ivy.

"Sure. Just as soon as I close up."

"I'm ready for a party," she said. "I need some diversion after today."

Gavin's expression grew serious. "This news about Madeline—the autopsy, the detective. We're the only ones who know this, aren't we?"

"Probably," said Ivy. "It won't be in the *Chronicle* until Monday—or even Tuesday, with the holiday."

"Jake knows," I said, "but he doesn't talk. My paper won't be out until Wednesday."

"I've been thinking," he said. "I'd rather not deal with this at the party."

"Oh, me neither," said Ivy. "Everyone would start pumping us for information."

"Then why don't we keep it to ourselves," I said.

"Let's make a pact," said Ivy.

"Okay," said Gavin. And the three of us made a deal.

"The carrot sticks are ready," I said. "Shall I stuff the celery?"

"That's all done," Jewell said. "I think we're about finished. Derek is setting up chairs on the deck."

It was Sunday afternoon and I was feeling relaxed, happy to be in the middle of a three-day weekend. There had been no word from Brooke or her mother so I figured the idea of coming to Shagoni River had been displaced by some other scheme. The sun was shining, the temperature was inching toward seventy degrees, and the Lavallens' party was getting under way.

"Hey Tracy, you wanna cruise?" Derek Lavallen stood in the doorway, a lanky kid in baggy jeans and a black tee shirt. His hair was short at the sides with the middle pulled back into a ponytail. "Dad says they've got room for one more."

"Go ahead," said Jewell. "You've worked hard enough."

I got my jacket and followed Derek down to the dock where *Jewell of the Sea* was waiting. The boat was about thirty feet long, with a small cabin up front and a green MSU flag hanging at the stern. The U shaped seating area in the back had two couples already in it. When I got in, the boat shifted under my weight and I sort of fell into the remaining spot. I'll never be a sailor.

Derek untied a rope from the dock piling and tossed it in. Paul shifted into reverse and we chugged away. Arrowhead Lake is lined with summer homes and it looked like every house, cabin or cottage had people spilling down into the water. We passed a catamaran with its sail going up, a young couple racing their kayaks and some plucky kids diving from a raft. Paul took us close to town for a peek at the holiday action in Shagoni River. Young sailors at the yacht club were lining up their Sunfishes for a race, accompanied by band music that drifted down from the village green.

Paul clearly enjoyed his role as captain, pointing out landmarks like the village water tower and Old Sawmill Point. At the west end of the lake, traffic grew heavy and we were surrounded by a variety of watercraft all maneuvering to enter the channel. Two guys on jet skis nearly collided in front of us and a speedboat careened so close that it splashed us with its spray.

"That's far enough," Paul said as he turned the boat around. "Too many crazies on the water." He took us back along the south shore where the view was high cliffs, cedar trees and not so many houses. As we approached Lavallens' house, the sound of voices and laughter came drifting out to us. Derek appeared on the dock, caught the lines and gave each of us a hand as we stepped ashore. I stood for a moment, trying to decide if the earth was moving. It wasn't.

"Guess I'd better get to work," Paul said with a glance toward the house. About a dozen people had arrived during our absence, most of the women in white slacks and the men in khaki pants. Ivy came walking down the steps toward us, cutting a colorful figure in her red halter-top and Capri pants.

"Guess I'm too late for a ride," she said to Paul as they passed.

"Sorry about that," he said. "Maybe next time."

Ivy and I made appropriate female bonding gestures. She surveyed my blue jeans and plaid shirt with a sad expression. "You really ought to let me take you shopping sometime."

I groaned. Ivy didn't understand that the mall experience was sheer torture for me, while it probably ranked close to chocolate and sex for her. The joy of shopping had somehow eluded me. Perhaps it was a missing gene.

"Maybe sometime. I'm short of cash right now."

"No excuse, you should get a credit card."

"I'll think about it."

"You're hopeless," she said with a sigh. Then she brightened. "Let's go find something to drink."

In a shaded corner of the yard we found a tub full of iced drinks and extracted a pair of wine coolers. The drinks were opened for us by a silver-haired man wearing a blue striped shirt and yellow bow tie. The man was Les Tattersal, the lawyer who had handled my grandfather's estate.

"Tracy," he said. How are you coming on those shutters?"

"I'm embarrassed to tell you, Les. I've only painted two of them."

"It's nothing to feel guilty about." Les had helped me take down shutters the previous fall and now spring had arrived with negligible progress. But I knew that Les probably didn't care about the shutters; he just liked to have a reason to visit the house where his old friend had lived. "Let me know if you need any help starting that lawnmower."

"I will, and thanks."

"Too bad about your friend Madeline. What a terrible accident."

I accepted his condolences and changed the subject. "Guess I'd better give Jewell a hand," I said. I gave Les a hug and headed for the house.

The deck was awash with cooking smells. Paul was presiding over two grills, one sizzling with salmon filets and the other oozing with hamburger patties. I carried condiments and dishes out from the kitchen while Jewell arranged plates, silver and hot dishes on the table. Then Paul gave the word and guests began to fill their plates.

After a few minutes I joined the line and came away with grilled salmon, bean salad, creamed asparagus, scalloped potatoes, cole slaw, and corn bread. I looked around for a seat and saw Ivy claim the last empty chair. For a moment I thought I was condemned to eat standing up. Then I spotted Derek Lavallen sprawled on the steps and using the deck as a table, so I joined him, grateful that I wasn't hampered by white pants. We talked about college life, finding a summer job.

"Was it rough moving here?" I said. "You must have been right in the middle of high school. I know what that's like."

"It was definitely the pits. But there was one big advantage. Smaller school, I got to play basketball instead of sitting on the bench. It made all the difference." He looked up. "Uh oh, what's Dad up to?"

Paul Lavallen was banging on a glass with his fork. The din of conversation slowly subsided. "Sorry to interrupt the merriment," he said, "but I have an announcement to make." Jewell appeared next to him and he put an arm around her. "After conferring with my wife, I've decided to become a candidate for district two county commissioner. Naturally I'd appreciate your support."

The party buzzed back to life with comments like, "Right on" and "It's time for some new blood."

"So your little bird was right," I said to Ivy when we met at the dessert table.

"Apparently the rumors were true," she replied with a secretive smile. "Oh look who's here." She turned to wave at Gavin who was walking across the lawn bearing a large white bakery box.

Jewell gave him a good-natured scolding. "Gavin, you didn't need to bring anything. We know you were working all day."

Gavin set his box on the table with a flourish. "No party is complete," he said, "without a chocolate cheesecake." He reached across the table to shake Paul's hand. "Just heard the news. I'll do what I can to help."

"Thanks," said Paul. "I'm not sure how much campaign I'll run. Depends on the competition."

Paul sliced and served the cheesecake. It was fantastic, probably a thousand calories per bite. People drifted in and out. A couple of Derek's friends showed up and ate enormous quantities of food, then all three of them left together. It was getting dark and only a handful of people was left when I told Paul and Jewell goodnight. Then my stupid car wouldn't start —wouldn't even turn over. Gavin offered me a ride and I gratefully accepted.

We were coming up on the Roadside Inn when Gavin said, "Want to stop?"

"Might as well, no work tomorrow."

A denim clad couple at the bar and two guys shooting pool were the only other customers. We sat in a booth. I ordered a beer, Gavin a screwdriver.

"That detective showed up at my store this morning," he said, keeping his voice low.

"So Ivy was right – about you being next. Did he scare any customers away?"

"He didn't stay that long. Just wanted the keys to Madeline's apartment so he could go in and search."

"That is such a violation of her privacy," I said with a shudder. I pictured a coarse looking guy rummaging through Madeline's undies, fingering her bras and teddies while he searched for clues.

"I guess when you're murdered, you give up your privacy."

Murder. Not a nice word but someone had finally said it. "What would he be looking for?"

"Phone bills, letters, bank records. Anything to give him an idea what was going on in her life. Remember, Phil said he did the same thing at the office."

"Did he ask you a lot of questions?"

"Just a few, said he'd catch me another time when I wasn't working."

We finished our drinks and stepped outside. The sky was clear except for a ring around the moon. We thought maybe we saw some northern lights but after all the alcohol and neon, it was hard to tell for sure. When we reached my house I was surprised to see light spilling from the living room windows, making yellow rectangles on the lawn.

"Look at that," I said.

"Did you leave your lights on?"

"No way. It was broad daylight when I left."

"Did you lock the house?"

"I told you, I don't even have a key. All I have is deadbolts."

"My god, Tracy."

"Gramps never locked the house. This is such a low crime area."

"Not any more, it isn't."

"Oh, you're right."

"How about I come in with you?"

"Good idea."

With Gavin behind me, I opened the front door. The television was on and a figure was sprawled on the couch, apparently asleep. As we entered the living room, the intruder stirred and looked up.

"Oh hi, Tracy, don't shoot. It's just me."

I struggled with disbelief as the identity of the young woman on my couch became clear. I tried to speak, choked. When I finally got some words out, my voice sounded like it belonged to someone else.

"Gavin," I said, "I'd like you to meet Brooke. She's—ah, she's a friend of mine."

CHAPTER SIX

I awakened to a strange smell and wondered for a minute if the house was on fire. Then I recognized the odor of fresh coffee, which seemed equally out of place until I remembered that I had a house guest. A house guest who had apparently mastered my filter drip coffee method. Brooke and I had stayed up talking until after two in the morning. First she explained that she had been *meaning* to call her mother but, with studying for exams and all, had never made contact. Then she discovered someone on campus that was driving to Traverse City and had room for a passenger.

"I just had to do it," she said. "It was like this was meant to be. They brought me right to your door."

So they had. And so I had found her on my couch. And according to her nineteen-year-old logic, this was all *meant to be?* For the entire summer? I felt like I had been blindsided. But she was so happy to see me and so thrilled to be in Shagoni River that I couldn't bring myself to dampen her spirits. I told her she would have to call her mother in the morning and we'd figure things out from there.

After that we made hot cocoa and fell into a dormitory-like gabfest. For Brooke, the intervening years had been a series of milestones. She told me about her first crush, her disastrous driving test, prom night follies and coping with college. Her description of the yellow dress she had to wear for her mother's wedding sent us both into paroxysms of laughter.

Then it was my turn, though I didn't have any major rites of passage to report. I recounted my grandfather's death, my latest career change and the travails of home ownership. My only exciting news had a gruesome twist. I told her about the dune ride that ended with my discovery of Madeline's body on the beach but the news did nothing to dampen her enthusiasm for spending the summer with me. Brooke responded to the revelation as though it were something on television. When we both started yawning, I ushered her upstairs to my old bedroom, the one with daisy wallpaper and ruffled yellow curtains.

It felt strange to have another person in the house. I climbed out of bed and made my way to the kitchen where I found Brooke sitting at the table with a cup of coffee. Even in her morning disarray, it was clear that the kid with braces had become a beautiful young woman. Startling green eyes looked out at me from an oval face brushed with freckles across the cheekbones. Long auburn hair tumbled over her shoulders.

"Morning, Tracy." She stood and gave me a hug, proving that she was nearly as tall as I was. "I sort of need a shower," she said, "but I didn't want to wake you up."

I reminded her of the promise to call her mother. She heaved a sigh and went to the living room to make the call. It was a dial phone, probably the first one she had ever seen, but she must have gotten through because I heard her talking with someone. A few minutes later she called me in and handed over the receiver.

"I can't understand why she doesn't want to come home," Jocelyn said after we had dispensed with the niceties, "but she seems to have ideas of her own. How do you feel about this, Tracy? I think she sort of dumped it on you."

It was true that her daughter had ambushed me, but when Jocelyn said it, I became suddenly protective. I told her that Brooke's arrival had not been a total surprise because we had discussed it beforehand (well, sort of), but I did want Jocelyn's approval.

"If she stays," said Jocelyn, "she'll have to get a job and help you with money. I don't want her freeloading."

I laughed. "Freeloading is not an option. I'm too broke to support a dependent."

"Do you think she can find work there?"

"Summer jobs are popping up like asparagus in May. If she's not particular she'll find some kind of work."

Jocelyn agreed that we would all give the situation a trial and insisted that I call her if we had problems of any kind. She sounded sincere. Brooke came out of the bathroom with a towel on her head and I reported my conversation with her mother.

"Does this mean I get to stay?"

"Trial period," I said, trying to inject a note of caution.

"Don't worry. It'll all work out, you'll see." She did a little dance. "I love to cook, and I'll find a job. I'll clean my room. I'm good at cutting hair. I'll even —."

"Take it easy. You don't have to scrub floors. Just try not to leave me with dirty dishes. I get very testy about that. As for your room, that's your business."

"Cool. Thanks, Tracy." She sat down and started drying her hair.

"Are you hungry? Do you want some pancakes?"

"I'm starved." She looked out from under the towel. "And I still remember your pancakes. They were wonderful."

This was unexpected news since her father had never thought much of my cooking skills. I went into the kitchen and produced a fair sized stack of pancakes while Brooke finished drying her hair. When we sat down to eat, I mentioned my conversation with her mother. "She seems hurt that you don't want to come home."

"It shouldn't come as a surprise. She knows I can't stand Walter."

"What *is* it about him?" I poured maple syrup, passed it to Brooke.

"He's a creep. A whole year with him was way too long. I couldn't wait to get away."

I felt like I needed Jewell's advice on how to phrase my next question. Lacking it, I blundered on. "Did he get funny with you—I mean, physically?"

"Oh nothing as dramatic as that." She cut into her pancake. "Walter just happens to be an overbearing asshole, excuse my language. He has an opinion on every subject in the world that lasts a full half-hour. He talks all the time. He tells me what to wear, what to read, what to think. Mom says he's just trying to communicate, but I feel suffocated. She thinks all that bullshit is brilliance. Go figure."

I wasn't sure how to respond to this barrage. "Your mother waited a long time to remarry. Maybe she needed someone who could, ah, give her direction."

"She needs him, she can have him." Brooke punctuated her remark with a fierce jab of her fork. "But I had to get out. So thanks for rescuing me." Then she moved on to the subject I had managed to avoid so far—her father. "What happened with you guys anyway? I cried a lot when Dad told me I wasn't going to see you any more."

"I don't know what to tell you Brooke, because I never understood either." I went to the refrigerator and pulled out a carton of orange juice. "Ending the marriage was never my idea. He gave me a hundred reasons why and none of them made any sense. As far as I can see, he just fell out of love with me."

"Do you think it was that airline stewardess?"

"Connie? No, he didn't meet her until after the divorce. I know, because I introduced them."

"Well, he didn't marry the stewardess, after all. He married a woman named Holly who groomed dogs. Then he moved to Atlanta 'cause that's where she had her business. Can you believe it?"

"I heard about the dog groomer and thought it was pretty ironic. Last I knew he hated dogs."

"She even kind of looked like a poodle." Brooke giggled, using her fingers to mimic a head of tightly curled hair.

I laughed too. She made Steve and his follies sound like a comic strip. I found two green tumblers, filled them with orange juice and passed one to Brooke. "Great color," she said, holding the glass up to the light. "Green-orange, grunge. Did you know that's where the word grunge came from?" More giggling.

It was refreshing to laugh, especially to laugh about Steve. But I felt he deserved some credit for trying to be a father. "Your dad always kept in touch with you, didn't he?"

"Pretty much—except when Holly left him. That was divorce number three and I guess it made him pretty depressed."

"So somebody dumped Mr. Perfect." The orange juice was tangy after the sweetness of the syrup.

"Dad sort of fell apart that year and he lost his job. I didn't hear from him for a while. Then he ran into a friend who was starting a radio station in Miami, so he moved down there and became an announcer."

"Steve always comes up with something, doesn't he?"

"Sure does. I went to see him over Christmas but I didn't like Miami and I didn't like his dinky little apartment. He's got another girlfriend now, that he says he's going to marry. If he does, she'll be number four." She took a swig of juice, wiped her mouth with the back of her hand. "What about you, Tracy? Do you think you'll ever get married again?"

I thought for a few seconds before answering. "I'm not opposed to the idea," I said at last. "But it doesn't seem to be happening. After the divorce I dated a few guys, but none of them really aroused my interest."

"No one who turned your crank, huh?"

"Guess that's one way of putting it."

"Are you bitter, do you think, about men?"

I poured myself another cup of coffee while I considered my answer. "Sometimes I think men are from another planet, but no, I don't think I'm bitter. The main problem right now is, I'm living out in the boondocks. And any guy in Cedar County who's single, believe me, there's a really good reason for it." I split the last pancake and took half of it. "Maybe it's me, Brooke, maybe I'm not feminine enough for today's market—or maybe I never really got over Steve." I stopped, suddenly embarrassed. Here I was, a month short of my forty-fifth birthday, baring my soul to a nineteen year-old-kid.

Brooke didn't seem to notice my discomfort. "Well, I think you're way cool, and Dad was a fool to leave you. I never liked any of his other women as well as you."

"Come on. You're just buttering me up."

"I mean it. Dad knows how I feel."

"Okay. I'll put that on my next job application—'*ex-husband's daughter says I'm the best.*'"

She laughed and forked the remaining pancake from the platter. "You cooked," she said, "so I'll do the dishes." As soon as we finished eating, Brooke followed through—she cleared the table and filled the dishpan with sudsy water. I explained about the cantankerous drain and told her to leave the dishwater for me to carry out to the flowerbed. "When I'm done," she said, "I think I'll walk down town and look for 'help wanted' signs. Maybe go to the beach. Want to come along?"

"Thanks, but I've got stuff I need to do in the house."

"I'll stay and help if you want."

"How about you just take your things upstairs?" I nodded toward the living room where her army-sized duffel bag had its contents disgorged on the floor.

"Sure, no problem." She finished the dishes, took her stuff upstairs and was out the door with a cheerful goodbye. The phone rang and it was Jewell, calling to tell me that I had left my salad bowl at her house.

"I had a major shock when I got home," I told her. "Brooke was here, practically moved in already."

"You mean she just showed up?"

"Found her on the couch."

"Were you ready for this?"

"Not a bit. Just ask Gavin—he'll tell you that I nearly fainted. But then we talked for a couple hours and now she feels like an old friend, more adult than kid."

"But she's still a kid. Believe me, Tracy, you'll have to set some limits for her."

"Limits?" I wasn't quite sure what Jewell was talking about. "Well, she's looking for a job so she can help with money—and she washed dishes without being told. So I guess we'll take it one day at a time." Then I remembered my car. "Jewell, I totally forgot, I have to deal with that useless vehicle I left at your place last night."

She laughed. "That's another reason I called. Gavin's coming out to talk with Paul. He said he'd stop by to pick you up."

Gavin picked me up ten minutes later. We arrived at Lavallens' and found my Honda sitting there as though nothing had gone wrong between us. I mumbled an incantation and slid behind the wheel. When it started on the first try, I almost cried with relief.

"Starters get unpredictable when they get old," Gavin said. "You'd better get your car into Sam's and have him check it out."

I told him I would, very soon, but we both knew that I'd procrastinate. Just then Jewell came out of the house. Gavin asked her how she felt about Paul's political ambitions.

"Okay so far." She smiled ruefully. "Running for county commissioner is a pretty low key situation. But the fact is, Paul sees it as a first step toward the state house."

"A state representative?" Gavin looked surprised.

Jewell nodded slowly.

"Are you ready to be a politician's wife?" I said.

"I think I can handle it," she said with a laugh. "I've been called worse."

"I suppose working with schizophrenics prepares you for just about anything," said Gavin.

"Right," said Jewell. "Even politics."

I arrived home determined to complete at least one major task before my three day weekend had slipped away. The chore I had in mind was a dirty one so I changed into a pair of ragged cut-offs and appropriated one of grandpa's long tailed shirts that hung almost to my knees. An accidental glance in the mirror told me that the shirt covered the cut-offs, making me look half dressed. But I wasn't trying for a fashion statement. I was dressed for a rite of spring—cleaning ashes out of the pot-bellied stove in the living room.

The job proved harder than it looked and my every pass with the long-handled shovel left a trail of ash on the carpet. I was working on the second bucketful and in no mood for company when I heard a knock on the front door. I ducked my head and kept working. But the knocking persisted and got louder.

Mumbling curses, I got off my knees and went to the front door. Through the frosted glass could I saw a man standing on my porch, and judging by what I could see, it was a large man. Curious, I swung open the door and stood face to face with a tall guy who had the broad shoulders and chest that made me think of Paul Bunyan. The plaid flannel shirt was worn and it strained a little across his belly. His jeans were faded and his hiking boots scuffed. I figured he was looking for directions.

"Can I help you?"

"I'm looking for Tracy Quinn." The voice was deep and sounded like gravel.

"Guess that's me."

"I'm Frank Kolowsky, detective with the Cedar County Sheriff's Department." He pulled a flattened wallet from his pocket and opened it to display an official looking card with a badge. I squinted at the card, then at him, wondering if he was for real. For all I knew the card could have come from a Cracker Jack box. "I'm looking into the death of Madeline Maxwell," he said, "and I'd like to ask you a few questions. If this is a good time."

It was not a good time. What with Brooke's arrival and Jewell's party and Madeline's funeral, I'd had my fill of talking to strangers – and I certainly wasn't dressed for company. But sending him away didn't feel like an option, so I invited him inside and led him straight to the kitchen, avoiding the ash-strewn living room. I offered him coffee, then wondered if this was acceptable protocol for being questioned by a detective. Was I acting guilty? Was I overcompensating? For what, for heaven's sake?

"Coffee would be great," he said, with a smile that revealed a gap between his two front teeth. While I put the coffee on to heat he just stood there, looking at me. Suddenly conscious of my weird get-up, I started to tie my shirttails together. But that maneuver was abandoned when I realized it would only reveal more of my legs. My winter-pale legs.

I fumbled in the cupboard for cups and said, "Have a seat."

"Thanks." He grabbed a chair and straddled it, leaning his elbows on the table. I poured the coffee and sat down, happy to hide my legs under the table.

"Want milk or anything?"

"Black is fine." Frank Kolowsky had an interesting face. Square jaw, just beginning to go soft at the jowls—a curved scar intersected the left eyebrow and the nose seemed a little out of line. His hair was salt and pepper, heavy on the salt. I pictured him going through Madeline's lingerie drawer, looking for clues.

He took a tiny notebook out of his shirt pocket. "You're the one who found the body?"

"That's right. Me and Mickey—the dune driver."

"So you're the reporter?" I nodded. "This conversation is not for publication, okay?"

"No problem. Jake does all the police stories, anyway."

"Fine." He started jotting in the notebook. "How long had you known the deceased, uh, Madeline?"

"We met last summer, shortly after I moved into town. She showed up at my door one day, wanting to list the house. You know she was in real estate." He nodded. "Well, she didn't get the listing but we became friends, both fairly new in town, both unattached. She used to come by and give me advice on fixing up the house."

"It's a nice old place."

"Thanks," I said. "My grandparents lived here. Anyhow, I never took Maddie's advice on the house because it always involved spending money, but that didn't seem to bother her. She liked her work. As soon as she met anyone, she told them what she did for a living." I stopped. "Is this the kind of information you're looking for?"

"Sure, I need to find out all I can about her. Did she ever say why she moved here?"

"She gave different reasons at different times. Either it was because Cedar County real estate was going through the roof, or she had been here on vacation with her family—and maybe there was a love gone wrong in Lansing. That's where she lived before she moved here."

"Did she ever say who the guy was—the one in Lansing?"

I shook my head. "She never mentioned a name. Just dropped hints of a bad break up. I guess she was married once, but I don't know anything about him either. There didn't seem to be any ex-husband at the funeral." I told him about the service, the family members we had met, the missing sister. It was fun to see someone else taking notes. His handwriting looked worse than mine.

He took a wooden toothpick out of his pocket and stuck it in his mouth. "Can you tell me about anyone she was involved with while she lived here?"

"You mean romantically?" He nodded. "There was no one she dated, in the sense of appearing with him at social functions." I hesitated. "There were some one night stands, usually tourists. And she said the real estate conventions were pretty wild."

"I've heard that too." He almost smiled.

I felt like we had stepped over a line, and I didn't want to talk any more about Madeline's sex life. But, as Gavin had said, when you're murdered you lose your privacy. "Do you think it was a—boyfriend—who killed her?"

"Let's put it this way." He put down the notebook. "We don't have a lot of violent crime in these parts—and when it does happen, it's almost never random. So, yes, we're looking for someone who knew her. When was the last time you saw her?"

"That Friday night. We played pool at the Belly Up, that bar in town."

"Did she mention her plans for Saturday?" He rolled the toothpick and started chewing on it.

"Nope. We both left about eleven. We talked about getting together for lunch during the week."

He picked up the notebook again. "Did she know anyone who owned a boat?"

"Of course she did. Half the people in town own some kind of water-craft."

"Lake Michigan boats?"

I could see where he was heading with this. Discounting the walk on the pier, Madeline had to get offshore in order for her body to wash up on the Lake Michigan beach. "She went sailing a few times with someone from Muskegon. But that was last summer."

"Nothing recent?"

"No. It's been too cold for the sailing crowd."

"I saw activity at the marina today."

"Charter fishing boats," I said. "They start early." He raised an eyebrow, the one with the scar, so I went on. "Two of the captains, Harley and Skip, are regulars at the Belly Up. Maddie and I used to play darts with them last winter, but it couldn't have been either of them —." My voice trailed off as I realized he didn't want my opinions, he just wanted the facts. His next question took a different tack.

"Did you ever see her with anyone who rode a motorcycle?"

"Definitely not her style, why?"

"That weekend was the motorcycle rally. How many bikers in town?"

"Five thousand, according to the article I wrote." The light dawned. "Oh, that sure muddies the water doesn't it?"

"Doesn't help, that's for sure. If someone wanted to blend into a crowd, there was a big crowd to blend into." He moved on. "Did she ever seem afraid of anyone, or nervous about anything?"

I thought hard. He didn't rush me. Talking to a detective wasn't as scary as I had expected. At least not this one. "I don't know if this is important," I said at last, "but there was one time at the Belly Up, when Maddie and I were playing pool, and this guy in a sport coat came in. I remember because we commented on his looks."

66

"Girls do that?"

"Women do that. It's called equal opportunity."

"Sorry. Go on."

"Okay, so we saw this guy sit down at the bar. A few minutes later, Madeline disappeared into the bathroom and didn't come out. Finally I went in to check on her. She said she had to leave. So I brought her coat, and she hightailed it out the back door. When I asked about it later, she told me her period had started and she felt lousy. But I got the feeling she was avoiding that guy."

"What did he look like?"

"In his forties, I'd say. Medium height. Pretty well dressed, that's why we noticed him. Sport jacket, dress pants."

"What about hair?"

"Hair?" I struggled to remember. "Well he wasn't bald—and it wasn't noticeably long. If it had been blonde or curly, we would have noticed. So just hair, medium length, medium color."

"Clean shaven?"

"No beard. I think he had sideburns. I don't remember a mustache."

"Anything else? Glasses?"

"Sorry. Can't remember."

"That's okay. When did this happen?"

"Probably around the end of March. I don't think I've seen the guy since."

He asked me where I was the night Madeline disappeared and I told him I was covering the United Way Dinner. After a few more questions he stood, still chewing the toothpick, and thanked me for my help. He handed me a business card and told me to call him if I remembered anything else that might be helpful. I walked with him out to the porch and decided to turn the tables.

"Can I ask *you* a question, now?"

"I guess so." He tossed the chewed up toothpick over the railing.

"Why are you working on Memorial Day?"

A smile pulled up one side of his mouth. "Two reasons. One, I don't want the trail to get cold, as they say." He pulled another toothpick from his pocket and started chewing on it.

"And number two?"

"Maybe I just need something to do. Thanks for your time, Ms.Quinn."

I had just finished cleaning the stove when Brooke came home and volunteered to cook spaghetti for supper. So I got to relax in the shower while she banged around the kitchen and filled the house with appetizing odors. We were still eating supper when a series of rumbles and rattles announced the arrival of a strange vehicle. Through the window I glimpsed a rusty pick-up truck. I was mystified but Brooke seemed to know what was happening.

"Oh Tracy," she said, "I hope you don't mind me leaving you with the dishes. I met this guy at the beach and he said he'd come by and take me for a ride." She smiled briefly, got up and disappeared into the bathroom.

Stunned by this development, I sat and stared at my spaghetti. I was barely adjusting to the presence of a house guest, and now I had to deal with a boyfriend? Jocelyn and I had not discussed boyfriends. What was expected of me? Was I supposed to screen her daughter's male friends? Set a curfew? Ask for references? Brooke was still in the bathroom and I was still contemplating my plate when the screen door rattled under a vigorous knock.

"Come on in," I yelled. "Brooke's in the bathroom."

The driver of the disreputable truck opened the front door, came down the hall and stood in the kitchen doorway. He was tall and gangly, with wrists hanging out of his MSU sweatshirt and knees poking through holes in his jeans.

"Yo Tracy," he said, flashing a familiar grin. "How's it going?"

"Brooke didn't tell me it was you," I croaked. Relief mingled with surprise as I recognized the caller.

"We wanted to surprise you."

It was Derek Lavallen.

CHAPTER SEVEN

"Sheriff Says She Didn't Drown!" was the headline on Tuesday's *Manistee Chronicle*. On Wednesday the *Shagoni River News* said the death of Madeline Maxwell had been ruled "suspicious" and was under investigation. Both papers used the term "possible homicide." Both stories concluded with a request for anyone with information to contact the Cedar County Sheriff's Department.

I was in Stanwood to cover a visit from state representative Kevin Collier and even there the buzz was all about Madeline. Leaving the courthouse, I overheard two men discussing the situation as they lounged against the civil war monument. One of them, dressed in head to toe camouflage, said he knew for a fact that all real estate people were involved with the Chicago Mafia. The other, with a ponytail hanging out of his baseball cap, said she died because she knew too much about drug smuggling from Canada. I shook my head and kept walking.

"How was the meeting with the Collier?" Jake said as I walked in the newsroom.

"Pretty good turn out. About a dozen guys in overalls and some women I wouldn't care to tangle with. The farmers complained about tree huggers in Lansing who make so many laws they can't farm their own land. Collier promised he would pursue everything to the full extent of his abilities —."

"——as their elected representative in Lansing."

"Exact words. You've covered him before?"

"Him—the others, they all sound the same."

"Jake, you've been doing this too long." I dropped my stuff on my desk. "Everybody's talking about Madeline. Is there any real news?"

Jake motioned toward his office. I followed him in and he closed the door behind us. "Couple things," he said taking a seat behind his desk. "But don't let this get out."

I nodded. "I saw Dupree this morning. He said the time of death had to be Saturday night or early Sunday, near as they can make it. Car keys, one set was in her apartment and the other in her car."

"I don't get that. Madeline never left keys in her car."

"Maybe she wasn't the last one to drive it. No fingerprints, anywhere. And the general talk over there—no one thinks it was random. Whoever did it must have known her."

"What about her Sunfish?"

"Her little sailboat is still in winter storage. And, oh yeah, her purse hasn't showed up. It wasn't in the apartment or the car."

"It's probably in the lake," I said. "Damn. It's creepy to think the guy is still out there."

"Guy or girl, Tracy. Aren't you one of those equal opportunity folks?"

"Isn't it a little late for you to start being a feminist?"

Jake managed a faint smile. He dismissed me and headed for Kyle's desk where he probably interrupted a game of computer solitaire. I moved into my corner and scanned the paper. My short piece about Paul's bid for county commissioner had made the bottom of page three. In 'Letters to the Editor' we heard from two writers who were not a bit happy with the Diamond D's powered parachute operation. One was a dairy farmer who said the noise was affecting his cows' milk production. The other was a woman with a swimming pool who said the low flying aircraft invaded her privacy. Didn't she wear a bathing suit? I dumped the newspaper on the floor and switched on my computer, determined to write up the Collier story before lunch.

An hour later my stomach was growling. I thought about visiting the Blue Bird Tea Room to see how Brooke was doing at her new job, but ditched that idea. My unannounced presence could only add to the stress of her first day at work. Besides, I had a tuna sandwich in the refrigerator. I ate lunch in the break room and worked until about four-thirty. Then I sneaked out.

Flagstone Real Estate, Madeline's erstwhile employer, usually closed about five. My plan was to catch Phil Cutter and see how he was coping with the latest round of publicity about his deceased employee. Walking down Hancock, I paused to admire the tubs of pink and white petunias that had blossomed overnight and was almost struck down by a kid on a skateboard. Fortunately, the real estate office was open. I stepped inside and was greeted by a white-haired lady named Irma Babcock.

Irma had worked at Flagstone real Estate so long that she had become an institution. Her hair is always backcombed into a silver halo and today she wore an immaculate powder blue suit. When she turned in her swivel chair, Irma revealed shapely legs in pale blue nylons and smart looking navy blue pumps. I would love to be as neat and well dressed as Irma when I reach her age. Actually I would love to be as neat and well dressed as Irma right now.

"Hello Tracy. It's good to see you."

"Irma, you're looking well. Is Phil around?"

"I'm just waiting for him to come in before I close up. Why don't you sit down and keep me company—if you've got the time."

"All the time in the world." I took a seat beside her.

"Maybe I'm silly," she said, "but I don't feel good being here alone, after the latest news about Madeline. Isn't it terrible? I just hate to think about it."

If everybody hated to think about it, why did they keep bringing it up? Still I couldn't fault Irma for doing it, she had worked with Madeline for over two years. It was the idle speculation from strangers that was beginning to annoy me.

"I'm happy to keep you company. This is such a wonderful old building."

Irma put away her work and gave me a quick history lesson about her workplace, a Victorian mansion built by Chesterton Mears, the logging baron who founded Shagoni River. The house had been scheduled for demolition sometime in the seventies when Seth Flagstone bought it to renovate as a real estate office. Irma pointed out the original wainscoting and elaborate woodwork. A large plate glass window faced the street, but all of the remaining windows were tall and narrow, draped with valences and lace curtains. Through a doorway, I could see the old kitchen that now served as a lunchroom with a planter of bright red geraniums filling the large bay window.

Irma opened a drawer and pulled out some yarn and a pair of long needles. "Do you suppose you could do me a favor?" she said as she began to make those rapid, esoteric motions associated with knitting.

"I will if I can."

"It's about your friend Mr. Macleod. Tell him I'm ready to sell that bureau and vanity that he looked at. There's even an old commode if he wants it."

"I'll tell him. But are you sure you want to —?"

"Sell that stuff? Sure I'm sure. There's no reason to keep it any longer." Her needles clicked. "My daughter and family are coming to visit this summer so I'm redecorating the guest room—getting rid of all that old stuff. It's a good idea, don't you think?"

I squirmed. What did I know about decorating? "It seems like a good idea," I said, "and Gavin will be thrilled to get your stuff."

"I know he'll give me a fair price. He's very trustworthy." She gave me a coy smile. "You and Gavin make such a nice looking couple. I just think you might be the one to —-. Oh goody, here's Phil."

Phil's arrival spared me from further speculation about my future with Gavin. Irma conferred briefly with her boss, then gathered up her things and slipped out the door, favoring us with the wave of a blue veined hand.

"Getting hot out there," said Phil. He dumped his briefcase on his desk, pulled out a handkerchief and mopped his brow. At five foot seven and two hundred pounds, Phil is not the fattest person I have ever known, but he does top the charts for flabbiness. His cheeks are soft, his neck hangs over his collar and his chin disappears into his jowls.

"Town's buzzing about Madeline," he said, "and we're right in the middle of it." He loosened his tie. "That friggin' detective was here again yesterday. I'm doing my best to cooperate, but the guy is getting on my nerves. Let's go in the back." Phil locked the front door and we moved into the kitchen. He opened the refrigerator, pulled out two diet sodas and handed one to me.

"I'm getting my craw full of that Kolowsky character." Phil settled his bulk on a plastic chair. "He was here again yesterday."

"Guess he's making the rounds. He caught me at home on Monday—but it wasn't too bad. What's he bugging you about?"

"Almost everything." Phil let out a sigh that turned into a burp. "He wanted us to locate a guy from Muskegon named Burt Plaxton. Madeline's calendar showed an appointment with Plaxton on the nineteenth to look at some property. But we don't know if they connected or not."

"If she kept the appointment, then he might have been the last person to see her alive."

"Exactly. So Irma and I have been trying all week to reach him. But there's no answer at his home and just a recording at his place of business. I forget what he does, some kind of one-man show. So Kolowsky took the guy's name and address to see if he could track him down."

"What house was she supposed to show? Would the owners know anything?"

"We thought of that. But Plaxton was looking at hunting property—a vacant forty acres out in Leavitt Township. I told him all that." Phil reached into a candy dish and popped a handful of jellybeans into his mouth. "So then Kolowsky wanted to see a record of Madeline's earnings."

"She worked on commission, didn't she?"

"Sure, we all do. You sell, you get money. You don't, you starve. Every two weeks Irma calculates the commissions, makes the deductions and issues checks, just like any place else. Except the pay check can be big or small." He held out the candy dish, a leaf shaped affair.

I waved it away. "Did that satisfy him?'

"Who knows? I gave him a record of all her paychecks for the two years she worked here. But then he came up with some dates and wanted to know if she had got any bonuses or commissions. I got the feeling he saw some deposits on her bank records he was trying to account for."

"Madeline always seemed to have cash. I borrowed from her a couple of times myself. Did she have an inheritance or trust fund or something?"

"Not that I knew of. My guess is he'll be asking her family about that." Phil ate some more jellybeans, washed them down with soda. "Then Kolowsky showed me Madeline's home telephone bill. She had a whole bunch of calls to Greenwood Realty in Manistee."

"Well, you guys all trade referrals, don't you?"

"Sure, if we don't have it, someone else might. But we generally conduct business from the office. At home, you don't have any files to work with—plus it's on your own nickel."

"So her calling from home looks strange?"

"Yes, it does. Plus the fact that those calls were pretty late at night."

"I guess Greenwood Realty will have a visit from Kolowsky."

"Lucky them. I gave Mark Greenwood a call so he wouldn't be taken by surprise." He finished off the jellybeans. "Then to top it off, the guy had the nerve to ask *me* where I was on the night of May nineteenth."

"Gosh, Phil, does this mean you're a suspect?" The thought of roly-poly Phil doing violence to anyone struck me as ludicrous.

"Not for long, I wasn't. Corinne was with me all evening." He finished his drink and tossed the can in the recycle box.

"But the spouse will always cover. At least they do on television."

"Tracy, you're cruel. How about I was at a soccer game, with about fifty witnesses?"

"Guess you're in the clear—unless you're paying off a bleacher full of soccer moms."

"Thanks for your faith in me." He burped again. "I tell you, I just want this guy to get caught so business can get back to normal."

"Me too." We stood to leave. "You know," I said, "Madeline was a little on the wild side, but I never imagined that her shenanigans would leave her dead on the beach."

"Neither did I."

"You worked with her for two years, Phil. Did you ever notice anything that seemed, well, not right—off center?"

Phil screwed up his mouth. "I'll tell you this about Madeline. She was a real go-getter—that's what I liked about her. After all, when she made money, I made money."

"Madeline always seemed to be working, no matter what else she was doing."

"All the time. She was sociable and she was attractive. And any woman who looks good is bound to use that to her advantage, why not? But sometimes —." He stopped.

"Sometimes what?"

"Sometimes Madeline overdid things. My wife didn't like her much." He opened the back door and we stepped outside into a soft June evening. "By the way, Tracy, if you'd ever like to sell real estate, we've got an opening."

"But I don't know anything about sales – or real estate."

"You could learn," he said. "And you'd make money. Everybody likes money."

When I got home, cooking smells came wafting through the screen door. When I paused in the hallway to savor the odors, Brooke came down the stairs so fast she nearly knocked me over. At least I think it was Brooke—my new housemate was dressed like a bag lady in training. Her sweatshirt was stained and ragged, her blue jeans had a patch on one knee and a hole in the other.

"Hi Tracy," she bubbled. "I survived my first day on the job – and they're gonna let me come back tomorrow." She laughed. "Supper's in the oven but I'm not sure I got the temperature right. Isn't the weather gorgeous? I swept the kitchen but I couldn't find a mop. Oh—how was your day?"

Her barrage threw me off balance. I was accustomed to coming home to a quiet, empty, unscented house. "It was okay," I said, and then realized I was supposed to reciprocate. "How about you? How's the new job?"

"So far, so good. I'm learning the menu, good thing it's short. They have a dress code so I gotta clean up my act tomorrow." She looked down at her tattered clothes. "I'm wearing my grubbies because I washed everything I own. Where's your dryer? I looked for it all over the house."

"The reason you can't find the dryer is because—there isn't any."

Her face registered absolute disbelief. "No *dryer? What do you do?*"

"I hang my clothes on that line in the back yard."

"But I washed *everything.*" Green eyes widened in dismay. "And I need my clothes *tomorrow.*"

I forced a smile, trying for patience. "There's a Laundromat in town. You can take your clothes there after supper."

"But everything's all soggy," she whined. "I can't carry them down the street."

"Oh, don't be so helpless," I snapped.

Brooke looked as though I had struck her. A big tear made its way down her cheek.

"Oh, Brooke, I'm sorry." I put an arm around her. "I'm just tired. We'll work something out. What are you cooking? It smells wonderful."

She wiped her nose on her sleeve. "Macaroni and cheese—Southwestern style. I hope you like it."

I assured her that I loved macaroni and cheese and we worked out a plan whereby I would drive her and the wet clothes to the Laundromat, and she would wait and carry them home (dry weight). She promised that in the future she would plan ahead and use the arcane device in the backyard called a clothesline.

Brooke made a salad while I steamed fresh asparagus. The macaroni and cheese came out of the oven so hot that we dished it up and ate our vegetables while we waited for it to cool down.

"I'm surprised you got a job at the tea room," I said. "I thought that place was going out of business."

"I guess it nearly was." She held up a stalk of asparagus as though it were an exotic plant. "I got the whole story today. See, this old lady, Mrs. Fritzell, was running the place and selling sandwiches and cookies and tea. But most of her customers died and nobody was coming in except a few old ladies in walkers. Then her daughter Leona came to town to help her. Now they serve capucinno and bagels and muffins, so things are picking up."

"Do they make a Reuben sandwich?"

"Twelve different sandwiches. Home made soup too."

"I thought I might come in for lunch tomorrow. If that wouldn't make you too nervous." I was picking up her habit of putting periods in the middle of my sentences.

"That would be great. And you can see the other stuff they've got for sale. Like jewelry and candles. Leona wants to call it the Java Shoppe but her mom doesn't want to change the name."

"You were lucky to find a job so fast."

"I know. It was only the second place I looked. But it's just three mornings a week, so I'll need to find something else too. At least it's a start. Um, could I borrow some change for the Laundromat?"

We finished supper and cleaned up the kitchen, then Brooke put her soggy clothes in a garbage bag and I drove her to the Laundromat. She hadn't mastered driving a stick shift so there was no question of her borrowing my car. Thank goodness. Back home I got ready for trash pick-up. Going through the landslide of old magazines and newspapers on the coffee table, I came across last week's issue of the *Shagoni River News*. It was open to my story about the motorcycle rally.

I glanced at the photo of two couples on motorcycles, remembering that it was the same weekend Madeline had been killed. And there, peering bleary eyed past his beer can, was the guy with Angel's sister who wouldn't give his name. Kolowsky's words ran through my mind. "Five thousand bikers in town. If a guy wanted to blend in —." The bashful biker wore mutton chop whiskers and wire rimmed glasses. He didn't look like a killer. On the other hand he didn't look much like a biker either. I folded the paper and put it in the recycle stack.

There was plenty of daylight left so I went outside and hauled the old lawnmower out of the garage. I filled it with oil and gas, pumped the choke button and yanked hard on the cord. Nothing happened. I fiddled with every visible widget, choked and yanked some more, still without results. Frustrated, I was about to call Les Tatersall when Derek's noisy truck arrived, bearing Brooke and her dry laundry home.

"You kids must have radar," I said as they climbed out.

Brooke laughed and walked into the house, her arms full of dry clothes. Derek grinned, looked at the mower. "Want me to try that thing?"

"Sure, have at it."

Derek gave the cord a couple of unsuccessful pulls, then asked me if there was any starting fluid around. We rummaged through the garage until we found a can. He directed a couple of sprays at the carburetor and the next time he pulled, the motor coughed to life.

"I'll try it out for you," he said and grabbed the handle of the mower so eagerly that I stepped aside. Brooke was watching from the porch, the lowering sun making a copper halo of her hair. I joined her there and we cautiously tried out the porch swing which made protesting noises as we rocked.

"I've got a chance for another job," she said.

76

"Already? Where's this one?"

"Out at the Diamond D Ranch. Derek's going for an interview tomorrow, and they told him to bring along anyone who wants to work."

"But that's six miles out of town. How will you get there?" I didn't relish the thought of playing chauffeur at odd hours.

"Derek said we'll be working together, so I can ride with him." Brooke looked at me and smiled. "Don't worry, everything will work out great."

Her breezy confidence unleashed an ugly feeling in me—I believe it's called generational envy. This kid had been in town, what – all of three days, and she already had two jobs and a boyfriend? But my ungenerous thoughts evaporated as we rocked gently together in the swing. We watched Derek as he circumnavigated the lawn in ever smaller rectangles and when he finished it was nine-thirty and still daylight.

The next day I went to the Blue Bird Tea Room for lunch. Brooke was there, looking very neat in her white blouse, navy blue skirt and track shoes which had also seen the benefit of my washing machine. She recommended something called a Denver sandwich so I gave it a try. The coffee was hot and freshly brewed. When all the other customers drifted out before my food came, I realized it was almost closing time and started to feel guilty about wandering in so late. But shortly after I started in on my sandwich, a gray-haired woman in a white ruffled blouse appeared.

"You just take your time," she said. "Leona and I stay here until almost three, so you don't need to feel rushed."

So I relaxed and soaked up the ambiance. There was classical music playing, fresh flowers graced every table and Audubon prints decorated the walls. When the petite lady brought my check, she said, "You're Tracy Quinn, aren't you? I've seen your name in the paper."

I acknowledged that I was.

She introduced herself as Daisy Fritzell and said, "Mrs. Quinn, we are so happy to have your daughter working here. She is such a dear child."

Despite myself, I felt a rush of motherly pride. Realizing that Brooke and I had the same last name, I tried to explain the distinction between daughter and stepdaughter. But the lady had other things on her mind.

"You knew Madeline, didn't you, that woman who got killed?" I nodded. Daisy Fritzell pulled up a chair and sat down with me. "Well, I saw her quite a lot. She used to come here for lunch and then she would try to get a listing on the place, but I kept telling her it wasn't for sale. I'm really glad I held out."

"I'm glad you did too, Mrs. Fritzell. Good for you." I laid my money on top of the check and pushed it toward her. She ignored it.

"Brooke told me a detective came to your house. Now that's exciting. I wish he would come and talk to me sometime."

I remembered Kolowsky's request for information. "Is there something you'd like to tell him?"

"Yes, and I think it's important." She took a deep breath and launched into her story. "It's about that Saturday night, the night she was killed. I live on Flagler, just a few blocks south of Mr. Macleod's duplex. Well, it was after one in the morning and I was wide awake. So I made some chamomile tea and sat on my screened porch to drink it—it's very good for sleep, you know, we sell it here if you want to try some."

I listened with half an ear, trying to remember if I was late for an afternoon meeting. "I was sitting there in the dark," she said, "when I saw this man walk by. He had his shoulders all hunched over and his head bent way down. Then a truck stopped and he got in and they drove away."

That was it? A guy got in a truck? I nodded, trying to be polite. Clearly this lady read too much Agatha Christie. "Well, it's a good thing you're keeping an eye on the neighborhood," I said, "but you know how it is. There's a lot of teen-agers out goofing around on a Saturday night, keeping very late hours. I know they shouldn't be, but they are."

"These were not teen-agers," she said sharply. "They were full grown men." She stood, raised her tiny chin and pursed her lips in a manner that let me know I had offended her. Daisy Fritzell started to walk away, then turned and stood with her hands on my table. "And furthermore," she said in a dramatic whisper, "the truck didn't have any lights on."

I should have paid more attention.

CHAPTER EIGHT

"Madeline's apartment is almost empty," said Gavin. "Her mother came by yesterday and took away a carload of stuff."

"I thought her apartment was sealed off."

"The police tape came down three days ago."

"Did Sheriff Dupree find any clues in there?"

"Maybe, but he didn't tell me about them."

Gavin and I were perusing the menus at the Wayside Inn, a spot so lacking in tourist appeal that it never gets overcrowded. A tired looking waitress with frizzy orange hair and matching lipstick delivered our beer, jotted down orders and relieved us of the menus.

"Dupree and Laman spent half a day in there and then told me it was cleared," Gavin said. "So I called Madeline's mom. She took what she wanted and told me to give the rest to charity. But I thought maybe you and Ivy would like to look around and see if there's anything you want. It's mostly kitchen stuff, books, magazines, and shoes. Lots of shoes."

"The books sound interesting. Sure, I'll take a look, tomorrow afternoon probably. I'll talk to Ivy—she'll go for the shoes."

"Thanks. I need to get the place cleaned up so I can advertise it."

The waitress reappeared and plunked down two orders of SeaFood Special without a word or a smile.

"That detective came to see me again," Gavin said, exploring the cole slaw.

"What did he want this time?" I made an experimental poke into one of my lumps of deep fried stuff. .

Gavin shrugged. "He went over the usual things, like how long had I known her and when did I see her last." He smiled. "But then he came up with something new."

"Such as—where were you the night of May nineteenth?"

79

"He got to that later. But get this. He wanted to know if my relationship with Madeline had gone beyond the usual—ah, 'landlord-tenant relationship' was how he put it."

I almost exhaled beer through my nose. "That's rich. What did you tell him?"

Gavin grinned. "I played him for a while. Said she wasn't my type, I had never thought of her that way."

"I guess that's all true enough."

"Here's the best part." He took a pull on his beer. "Kolowsky kept at me. He leaned in real close and said, 'Why not? She was attractive, single, right next door. Why turn it down?'"

I nearly choked on a clam. "How long did this go on?"

"Not too long. I finally looked him in the eye and said, 'Sir, you're a detective. Haven't you figured out that I'm gay?' He probably jumped two feet."

I tried to imagine the look on Frank Kolowsky's face when he got the news. "Do you think he believed you?"

"I don't know. Maybe he thinks I made it up to throw him off the trail."

"Where did he go from there?"

"He popped the big question—where was I the night she died."

"Out of town, weren't you?"

"Right. I went to Grand Rapids for an antique show and stayed over with a friend named Jim Diangelo. Of course Kolowsky wanted his phone number and address."

"Do you think he'll track Jim down to confirm your alibi?"

"I hope so."

"Really?" He nodded. "Why?"

"After he meets Jim, the detective should have no doubts. Jim is, shall we say, out of the closet. And I mean way out."

"I guess that's all I want out of here," said Ivy, looking at a cardboard box packed with plates, cups, a fur hat and footwear. Ivy had scored three pairs of shoes from Madeline's closet and she was welcome to them. They were not my style, since I couldn't think of any reason to add three inches to my height.

"I'm about done too." My box held a straw hat, magazines, an eggbeater and half a dozen books. "Let's drink our tea on the patio."

Tea was an optimistic term for the lukewarm beverage we had created from tap water and a jar of brown crystals we found lurking in the kitchen cupboard. Ivy added some skinny ice cubes and we took our drinks outside.

We moved the plastic chairs so we could catch a little of the afternoon sun during our tea party. The back yard looked as good as most people's front lawns, with lush green grass bordered on two sides by purple and yellow iris that stood like guards against a wooden fence.

"I feel a little guilty about looting Maddie's apartment," I said.

"You shouldn't. Madeline's been gone for two weeks now. At this point it's us or the Goodwill store."

"Guess you're right. Gavin says we're doing him a favor."

Ivy inspected her nails for damage from the afternoon's foray. "That detective is single, you know."

"Kolowsky? Single? How did you find that out?"

"I asked him, silly. When he finally got around to interview me." She sighed. "I guess I should be insulted that I was so far down on his list. But at least he didn't ask me to account for my whereabouts 'on the night of.'"

"Guess he doesn't think nice girls like us could be killers."

"So anyway, Tracy, this guy is single, divorced actually. You should make a play for him."

"Me?" I choked on an ice cube. "Not interested. And even if I was –."

"Aha, I detect a glimmer of interest."

"Even so, I have no idea —. "

"Don't be a dolt. He gave you his card, didn't he? Call him up, tell him you have information."

"But I don't."

"So fake it. He'll be flattered."

"I don't think so."

"You're hopeless—no imagination."

"You seem to have this all figured out. Why don't *you* go after him?"

"Not my type. Flannel shirts don't turn me on."

"You can't fool me." I waved a fly away from my drink "You're seeing Greg Wetherell again."

Greg Wetherell, a lawyer from Whitehall, had been Ivy's on and off love interest for as long as I had known her. In the past year I had counted at least three breakups, and every time swore it was The End.

Ivy's cheeks reddened. "Screw Greg Wetherell. He's a womanizer and a sleaze. We have no future. It's finished."

"So who *are* you seeing? Or did you take a vow of celibacy?"

"The only vow I've taken is to stay away from that bastard. As for my private life, let's just say I'm not suffering. But you, Tracy, you definitely need to get laid. Oh hi, Gavin. Come join us."

Gavin emerged from behind the wooden fence that separated the patios, coiling a length of garden hose. He finished with the hose and joined us.

"Gavin. I'm trying to get Tracy here to make a play for the detective."

"I know ladies, I heard you."

"Eavesdropper."

"Sorry, but it's pretty hard *not* to hear what goes on over this fence. The privacy is strictly visual. A couple of summers ago I had to listen to drunken parties out here almost every weekend."

"That was before Madeline?"

He nodded. "It was a relief when Madeline moved in. Finally I had a tenant who paid her rent on time, didn't break things and wasn't inclined to wild parties."

"Didn't her overnight guests ever annoy you?"

"Hey, I kept my nose out of her sex life and she did the same for me."

"Wasn't there one guy who seemed to like both of you?" said Ivy.

"Oh that." He grinned. "Well, Victor did create a bit of tension. But we worked things out. As a rule, Madeline was quiet and so were her guests. Except for one time."

"When was that?" I said.

"I told Kolowsky about it. Early this spring, I was working out back when I overheard Madeline and some guy yelling at each other."

"Really? What were they yelling about?" said Ivy.

"It was pretty intense—but it didn't sound like a lovers' quarrel. The guy was telling her to leave something alone and she said, 'I didn't come here to leave it alone.' Then I coughed to let them know I was around and they went inside."

"Who was the guy?"

"I didn't recognize his voice. I was trying hard not to be the nosy landlord. Of course by the time Kolowsky questioned me, we both wished I had been a whole lot nosier. Are you two finished with your scavenger hunt?"

We showed him the cardboard boxes we had filled. Gavin refused our offer of tea, saying he had to get down to the store. He told us how to lock up the apartment and a few minutes later, we heard his car in the driveway. Ivy and I lingered.

"Talking to that detective got me to thinking," she said.

"About what?"

"About Madeline. You know she did smoke a little pot."

"Sure. We all did, on occasion."

"Right, but it was always her stash. I mean she's the one who bought the stuff. Dealt with the underworld, so to speak."

"True. But I don't think people get offed over marijuana deals gone bad." I drained my glass. "Do you?"

"No, the stakes aren't high enough." Ivy peered at me over her sunglasses. "I didn't mention any of this to Kolowsky, did you?"

I shook my head. "Didn't seem like any of his business."

"Right. But then I started thinking. What if Madeline saw something, or heard something—that she wasn't supposed to?"

We explored that line of thought. I told Ivy about the incident at the Belly Up when Madeline freaked out and went into hiding at the sight of a guy in a sport coat.

"So that guy," she said. "Maybe he was the one Gavin overheard yelling at her."

"Maybe it was her ex-husband —"

"—or a creditor."

"—or a dealer."

"—or a jealous lover."

"—or the Chicago real estate Mafia."

Ivy fiddled with the leather strap on a shoe in her box. "There's something I've been wondering. What shoes was Madeline wearing when you found her?"

Reluctantly, I replayed the scene in my mind. "One foot was bare—but the other one had a shoe, mostly dangling by the ankle strap. It was cream colored with a wedge heel. Remember the pair she wore with her yellow suit?"

"I remember," said Ivy. "And you know, Madeline always had to have the right shoes for every occasion."

"That she did. So what was the occasion for the cream colored wedgies?"

"Seems like she wore those when she was negotiating a deal—said they brought her luck."

"Didn't work this time."

"That's for sure."

"It's almost like a fairy tale." Ivy held the shoe up by its heel. "Maybe if we could find the other shoe, we could find the killer."

"Nice touch. But the shoe is probably at the bottom of Lake Michigan, along with her purse."

"You're right." Ivy dropped the shoe back in the box.

We washed our glasses, locked the door and carried our boxes out to the car. The space we left behind us was just an empty apartment now, waiting for another tenant.

I arrived home to find Brooke getting ready for her second evening of work at the Diamond D. She stood in front of the hallway mirror modeling a pair of tight black jeans and a red shirt with a black yoke. Her unruly hair was confined in two braids and a metal star that read 'Deputy' was pinned to her chest.

"Pretty neat, don't you think?" She did a turn, revealing a large red 'D' stitched on each rear pocket of her jeans.

"Pretty neat," I had to agree. "Did they give you the outfit?"

"Not exactly. It's free if I stay all summer. Otherwise they take it out of my pay. But the tips are good. Much better than the tea room." A rumble in the driveway announced the arrival of Brooke's transportation. "Oops, gotta run."

"How late do you work?"

"Around one, I guess."

"Do you have your key?" We now had a lock on the back door.

"Yep, got it. See you later." Brooke grabbed her purse and was gone. Seconds later the door opened and she stuck her head inside. "Tracy, I washed some clothes and hung them on the line. Could you bring them in, please, when they're dry? Just throw them on my bed."

"No problem. Have a good evening."

The house was blessedly silent. I wandered into the kitchen and cooked up a mushroom omelet with lots of cheese, then took my supper to the picnic table in the back yard. The solo meal was a welcome change. Brooke had only been with me for a week, but I was already getting tired of negotiating things as simple as what to cook for supper.

Then, while I ate, a voice in my head started speaking. *Tracy Quinn*, it said, *you have lived alone too long. The fast track to spinsterhood is dead ahead. You might as well start collecting those cats.* Okay, I decided, maybe Brooke was good for me.

It was full daylight when I finished supper so I hauled a pair of shutters out of the garage and laid them on the picnic table. After scraping off the worst of the dead skin, I applied a coat of paint called New Hampshire Brown. When I finally finished I stepped back and congratulated myself, picturing the shutters mounted and flanking my windows.

But the fantasy quickly went sour. The shutters would only make the house with its flaking paint look even worse by contrast. Maybe this home improvement stuff was beyond me. Maybe it was time to give up and sell the house. Grumbling, I put away the paint and brushes and cleaned myself up.

I was in the back yard taking down Brooke's laundry when Jewell appeared. She was in her running mode, shorts and sweatshirt, hair plastered to her forehead. But her normal, carefree expression was missing.

"Jewell, you look – upset. Is something wrong?"

She sighed. "Yes, very wrong. I need to talk."

I gave her a hug. "Let's go get a drink. You look parched." In the kitchen I filled two glasses with lemonade and we took them to the front porch.

"What's going on?" I said as we sat in the big wooden chairs.

"I'm worried sick. That detective came to question me and Paul."

"Oh that – it's all routine," I assured her. "He's talking to everyone who knew Madeline. All of us ——Phil, Gavin, me, Ivy."

"I know, but this is different. He's zeroing in on Paul because of the boat."

"The boat?" I looked at her in disbelief. "That's the dumbest thing I have ever heard. I told Kolowsky that half the people in town own boats of some kind." Now I was getting angry. "Why should he pick on Paul?"

Jewell looked down at her clenched hands. "Well, for starters there's the alibi thing. Or lack of it. I was out of town, so I can't vouch for Paul's whereabouts."

"Where was he?"

"Home alone, is what he said. When I got back from staying with my parents, he said he was alone all weekend and really missed me."

"So the guy is way off track."

"I want to believe that, Tracy, but here's what came next. Paul and the detective went into the study, but I listened, so shoot me. Now I knew that Paul had talked to him before at his office in town, he told me about that." Jewell started to sniffle. "Bear with me."

She took a swallow of lemonade. "Okay. So the first time around, Paul said he was home all evening and didn't go anywhere. Then yesterday in the study, Kolowsky showed Paul something, I think it was a gas receipt for the boat, dated May nineteenth. So then Paul changed his story, said he just went out to buy gas and came back home." She looked at me. "So why did he lie the first time?"

"Maybe he just forgot."

"Maybe. But here's what came next. Kolowsky told Paul that someone had seen 'Jewell of the Sea' going out through the channel around sunset. How could he forget going onto Lake Michigan?"

"Damn, that's different. What does Paul say?"

"Nothing, and that's the worst part. He refuses to discuss it. Can you believe that? He says stupid things like, 'This is a murder investigation, and I'm not allowed to talk about it.'"

"There must be some explanation," I said, trying very hard to think of one – other than Paul taking Madeline for her last boat ride.

"That's what I keep telling myself." Her eyes brimmed with tears. "But I can't think of any. Why did he lie if he had nothing to hide? That's what I can't understand. And ever since then he's been acting so nasty that it's hard to even be around him. If he's innocent, then what's his problem?"

While Jewell struggled for control, I sat beside her feeling clueless. For once my friend had come to *me* with a problem and I hadn't the slightest idea what to do. Feeling like a ninny, I went inside and got a box of tissues, put them on the arm of her chair. I stood with a hand on her shoulder while she cried. What could I say? Like her, I was devastated by the suggestion that Paul might be involved in Madeline's death. The thought was utterly incomprehensible. But his silence made it clear that *something* was wrong.

As the sun made its way to the horizon, I remembered summer evenings, many years before, when I had sat and cried on this same porch. And I finally understood just a fraction of what my grandparents had gone through as they struggled to help that teen-aged Tracy deal with the loss of her mother. And that's when I knew what to do.

"Jewell," I said, "let's go to Lake Michigan."

She looked up at me, teary-eyed.

"We'll walk on the beach—watch the sunset."

She blew her nose.

"I'll buy you an ice cream."

.She wiped her eyes, managed a smile. "Sounds like a plan."

We drove to Fisherman's Point where I slipped the Honda into the last of the legal parking spots. Jewell and I walked single file along the north wall of the channel that connects Arrowhead Lake with Lake Michigan. The traffic in the channel was heavy—sailboats and powerboats, some heading out to the Big Lake, some returning home. On the other side of us, people relaxed in lawn chairs or worked their flowerbeds, completely at ease with the pedestrian traffic in their back yards.

When we reached Lake Michigan, the channel wall widened into a pier that jutted out into the lake and allowed us to walk side by side. Around us, people of all ages were enjoying the warm evening. Old men with fish poles sat in folding chairs, paying minimal attention to their lines. Young couples strolled, arm in arm, hip to hip. Three boys in bathing trunks shouted dares to one another as they ran straight off the pier in horizontal leaps that ended with magnificent noisy splashes in the channel. A sailboat dropped its canvas and came in under power.

Jewell and I reached the end of the pier, then turned and walked back to the beach where we took off our shoes and plunged bare feet into the sand. The sand was warm on top but cool underneath. Carrying our shoes, we waded through the gentle surf, squealing when an unexpected wave reached up to splash our pantlegs. We passed the lifeguard stand, then turned and headed for the boardwalk where we claimed an empty bench. Jewell held our seats while I walked to the concession stand and returned with a pair of ice cream cones, one mint and one chocolate chip.

We watched quietly while the sky above the lake began to change color. Around us an audience of campers, bikers, joggers, and teenagers began to appear, drawn by the promise of sunset theatrics. Dog-walkers averted their eyes as they passed the "No Dogs on Beach" sign. Some children were in strollers and other toddlers insisted on walking despite repeated falls onto padded behinds. A girl with long brown hair sat on the bench next to us and began to strum a large red guitar. Another girl, this one wearing a studded dog collar, joined her in singing "On Top of Old Smoky" until they ran out of verses.

When "Old Smoky" finally ended, the crowd applauded. As if on cue, the sun touched the lake, creating a path of shimmering orange that led straight to the beach. Soft underbellies of clouds turned purple and vermilion as the sun slowly diminished to a half circle and then disappeared into the lake. Twilight was leaching color from the world as Jewell and I walked slowly back to my car. We were tired of speculating about Paul, so our conversation took other directions. We talked about Brooke and Derek, their jobs at the Diamond D, and what kind of flowers might do well in my back yard. I drove her home.

"You're welcome to stay at my place," I said as we approached her house.

"I feel like I can handle things now," she said. "Thanks for being my shrink."

"I'm glad I could help."

Jewell promised to call me if she needed to talk and I promised to call her with any new information. When I got home I tried to watch television but soon gave up and went to bed. Then I couldn't sleep. I kept struggling to get my mind around this latest turn of events. Paul Lavallen was one of the kindest people in the world—he couldn't possibly be involved in a murder. But then why didn't he explain? Nothing made a bit of sense. And I knew that whatever I was feeling, Jewell must be feeling a hundred-fold. Even my dreams were restless.

The clamor of the telephone jarred me awake. A peek my watch told me it was only six—thirty so I pulled the covers over my head. But the ringing didn't stop so I dragged myself out and picked up the phone.

"Tracy, this is Jewell." Her voice sounded hoarse. "Derek hasn't come home. Is he at your place?"

I looked around. No long body on the couch, or behind it. "Hold on," I said.

I laid down the receiver and went upstairs. Brooke's bedroom door was closed. Feeling very uncomfortable, I knocked, coughed loudly and knocked again, all without response. Finally I eased the door open and found nothing except an unmade bed and the clothes I had brought up earlier. The spare bedroom yielded an empty set of bunk beds. I went back downstairs.

"There's nobody here," I said. "Do you think they had engine trouble? You know that truck of his —."

"I know. It's not very dependable."

"At least they're together." I wasn't awake enough to judge the severity of this crisis. Did I do stuff like this when I was nineteen? Probably.

"Let's give them a few hours," she said. "If nobody shows up I'll call some of his friends."

I crawled back into bed, but the damn birds were singing and sleep was elusive. Finally I dozed off, only to be awakened again by the telephone. This time it was twenty past ten. Hearing Jewell's voice, I figured Brooke and Derek had arrived. But I was wrong. The kids were still missing and Jewell had a new crisis on her hands.

"Sheriff Dupree and the marine officer are here," she said. "Paul's having a fit because they're trying to take his boat. I'm afraid he's going to do something stupid."

This time I was awake. "Hang on," I said, reaching for a sweatshirt. "I'm on my way."

CHAPTER NINE

Following the sound of angry voices, I walked around to the back of Lavallens' house and discovered three men standing near the dock. Paul Lavallen was in sweatpants and tee shirt, his hair uncombed; Sheriff Benny Dupree was in a brown uniform with a holster on his belt and the third man was also in uniform so I figured he was the marine officer.

Jewell was on the deck hugging herself as she watched the scene unfold. I went and stood beside her.

"Thanks for coming," she whispered.

Paul's voice was taut with anger. "You have absolutely no right to barge in here and try to seize my property," he said.

"My marine officer can," said Dupree. "He has the right to search any vessel."

"But we're not on the seas. This is my home and my private property." Paul glanced toward the house, noted my presence with a scowl.

"We can search a boat if we have reasonable suspicion of a crime," said the other officer. He was barrel chested, with a beefy face and sand colored hair.

"Who's that?" I said to Jewell.

"I think his name is Malik—Bernard Malik."

"You guys have no reason to suspect me of anything." Paul's voice rose, threatened to crack.

"Judge Vanderhill thinks we do." Dupree pulled a paper from his pocket, unfolded it and waved it at Paul. "This is a search warrant for your boat and we want to conduct the search down at the village marina."

Paul took the document and scanned it. When he finished, he had the look of a man in a corner. "This is ridiculous," he sputtered. "What are you guys looking for—a bloody hammer?"

Malik and Dupree traded a look.

"Paul, we'll do this as quick as we can," said Malik. "I'll have your boat back by the middle of the week. All you're going to miss is one Sunday on the lake. Just gotta get this cleared up."

Was this the good cop/bad cop routine? Whatever it was, it seemed to be working. Paul shrugged and walked to the house, ignoring Jewell and me. For a moment I wondered if he kept a gun in the house. But he emerged minutes later, carrying nothing more ominous than keys on a chain. Paul handed the keys over to Malik.

"You'd better not put a scratch on it," he said, "or I'll sue."

"I'll be careful," said Malik.

The three men walked onto the dock and the marine officer boarded the boat. Paul appeared to give him instructions and then Malik started the engine. Paul and the sheriff untied mooring lines and threw them aboard, then stood watching as *Jewell of the Sea* pulled away. The two of them engaged in a brief conversation that I couldn't hear. Then Dupree turned and walked toward his car, with a curt nod to Jewell and me as he passed.

The next scene was painful to watch.

Jewell walked down to where Paul was standing and tried to put an arm around him. He shrugged her off. She spun around and stood in front of him, arms folded across her chest. "Tell me what's going on," she said. "What kind of evidence do they have?"

"I don't know what those idiots are thinking." Paul's face darkened from pink to livid. "The judge who issued that warrant is a moron." He tried to walk past her.

Jewell sidestepped, blocking his passage. "I don't believe you," she said angrily. "There's something you're not telling me."

"Now you're calling me a liar," Paul's voice rose. "That's all I need, is you turning against me. Don't you trust me?" His arms hung at his sides, fists clenching and unclenching.

I watched in horrified fascination, wanting to be somewhere else. But suppose Paul *had* killed Madeline. Could he now turn that anger on his wife?

"No, I don't trust you," she said, "and I don't think I can go on living like this."

"If you don't want to live with me," Paul snapped, "maybe it's time to —."

He stopped mid-sentence and looked toward the house. Sounds were coming from the driveway. There was the roar of a truck, but not loud enough to be Derek's truck, the slamming of vehicle doors, high-spirited voices, laughing. Three figures appeared at the crest of Jewell's terraced rock garden. Derek and Brooke were home and they had a friend with them.

"Well, see we got off work about one-thirty, and then Travis was having this party out at his folks' cabin." Derek was telling the story between bites of

French toast. All six of us were sitting in Lavallens' kitchen having a noontime breakfast. The ugly hostility between Paul and Jewell had dissipated upon the arrival of our errant teenagers.

"You should have called to tell us what you were doing," said Paul.

"We thought about it," said Brooke, "but there isn't any pay phone out there and the one in the kitchen is strictly off limits."

"The management out there is not exactly friendly," said Travis, a baby faced kid with a dragon tattoo on his left bicep.

"Travis, did your folks know about this party?" asked Jewell.

"Sure. I mean they're out of town, but they said it was okay. I had the key, so it wasn't like we broke in or anything."

"It's a cool place," said Brooke. "The dunes are right in the back yard. We built a bonfire, the moon was out."

Jewell looked at me and raised an eyebrow. Surely a case of beer was involved, but no one seemed inclined to make that an issue. Certainly not me. We were into the second pot of coffee by the time we heard about the end of the party when everyone had left except the three of them, and Derek's truck wouldn't start.

"So we all got in Travis' truck, but he sort of backed up into a wet spot."

"It's a real bog out there."

"A swamp."

"A marsh."

"Anyway he was dug in good. And there we were with one truck dead, one in the swamp, and no phone in the cabin. So we got a few hours sleep."

Travis took over the story. "This morning we walked to a neighbor's. Ed Foley lives about a mile down the road, and he came over with his pickup and a tow chain. Ed nearly got stuck himself, but with three of us pushing we got him out, and then he got us out. He let us borrow the tow chain to bring Derek's truck home."

"I'm pretty sure I can fix it," said Derek, "probably just the fuel pump." He glanced out the window at the empty dock. "Hey Dad, where's the boat?"

Paul coughed and said it was "in for repairs." And we tell these kids not to lie.

Jewell changed the subject, asking Paul if they could let Derek take the cell phone when he worked evenings. Paul said they would talk about it.

On the way home I kept thinking I should give Brooke some kind of lecture, but I was too scattered to locate my parental mode. When we got inside I made an effort in that direction. "Brooke," I said, "you probably think we're just a bunch of old farts for worrying, but we really had no idea where you were."

"I'm sorry we freaked you guys out—but I was with Derek, so I just went along with him. I mean what else could I do?"

"Probably not much. But keep in mind, we're a little jumpy around here because we had a friend go missing, and she showed up dead on the beach." I gave her a hug. "So keep us informed, okay?"

She promised that she would. Brooke steamed up the bathroom with an extra long shower, then excused herself and went upstairs for a nap that lasted until supper-time.

By then it was mid-afternoon and the day was feeling like a lost cause. I was too tired to tackle any major project and too worked up to join Brooke in snooze land. Finally I decided that unpacking the box of stuff from Madeline's apartment would be a suitably non-challenging task. So I moved some of grandma's nick-nacks to make room for the books, except for two cookbooks which I filed on a shelf in the kitchen.

The magazines in the box were mostly Cosmopolitan and Vogue. I flipped through a couple but couldn't find any fashion tips that promised to work well in Shagoni River. Then I came across one that didn't seem to belong. It was called "CollegeCuties" and featured nothing more than page after page of women in various stages of undress.

I was ready to throw the magazine in the trash when I decided to take a closer look. Clearly, the target audience was males with erotic fantasies that combined brains and boobs. Each girl was pictured in a two or three page layout, wearing a get-up that became scantier in each photo, like she was having a really bad day at strip poker. Each "profile" had a little bit of text, giving the girl's name, hobbies, her college major (give me a break) and some quote like, "I love my body. I think nudity is healthy." It was all so inane I wondered where I could apply for a job writing this stuff to pick up some extra change.

Then came one that stopped me cold. The woman had bottle blonde hair and started out wearing overalls, plaid shirt and a straw hat. I noticed the hat, because it resembled the one I had rescued from Madeline's apartment. Then I noticed the model because she resembled Madeline, at least a somewhat younger Madeline. Looking closer, I had no doubt that it was her—a tiny mole on the upper lip gave her away. The most risqué pose had her in the bottom half of a string bikini, bending over to drink from a garden hose—ooh phallic. The profile called her Mitzi and said she was studying to be a dietitian.

I stuck the magazine in the bottom drawer of my desk and went for a walk to think about what this could mean. So Madeline had posed for a low budget girlie magazine. So what? The act seemed slightly out of character with the Madeline I knew but didn't strike me as having anything to do with her death. Or did it? A model had recently been done in by her photographer on a shoot in the mountains outside Los Angeles. The photo business does give a near stranger good reason for taking a woman alone to a remote spot. How about for a boat ride? But Madeline at thirty-four struck me as a bit too old to be selling her skin via camera.

Still, I rather liked the idea of Madeline being offed by a sleazy photographer. At least it would get Paul Lavallen off the hook.

The workweek started out badly, with Marge accosting me before I even got to my desk. "You can't wear that in here," she said, pointing a stubby finger at my chest. Just for the record, Marge was wearing an orange chemise that made her look like a fire hydrant.

I paused to consider my ensemble, which I thought was no worse than usual—clean blue jeans, white shirt and a navy blue blazer. For the life of me I could not identify the offending article.

Marge helped me out. "That," she said, indicating a button pinned to my lapel. The button said, "Paul Lavallen for District Two." Marge unpinned the offending article and handed it to me, point first. "And furthermore, you are not to wear any sort of campaign material when you are covering events or otherwise representing the paper."

"Okay." I dropped the button in my pocket. "But why?"

"Because this newspaper is politically neutral. We must never be perceived as favoring one candidate over another. Furthermore, if you participate in Lavallen's campaign, you are not to write a single word about him in the paper."

"But Marge, in the good old days, people founded newspapers for the express purpose of bashing their political opponents."

"That," she said, "is precisely the legacy we are determined to overcome."

"Okay, point taken."

"Good." She shouldered her bag and headed for the door where she paused with a hand on the doorknob. "From what Jake tells me, your friend Lavallen is in a heap of trouble."

"And I suppose we'll read all about it on page one."

"Why not?" she said. "It's news."

Marge was out the door before I could call her the bad word I was thinking. I pinned the campaign button back on and that made me feel so good that I finished three stories by noon.

After lunch I drove to Wexford Hospital and interviewed the head of radiology about their new CAT scan equipment. I was hoping to run into Jewell but she had the day off. It was after five when I got back to town so I bypassed the office and went straight home. I was less than thrilled to find a Shagoni River police car parked on the road in front of my house.

Brooke was there in shorts and a tank top, talking to a policeman who didn't look old enough to drive, let alone keep order in the village. I parked in my driveway and walked down to meet him.

"Can I help you?"

"Are you the homeowner here?"

"I suppose I am."

The policeman cleared his throat. "Well, you see, the village council is on this clean-up campaign and your place has been cited." Either the guy had naturally pink cheeks or he was embarrassed that he didn't have bigger criminals to pursue. "See, the vegetation here is more than seven inches high."

He pointed to the weed-covered slope where my lawn ended. The area was so steep as to be nearly vertical, and so had escaped Derek and the lawnmower. "It's pretty hard to cut this stuff," I said.

"Probably you need a weed trimmer."

"Well yes, but —." I had no intention of buying a weed trimmer.

"Oh, but look here," Brooke interrupted, pointing to a plant with pale green leaves. "Most of this stuff is milkweed. And no one should *ever* cut milkweed."

"Why's that?" said the cop.

"Because milkweed is the only food of the Monarch Butterfly caterpillar." She ripped off a fuzzy leaf and held it up for his inspection. "Monarchs used to cover the entire country but they're now in danger of extinction."

She now had his undivided attention.

"The Monarchs are endangered," she said, "because people are so obsessed with the concept of lawnmowing." The way she said the word made it sound like a perversion.

He shook his head, started writing. "Okay, I'll report this to my boss. What butterfly is that?"

"Monarch," she said. "M-o-n-a-r-c-h."

The blushing cop finished his report, smiled sheepishly at Brooke and then climbed into his vehicle where he paused to consult a list, probably hoping the next offender would be more compliant. Brooke waved as he pulled away.

"That was really impressive," I said. "How did you know all that?"

"I had a really good science teacher in high school." She held the soft leaf against her cheek. "He made us go out and look at stuff."

"Have you ever considered a major in biology?"

"Well no, because I didn't like cutting up frogs—." She glanced toward the house. "Oh, yikes, I've got something in the oven. I'd better go check on it. I'm making noodles and tuna. I hope you'll like it."

"I love noodles and tuna. I'll cook some asparagus."

She started toward the house, turned back. "I invited Derek to have supper with us. Is that okay?"

"Sure. I like Derek."

"Thanks a lot." She came back and gave me a quick hug. "He says things are kind of weird at his place."

I figured that was probably an understatement. I wondered how things were going at the Lavallen household since the eventful Sunday afternoon. I hadn't heard a word from Jewell.

"Lavallen Questioned in Murder Probe."

The headline was splashed all over the front page of the Shagoni River News. Seeing it there made me feel like I worked for some ugly tabloid. I scanned the lead—'Paul Lavallen, recently declared candidate for district two county commissioner, had his boat seized Sunday by the Cedar County Sheriff's Department in connection with the investigation into the death of Madeline Maxwell...' I stopped reading because I felt like I might throw up.

The story was true, of course, and I couldn't expect Marge to ignore it. But did she to make such a big deal of it? Did the headline have to be two inches high? She was enjoying this, I knew, because Paul was my friend. I seethed quietly until Jake showed up, then followed him into his office.

"Jake," I said, "what's going on? What do they have on Paul? How did Dupree get the search warrant?"

"Tracy, please." Jake dropped his briefcase on his desk, rubbed his back. "Just give me a minute, okay?"

"Okay, sorry."

Jake went out and returned with a cup of coffee, sat down behind his desk. "If I had any answers," he said, "I'd tell you. But I don't."

95

"But you're the one who wrote the story—about his boat being seized."

"Sure. I took it off the police report. Beyond that, all I know is that Judge Vanderhill swore out a warrant because—let me see." He pulled out a notebook and flipped it open. "The search warrant was issued 'based on witness reports about seeing boat at time and place to connect it with homicide.'"

"Read that last part again—please."

He looked at me over his spectacles, then repeated, "——witness reports about seeing boat at time and place to connect it to homicide."

"So who were these witnesses?"

"Nobody's talking. I hung around the sheriff's office for two hours and couldn't pick up a thing."

"Did you talk to the marine officer?"

"Malik? Sure. He said they have Paul's boat and they're searching it."

"Nothing else?"

"Nothing. Everybody is tight-mouthed as a clam."

"Well, they're not going to find anything," I said vehemently. "They're on the wrong track."

"Come on, Tracy. Don't you want the bad guy to get caught?"

"Of course I want the bad guy caught. But not —."

"Not if it's a friend of yours—right?"

"Damnit Jake, it was a friend of mine that got killed."

I turned and stalked out of his office.

Somehow I got through the day but as soon as it was over I went straight to the Treasure Chest. Just walking into the store made me feel better. The place smelled of cinnamon, Billie Holiday was singing "Georgia on my Mind," and Gavin was showing an antique doll to a lady with blue hair. I laid a copy of the *News* on the counter and gestured to Gavin that I was going to his office in back to use the telephone.

Jewell answered on the second ring.

"Have you seen today's paper?" I said.

"No, but I heard about it. Probably I don't want to read it."

"Believe me, you don't. I am so sorry about this."

"Tracy, there was nothing you could do to stop it."

"Sure, the public has a right to know—all the gory details. But I hate myself anyway. How is Paul taking it?"

"I have no idea. He left a message that he was working late, which is nothing new. I rarely see him any more."

"Then how about coming into town for supper? We could get something at the Park Deli and eat outside."

"There's an idea," she said. "We could rent bikes afterward."

"Oh no. Not exercise."

"Come on – we both need it."

"No, I'm the one who needs it. You actually like it."

She laughed. "It'll do us both good."

I decided I could make the sacrifice for Jewell's mental health. "Okay, but let's keep it short."

"Only a couple of miles, I promise."

"Okay. I'll meet you there."

Up front, the blue haired lady was gone and Gavin was reading the newspaper. He looked up at me and scowled. "Tracy, this is nasty."

"Nasty, but true." I gave him a quick run down on the scene I had witnessed Sunday at Lavallens'.

He shook his head. "This is starting to look bad. If Paul doesn't get out from under it, he can forget about his political future." He laid down the paper. "What kind of evidence do you think Dupree has?"

"Something good, or he wouldn't have gotten the search warrant. But even Jake can't find out what it is."

"I wonder if this could be connected—someone trying to ruin Paul's credibility?"

"Now there's an idea. In a way it would be a relief to think so."

"Think about it. One week he declares his candidacy—and the next week he's on the hot seat in a murder investigation. Is that coincidence or sabotage?" He started his closing routine—turned the sign over, switched off the lights.

"But who could it be? No one else has even declared as a candidate."

"There's plenty of time. Maybe someone wants to get Paul out of the way, then step in to fill the gap."

"Can you think of anyone in district two with political ambitions?"

"I heard that Tom Halladay might run." He picked up his jacket.

"That's a joke. No one would vote for him—would they?"

"Hard to say." He glanced at his watch. "Sorry to rush, but I've got to be in Grand Rapids by seven."

"No problem. I'm meeting Jewell for supper and a bike ride."

"Give her my best. Tell her to hang in there."

Jewell was waiting for me at the Park Deli. Her normally sunny face had taken on a haunted look—there were creases I had never seen before. We ate our sandwiches at a picnic table that overlooked the public beach on Arrowhead Lake.

"I hope I can remember how to ride a bike," I said. "It's been years."

"Don't worry. Once you learn, it always comes back to you. It's like —."

"Like having sex —?"

"Something like that."

"I've probably forgotten that too."

At least that made her laugh. Seeing Jewell so unhappy made me realize how much I depended on her to keep my spirits up. After supper we went to the bike rental shop behind the deli where the owner fitted us out with user friendly three speeds. I was pleased to find that I had no problem staying upright. Together we set off along a wooded trail that had once echoed with train whistles and the clang of metal wheels. The linear park was a railroad right-of—way that had been converted to bicycle trail after the tracks were abandoned.

The wisdom of the conversion was soon evident. The trail we pedaled had almost no hills and was just wide enough for us to ride abreast and carry on a conversation. We rode through a forest of birch trees with peeling white bark, tall singing pines, and occasional clumps of cedar that made the air smell like my grandma's linen chest.

"How are things at home?" I said when I had enough breath to talk.

"Not very good."

"How not good?"

"When Paul's home, which isn't often, he's either super-critical or sullen. If I ask the most innocent question, he accuses me of prying. Some days I have fantasies about—just walking out."

"Really?"

"Just fantasies, of course. I'd never actually do it."

"Doesn't he say *anything*?

"Not a word." I fell behind her as we met opposing traffic, a young couple in shiny black biking outfits. "I just don't know what to think," she said when I caught up with her again. "Nothing makes a bit of sense."

It didn't make sense to me either. "I can't imagine Paul hurting Madeline—much less killing her."

"I can't either. But then why won't he talk to me?"

"Could he be covering for someone else?"

"I guess that's possible. But who, and why? I don't know what to do. Should I be more supportive? File for divorce? Sleep with a baseball bat? We're already in separate beds."

"I wish I could do something."

"I guess there's nothing anyone can do."

We rode in silence for a while. The exercise had set my blood to circulating and somewhere in my brain the nucleus of an idea emerged. The idea slowly grew into something like a plan. At the three mile marker, I stopped and said, "Jewell, I've got an idea."

She stopped and looked me, her face hopeful. "Let's hear it."

We turned around and started slowly back. I could hardly believe what I was proposing, but these were desperate times. "Okay, here it is. The other day Ivy came up with this wild notion. She said I should call detective Kolowsky and tell him I had some kind of information—I don't know what it would be."

"We could think of something."

"Okay. Fine. Then I feed him dinner."

"And ply him with wine —."

"Right. And then he tells me what they've got on Paul. Well, at least he tells me something—anything at all—about what's going on."

"I like it." Her voice took on an edge of excitement.

"You do?"

"Of course. This is so much better than sitting around and agonizing. At least we're doing *something*. I'll be forever in your debt."

"Hey, I haven't done anything yet."

"But you will, won't you?"

"I guess so. If you think it's a good idea."

"I think it's a great idea."

"You may not like what I find out."

"I don't care how bad it is," she said with an air of determination. "Once I know the truth, I'll deal with it. Anything's better than being in the dark."

By the time we got back to town the sun had disappeared among the trees and we had refined our plan. I could only pray that I would have the guts to carry it out.

CHAPTER TEN

Frank Kolowski was waiting on my porch Friday when I got home from work. He came down the steps to meet me as I approached the house with a grocery sack in each hand

"Thanks for coming," I said as he claimed one of the sacks. "I didn't know if you could make it on such short notice."

"I managed to work it into my schedule," he said past the toothpick in his mouth.

Frank was wearing a necktie. The tie was black and so were his shirt and pants so now he looked a bit like Zorro except for the high top track shoes. He followed me into the house and back to the kitchen where we deposited our grocery bags on the counter.

"I haven't eaten since breakfast," I said, "and I'm starving. How about having supper with me while I get my thoughts arranged?"

"Never turn down a free meal."

"I've got some fried chicken here from the deli." I pulled out a paper carton and put it on the table, added a plastic container of potato salad. Next I took some cheese and pickles out of the refrigerator, babbling all the while as though it were a normal occurrence for me to find a detective on my porch and invite him to supper. Finally I added plates, glasses, bread and butter plus half a bottle of wine.

"Nothing fancy," I said.

"Looks good to me."

As soon as we sat down I felt a wave of nausea. What on earth had made me think I could pull this off? Instead of feeling suave and Mata Hari like, I was nervous and sweaty. Not to mention a little dizzy. I took a deep breath and let it out slowly.

"Rough day?" Frank gave me an inquiring look.

"Oh, yeah. I'm just, ah, winding down." I took a sip of the wine.

Frank, not a bit nervous, was filling his plate. He discarded the toothpick he had been chewing and caught my quizzical look. "I quit smoking about three months ago. I guess these things are my crutch."

"That's okay. A toothpick is probably healthier than a cigarette."

"Unless I swallow it." He picked up a chicken leg and disjointed it with his hands. "Did you ever smoke?"

"For a couple of years," I said, relieved to have a topic of conversation. "Until the night I burned a hole in my dress while dining in an upscale restaurant. That's when I quit—figured I was too clumsy to pull it off."

He laughed. "Lucky you quit when you did. I've got a thirty year habit I'm trying to kick." He gulped his wine. "Started when I was in the service. Cigarettes were so cheap it seemed like a waste not to smoke. Of course that was before we knew how bad they were. So now, I'm off tobacco." He patted his midsection. "But I probably eat too much. Can't win. This is good, by the way." He waved the drumstick at me.

I gave up on niceties and started gnawing on a chicken wing. "How did you get to be a detective?"

"Too dumb for college. Not quite dumb enough to stay in the army. I applied to the Detroit police force and got in with extra points for being a veteran. Worked my way up to detective in about fifteen years."

"So you've been chasing bad guys for a long time."

"Long enough to get pretty beat up."

"Sounds kind of rough. Has it made you cynical?"

"Cynical? Sure. After a while you start suspecting your own mother." He speared a pickle from the jar. "It was probably good for me to get out of the city."

"Being out here must feel like living in another country."

"Another planet is more like it. People actually sleep at night." He refilled his glass.

"How did you wind up in Cedar County?"

"Divorce." He reached for another piece of chicken. "She got the house, I got the hunting shack. I always liked coming up here, so it worked out okay. You been married?"

I nodded, mouth full. "Divorced. Almost ten years now. I quit counting."

"Guess we're both into our second lives. My pension doesn't start for a few years, so I have this job. But it doesn't even feel like work, no one shoots at me."

"Any kids?"

"One of each, Jason and Sandra. I don't see them enough, but that's my own fault. Sandra's married, got two little boys."

So I was dining with a grandpa. A pretty fit looking grandpa I had to admit. I told him about the jobs I'd held before I became a reporter and he told me some hair-raising tales about misadventures on the mean streets of Detroit. Between us we consumed almost everything on the table so then I made coffee and found some windmill cookies for dessert. If Frank was wondering when I was going to cough up the information I had promised, he didn't show it. I really did have some tips to share but I didn't intend to give them away—what I had in mind was a trade.

Over coffee and cookies, I decided to begin negotiations.

"About this Madeline business—I have something to show you." I brought out the May 25 issue of the *Shagoni River News*, opened it to my story about the motorcycle rally, and showed him the photo. "This guy here wouldn't give his name." I pointed to the bleary eyed biker. "And then I remembered what you said about it being the same weekend that Madeline was killed."

He looked at the photo and read through the story. "This might be worth checking out. Can I have this paper?"

"Sure, take it."

Supper was over, the wine was gone, but I still hadn't learned anything about the case against Paul. "We could take a walk," I said. "Have you ever hiked up Old Baldy?"

"No, but I'm willing. Probably need some exercise."

I put on my hiking shoes and we walked to Centennial Park, a tiny patch of greenery that offered a few swings and benches at the foot of a steep, tree covered hill. An arrow pointed to the beginning of a foot-trail that disappeared into the trees.

"This is it," I said. "In the winter we used to hike up here and slide down the other side. Half the time we didn't even need sleds."

We fell into single file and started climbing. I let Frank take the lead because I preferred a view of his backside to having him look at mine. The trail was narrow and ascended sharply, alternating between packed earth and flights of wooden steps. We were the only humans on the hill, though I heard various small creatures scramble for cover as we passed. After about ten minutes of climbing we reached a hexagonal wooden platform which commanded a panoramic view of downtown Shagoni River and Arrowhead Lake.

Frank stood and looked around. "This is nice," he said, catching his breath. "I should do this more often. Getting out of shape."

"Not enough bad guys for you to chase."

"Damn cigarettes didn't help."

The platform had a railing around the edges and benches on three of the sides. Frank and I looked down at the lake, leaning casually against the railing as though we were passengers on a cruise ship. I told him about Mrs. Fritzell of the Blue Bird Tea Room, and the men she had seen outside her house on the night of the murder.

"Her story seemed kind of silly," I said, "but I promised to pass it on if I saw you again."

He took the information seriously enough to write down her name and the address of the tearoom. We made small talk and watched boats on the lake below us as they motored into their slips at the marina. It felt good standing next to Frank – his bulk made me feel almost petite. Well that was a stretch, but at least I didn't feel ungainly around him. But such thoughts were not on my agenda—it was time to try for the swap. I screwed up my courage and took the plunge.

"I was out at Lavallens' when the sheriff took Paul's boat. I'm just wondering how he got a search warrant." He didn't say anything so I stumbled on. "I mean, everything I heard was pretty benign."

Frank was quiet, clearly weighing his words. "Well the thing is," he said at last, "Lavallen denied taking his boat out that night ———but at least two people saw him cruising. The situation looked a little fishy."

"Who saw him – the guy where he bought gas?"

"That was one of them."

"Well okay. But an evening cruise on the lake is hardly a crime."

"Of course not, but the fact that he denied it looks bad. Plus, the owner of the Brown Bear swears he saw him going out the channel." Frank turned to look at me. "I know Lavallen's your friend," he said, "but the sad fact is that most murders are committed by friends or family, not strangers."

I was tempted to defend Paul, but figured that wouldn't help me learn anything. We were quiet for a bit, watching clouds change from pink to vermilion as the sun slipped toward the horizon. Then I tried a different tack. "Madeline's boss, Phil, told me about a guy named Burt Plaxton. Did you ever locate him?"

His forehead furrowed. "Burt who?"

"Plaxton. Madeline had an appointment with him the afternoon she was killed."

Frank's eyes narrowed. "This isn't going in the paper, is it?"

"Of course not. I tell people when they're on the record."

"Okay. The answer is no. I went to Muskegon, located Plaxton's apartment and found it empty. There was a pile of newspapers in front of the door. Neighbors said he was there one day and gone the next."

"Do you think he could be the killer—and now he's on the run?"

"That's one possibility. Or try this. Maybe somebody killed them both and the second body hasn't washed up yet."

"Oh, double murder. You are from the big city."

"I'm looking for Plaxton's relatives. I won't jump to any conclusions until I talk to them."

I felt like I was on a roll. "What about the Manistee connection?"

"Manistee? Where did you hear about that?"

"From Phil." He got that look in his eyes again. "Hey, we talk among ourselves. You couldn't expect us not to, could you?"

"No, I guess not."

"Okay. Phil told me about Madeline's phone calls to Greenwood Agency, the calls she made from home."

"Oh that. Well the owner, Mark Greenwood, claims the calls were all legitimate. Said his staff works a lot of evenings. But he looked a little surprised when I told him the calls were between ten and midnight. He said he'd question his people and get back to me. We'll see if he does."

I was out of words but keenly aware of his presence. A pair of squirrels, one black and one brown, chattered madly as they chased each other around a large tree trunk "Guess we'd better head back," I said.

Frank smiled. "Thanks for bringing me up here."

"Thanks for coming."

Single file and dodging branches, we walked down the hill and back to my house. I told him about my mother's death, my grandparents taking me in, and how I came back when my grandfather died. When we reached the house I said, "This is a little embarrassing, but I've got something else to show you." We went into the living room and I pulled the CollegeCutie magazine out of my desk.

I handed him the magazine. "That's her," I said, "Madeline a few years ago." Frank sat on the couch and studied the photos of Madeline, then flipped through the rest of the pages, checking the publisher and date. "Think it means anything?"

"Maybe, maybe not. Sometimes the gals who do these shots are small time hookers, consider this a little advertising. Do you think your friend ever turned tricks?"

I thought about his question. "Madeline had this way of meeting strangers," I said at last. "She'd act very friendly, strike up a conversation, and then bring it around to business. She did it anywhere, on the street, in a restaurant, at the bar or beach."

"Sounds like a pro."

"Right, but as near as I could tell, the business was always a second home, cottage or condo." I mentioned the Los Angeles case where the photographer had killed the model. "Do you think it could have been something like that— photographer turned killer?"

"Possible, but not likely. Cases like that get publicity just because they are so unusual. Okay if I take this magazine?"

"Go ahead," I said. He rolled it up. "You're not going to pass it around the station, are you?"

"Wouldn't think of it." He stood and stretched. "Guess I'd better be going." I walked with him out to the porch, steering him around the loose board. "You must be good for me," he said.

"Good for you—how?"

"No toothpick. Forgot all about it since supper. Now that's progress." He flashed me a smile. "Good night and thanks for supper."

After he was gone I sat in the creaking porch swing until after dark, reviewing our conversation and wondering what kind of impression I had made on Frank Kolowsky. Not that it mattered, of course. The important thing was the information I had gleaned about the case against Paul Lavallen – and what I was planning to do with it.

Saturday morning I didn't waste any time. After a quick cup of coffee, I went straight to the village marina where I found the manager, Parnell Weeks, unlocking his office. Parnell turned to greet me, displaying a guileless face and a friendly smile. He wore a gaudy Hawaiian shirt that almost reached the cargo pockets of his shorts which bulged with mysterious contents. Parnell and I had met last summer when I did a story about the marina expansion. I asked him how things were going, then brought up the visit from detective Kolowsky.

"Guess maybe I stirred up a hornet's nest there," Parnell said as he let us into the office, "but I couldn't lie. I work for the village and all our transactions are public. Paul was here that evening. Paid for his gas with a credit card, so there was a record of everything—date, time, amount."

"Did Paul say anything when he bought the gas?"

"When I dug up the receipt, that's when I remembered what we talked about." Parnell ran a hand over his round head. "Paul asked me if I'd heard the marine weather report. I told him the forecast was for light wind and waves no more than two feet."

"Did he say he was going onto Lake Michigan?"

"That's the impression I got."

Through the smudged window I saw a man in white pants waiting outside, and realized that Parnell had work to do. "Well, thanks," I said, "I just wondered how they justified grabbing his boat."

"I'm pretty sure they plan to release it today."

"Have you heard if they found anything?"

"Zilch. Nobody's talking. Never saw Dupree and Malik so tight lipped."

I moved toward the door. Parnell motioned me back. He leaned across the desk and spoke quietly. "There's another thing, something I didn't tell that detective."

"What's that?"

"Paul wasn't alone on the boat. I heard him talking to someone in the cabin—but whoever it was stayed out of sight."

My mind raced with unwelcome thoughts as I drove around Arrowhead Lake to the Brown Bear and I was relieved to find Hank Shober there alone. I ordered coffee and scrambled eggs, figuring he deserved some business in return for letting me pick his brain. Hank was washing glasses so I ate at the bar and talked to him while he worked.

"I understand you had a visit from Detective Kolowsky."

"You heard right. He was up here was here last week, had a couple beers."

"Did you know Dupree impounded Paul Lavallen's boat?"

Hank stopped washing. "No. I didn't know that."

"Were you the one who saw Paul heading out the channel?"

"Hey, I didn't mean to get anyone in trouble, but my son and I both saw it. Buzz was helping with supper, and when things slowed down we took a break on the deck. Buzz looked out and said, 'There goes *Jewell of the Sea*.' I looked up and saw Paul's boat heading into the channel."

"But how could you guys be sure? There must be a dozen ChrisCrafts about that size."

"Yeah, but they don't all have that green MSU flag on the stern."

Shit, he was right. I put some marmalade on an English muffin. Drank some more coffee. Didn't want to ask the next question. "Was he alone?"

"No, he wasn't. Someone was standing beside him. Looked like a woman."

Hank was silent for a moment, then looked away as he said, "It didn't look like his wife. Too tall for Jewell."

I spent the afternoon in Stanton covering the Asparagus Festival and went to bed early though it took me a long time to actually fall asleep. Sunday morning I woke up and wondered what I was going to tell Jewell. All the facts I had uncovered pointed directly to Paul Lavallen being on lake Michigan with a woman in his boat the night Madeline was killed. This was not the kind of news I had been looking for—and definitely not the kind of news I wanted to share with Jewell. I decided to stall.

By early afternoon Jewell called me. "Malik returned Paul's boat yesterday," she said.

"That's good news—right?"

"Right. Because now Paul can take the boat and disappear. That's where he is now. Have you found out anything?"

Reluctantly, I told her about my supper with Frank, my visits to Parnell and Hank. "Worse and worse," she said with a heavy sigh.

"I know it looks bad, but it still doesn't mean he did it. There are other leads and Frank is looking into them. Do you want to get together this afternoon?"

"Thanks, but I'm just packing. I've got tomorrow off so I'm heading to Ann Arbor to spend the night with Sarah."

"Good. You need a change of scenery."

"I do. Plus Sarah needs to know what's going on and I feel like I should tell her in person."

"Remember my guest room is available."

"Thanks for the offer. But right now Paul and I have fixed our schedules so we hardly see each other. It works for us, but it's pretty hard on Derek. I hope you don't mind him being at your house so much."

"Derek's easy to have around," I said. "And he's helpful. Yesterday he unplugged my kitchen drain."

"I wish he'd do stuff like that at home. Anyway, thanks for trying to help me."

"I only wish I could have come up with some better news." I hung up, feeling depressed and foolish. My meddling hadn't helped Jewell at all—it had only made a bad situation worse.

"So this is the lovely Brooke," said Ivy. "I've heard so much about you."

Ivy and I were having lunch at the Blue Bird Tea Room, a date we had scheduled so she could meet my stepdaughter.

"Nice to meet you," said Brooke. "Tracy talks a lot about you, too. The special today is squash soup with a salmon salad, if you'd like to try it."

We both ordered the special and Brooke moved on to the next table where a party of six women had just arrived. Ivy leaned toward me and whispered, "She is just lovely, and you are so lucky. I tell you, I hear my biological clock ticking."

"I didn't know you had a clock. You mean you really want to —."

"Well, it would be nice. Company in my old age, someone to swap clothes with. Look at you." She pointed to the red silk shirt Brooke had given me. "You are wearing much better colors since Brooke came into your life. She's good for you."

"Don't let me discourage you from reproduction," I said, "but realize, it's pretty hard to place an order for a nineteen-year-old female. Kids come in two sexes, and all of them arrive with bare butts, kicking and screaming."

Ivy grimaced. "I forgot about that messy diaper business." She pulled out a compact, inspected her make-up. "And then there's the problem of choosing a father."

Brooke served up two bowls of thick golden soup that smelled a lot like pumpkin pie.

"Paul Lavallen is making the news." Ivy clicked her compact shut and blew on a spoonful of soup. "He's been in the Chronicle three times this week, and all three stories mention the murder investigation."

I groaned. "This can't be good for his campaign."

"Not one bit. The whole situation stinks. Have you seen them lately?"

"Jewell and I went for a bike ride the other day. It's hard on her but she's coping."

"Jewell's a survivor."

"Yes, she is."

Ivy tasted the soup, then arched an eyebrow at me. "You weren't at the Belly Up Friday night. Hot date?"

"Not exactly," I stammered. "But maybe. Sort of."

"Aha. You're holding out on me. Come on, give."

"Well, I sort of took your advice. I had Frank Kolowsky at my place for supper."

"The detective?" She did a little handclap. "Good for you. It's about time."

"This was strictly business, mind you. I wanted to find out what they had on Paul."

"So you got the detective drunk and took advantage —."

"I doubt if anyone takes advantage of Frank Kolowsky. But I did find out who he'd been talking to."

"You are so devious. What did you find out?"

So I told her about my visit to Parnell Weeks, and what Parnell had told me about Paul. Ivy stopped eating and glared at me. I continued, oblivious. "Then I talked to Hank Shober at the Brown Bear. Hank told me he saw Paul going out the channel with a woman in his boat. So then —."

"Tracy, what in hell did you think you were doing?"

I looked at her, baffled. "I was just trying to help Jewell. She wanted to know —."

"For heaven's sake, will you lay off this amateur detective business? You're making everything a hundred times worse." Ivy's mouth contorted as she fumbled for her purse.

"Ivy, what's bugging you?" I had never seen her like this.

In a sudden jerky motion, Ivy stood, nearly tipping over her chair. She bent down and hissed at me, "Just stay out of this, okay?"

Then she turned and bolted out the door, leaving a dozen ladies staring open mouthed at her back. I stared too, completely mystified by her dramatic exit.

Brooke reappeared with our sandwiches. "Gee, your friend left already? I was just going to take a minute to talk with her. She seemed real nice."

"She had an emergency," I lied. "But she said the food was really good."

Only then did I realize that Ivy's unscheduled departure had left me stuck with her bill. And of course I would have to leave a larger than average tip.

CHAPTER ELEVEN

"Tracy, hi there. Got a minute?"

The voice came from behind me. I paused on the courthouse steps and Frank Kolowsky appeared at my side, so close I could smell his aftershave—something with hints of lemon and spice.

I checked my watch. "Sure—got about twenty minutes."

"Let's go over there." He gestured toward a picnic table on the far side of the courthouse lawn. The grass felt spongy under my feet as we walked past the civil war monument and took opposite seats at a wooden table in the shade of a maple tree. There was no one around except a robin in search of worms and a jail trustee doing some yard work.

"Hey, you look nice today," he said.

I glanced down at the crocheted lavender top I was wearing. "Thanks. My, uh, Brooke gave me this."

"How was your weekend?"

"Busy." I swatted an imaginary mosquito. "I spent all day Saturday covering the Asparagus Festival." This was mostly true. I sure wasn't going to tell him about my visits to Parnell Weeks and Hank Schober.

Frank grunted, pulled a little spiral notebook out of his pocket. Also a toothpick.

"Uh oh. The dread notebook."

He grinned sheepishly. "Sorry, but this is kind of important."

"So that small talk was just to prime the pump."

"Boy, you sure are defensive." He put the toothpick in his mouth.

"Okay, forget I said that. What do you want to know?"

He smiled with one side of his mouth. "Does the name Greg Wetherell mean anything to you?"

"Lawyer from Whitehall?" He nodded. "Sure. I've met him a few times."

"Business?"

"Socially. Through my friend Ivy."

"Who?"

"Ivy Martin. Remember, the one with the long black hair?" Oh boy, wouldn't Ivy be rankled to know she had made a less-than-indelible impression?

"Oh yeah, her." He chewed on the toothpick. "So he and Ivy were—a couple?"

"Short answer, yes." I wasn't eager to delve into Ivy's complex love life so I didn't elaborate. But Frank just sat there looking at me, so I continued. "Long answer, Ivy and Greg have been in and out of a relationship for at least two years—maybe longer. I guess you'd call it stormy."

I waited for Frank to respond but he just chewed on the toothpick, apparently lost in thought. When I couldn't stand it any longer, I said, "This must have something to do with Madeline, right?" He didn't answer. "Come on, I've been helping you."

Frank rubbed his chin. "None of this goes in the paper, okay?"

"Promise."

"Okay. I found Wetherell's phone number on Madeline's phone bill."

"*Madeline?*" I echoed. "Madeline had calls to Greg?"

"Several calls, in fact." Now it was my turn to be silent as I stared at him, completely dumbfounded. Finally he filled me in. "I made a surprise to his office—to ask him what he and Madeline had talked about. First he claimed the calls were business. Then he acted kind of nervous and asked me to come back later, meet him after work. So I went back that evening to a place called the Twilight Zone."

"That place is well named."

"It is pretty dismal. Anyway, he got there ahead of me and he'd been at it for a while."

"Greg does like his scotch. What happened?"

"He admitted to having an affair with Madeline. A 'little fling' was how he put it."

I stared at Frank, my jaw hanging, no doubt. "Really? Greg Wetherell and Madeline?"

Frank nodded and things started to fall into place. So this was the affair that Ivy had been moaning about the afternoon we were in Madeline's apartment. The revelation brought up a lot of questions and I asked the first one that came to mind.

"Do you think Greg could have killed Madeline?"

Frank rolled the toothpick. "Probably not. His alibi was a fund raising dinner in Muskegon and it checked out. Plus, I don't see much in the way of motive. They were both adults and both single, after all. No real scandal there." He was quiet for a moment, abusing the toothpick and then said, "Did your friend Ivy know about them?"

"She knew there was someone," I said and then recapped our conversation in the apartment. "I really don't think she knew who it was."

"If she knew, do you think she would have told you?"

"She would have told me—in very colorful language. Ivy's not bashful."

Frank chewed his lower lip. "Unless she was hiding something."

"Hiding something? Like what?"

"Who knows?" He flipped the notebook shut. "Guess I'll have to pay her another visit."

Frank walked with me to the parking lot. When we reached my Honda, he tossed his toothpick, leaned on the hood and said, "You've been a big help, Tracy."

"I just hope it does some good." I opened the car door and slid inside.

Frank moved and stood with a hand on the open door. "Can I ask you a personal question?"

I fumbled with my keys. "I guess so."

"Are you, ah, seeing anyone?"

"No one in particular." I looked up at him, trying hard for an enigmatic smile. No use mentioning that I hadn't had a date in a year.

"Could I, maybe, take you to dinner some time?"

"Sure—I mean, I guess so." Was I sounding too eager?

"Good." He smiled, showing the gap between his teeth. "I'm heading out of town for a few days. But I'll call you as soon as I get back."

By the time I pulled out of the parking lot I was running late. Then I got trapped behind a monstrous piece of farm equipment lumbering down the road, so I crawled at forty miles an hour while my mind went racing. I was thrilled that Frank had finally made a move on me. But I had a nagging suspicion that our 'date' might be part of his investigation. I could just see it on his expense account—"Entertaining single female—friend of deceased —."

On the other hand, what could I say about ulterior motives? I certainly had one when I fed him supper at my house. So maybe we were just using each other. Tit for tat. Quid pro quo. And then there was the news about Madeline and Greg. What would Ivy say when she found out? I sure didn't want to be the one to tell her. I wondered if the affair had anything to do with Madeline's death. And where was Frank Kolowski heading off to anyway? Would he call me when he got back? And if he did, what would I wear?

"Wind power is the fuel of the future. You can start a green energy revolution right here in Cedar County that will earn you the gratitude of future generations."

The scene was the Shagoni Township Hall, packed to near capacity on a sultry June evening. The speaker was Kevin Carmicheal, partner in a company called GreenEnergyWorks. He was tall, thin and slightly hunched, creating an Abe Lincoln impression. Despite the heat, Carmichael was wearing black pants with a long sleeved white shirt and a necktie.

In deference to the sweltering weather I had arrived in modest shorts. But after ten minutes on a folding chair, I tried to move and found my thighs adhered to the metal seat. All of the windows in the ancient building were open to catch any possible breeze, but the night was still and the creaking overhead fans did little to move the tepid air. I unfolded the agenda I had been using as a fan. It said that Carmichael and his partner wanted to erect wind generators on land that was zoned agricultural. The meeting was their opportunity to request a permit.

Carmichael finished his spiel and invited questions. A man in the audience asked how the turbines would affect bird migration. Carmichael's partner, Jonah Flynn, stood up to answer. Flynn was barrel shaped and dressed exactly like his partner, giving them the appearance of Mormon missionaries. Flynn said the turbines presented no danger to wildlife. A woman in flowered shorts wanted to know if the turbines would be running all the time.

"Only a few hours in the morning," said Carmichael, "and again in the evening. And they're very quiet."

A white-haired man asked why they had chosen Shagoni Township for their project. Flynn said the township was one of very few places in Michigan that offered the right wind currents.

This comment was greeted by a derisive snort from the back of the room. Turning around I saw Tom Halladay, easily identifiable in his red shirt and black hat. Roxanne was beside him, looking hot in a red tank top and shorts.

"I think you folks are asking the wrong questions," Halladay said. "You should ask what effect these machines will have on your property values." People started turning around to look at him. "I've seen these turbines in operation and they're not a pretty sight. They are, in fact, monstrosities that stand four hundred feet tall and sound like threshing machines."

Halladay gathered steam. "We all know that scenic beauty is our greatest resource in this county. Hell, it's the reason a lot of us moved here. But these machines will destroy all that. They'll be an eyesore that will cause property values to plummet, and tourism to dry up." He gestured toward Flynn and Carmichael. "These two have told you that no other place has the right wind currents. Well that is a downright lie."

Halladay spoke slowly now, his voice rising in volume, like a preacher. "I'll tell you why they chose Shagoni Township. They think we're a bunch of hicks who don't have the guts to say no. Well, I'm against this project. And I think anyone who gives it serious thought will agree with me." Somebody clapped as Halladay sat down and the applause grew until it filled the room.

When things were quiet again, Mat Bryant, a retired lawyer stood up. "This is a brand new company," he said. "If they go broke they could leave us with an ugly pile of rusting scrap metal."

Flynn and Carmichael both stood and interrupted one another as they tried to answer. But the mood in the room had shifted and all responses from the Mormon team were met with scornful mutters. The meeting deteriorated into a dozen private conversations and the chairman adjourned, promising another hearing in thirty days. I rose to leave and found myself once again glued to the chair.

"Tom Halladay is the biggest hypocrite this side of the Mississippi," Marge said when I told her about the meeting. "He's the one who moved in with major development and now he's crying about city folks trying to take advantage. What a laugh." Marge was wearing a ruffled yellow dress that reminded me of a second grade musical where we all dressed up like flowers.

"I think some of the people were in favor of the turbine project," I said. "But after Halladay's tirade they were afraid to speak up."

"How close is the ranch to the proposed site?"

"Pretty close. I think it adjoins at some point."

"I can see why he's scared. " She snapped on a pair of yellow plastic earrings. "He's put a bundle of money into that ranch, and those generators would mar the vision of rustic beauty he's peddling." She sorted through a stack of papers on her desk until she found a letter which she handed to me. "And get a load of this."

It was a press release. I read aloud, "To all media outlets. The Diamond D Ranch will host a Celebrity Golf Tournament on August 12 with all proceeds going to local charities. Owner Tom Halladay said —." I quit reading and dropped the letter back on her desk. "Great publicity stunt. It's just a cheap way to get the Diamond D name into all the newspapers."

"Not to mention TV and radio. Want to cover it?"

"Please, no golf. I'm the one who thinks high scores should win."

"Okay. I'll send Kyle. Did they ever get that liquor license?"

"It's still in process. Dirkse told me that Halladay is leaning hard on the township to give it their approval."

"That figures. The charity golf tournament is probably part of his campaign to win over the township board."

"Do you think it will work?"

"Depends on who you ask. People seem to either love or hate the Diamond D."

Marge stood, shoving things into her purse. "I'm off," she said. "Don't forget you're covering the 4H Folk Festival. Get plenty of photos. And please, Tracy, for that Garden Club Luncheon tomorrow —."

"Yes?" I paused in the doorway.

"Try to dress up a little."

The Folk Festival was rife with photo opportunities. A hefty woman in a long dress was bent over a tub of soapy water, demonstrating the use of lye soap and a washboard to a group of gum chewing school kids. She got one of the kids to help her wring water from a shirt and then pinned it to a clothesline strung between two trees. I chuckled to think that my current clothes drying technique was part of an historic exhibit. Brooke would love that.

A muscular, bearded man was hammering a horseshoe and stopped long enough to tell me that nobody spelled farrier correctly and I promised to get it right. I stepped inside the exhibit hall and was immersed in sound. Dozens of men and women were talking as they demonstrated corn-shellers, churns and muzzle loaders to kids who were laughing and poking each other. In the midst of the cacophony I was relieved to see a familiar face.

Les Tattersal was whittling on a piece of wood, wearing his impeccable blue shirt and yellow bow tie. He sat behind a table laden with carvings of fish, birds, wolves and other shapes that I couldn't immediately identify.

"Hello, Les. I didn't know you were so talented."

"Good to see you, Tracy." Les came around the table and gave me a hug. "Yeah, there's a few of us old farts who do this. It keeps us out of trouble." While we chatted he whittled a boutonniere and tucked it into my lapel.

I got a photo of Les and his woodcarvings and then moved around the room snapping pictures of women quilting, a girl weaving baskets, and a man working a large loom. A small lady in a high necked blouse was twisting strands of yarn while she pedaled a spinning wheel bigger than she was. The spinner was Daisy Birdsall from the Blue Bird Tea Room and the minute she saw me she laid down her work.

"Oh, it's Tracy Quinn," she said. "I'm so glad to see you." She looked around and then lowered her voice to a conspiratorial whisper. "That detective fellow came to see me last week. It was so exciting. And he seemed very nice. I do hope he can catch that person, whoever it is. Oh, did you want a picture of me with the spinning wheel?" She fluffed her hair and moved back into position.

As I took her picture, Les Tattersal appeared beside me. "Miss Daisy has agreed to join me for coffee. Would you like to come with us?"

The three of us went to the food court where the coffee came in Styrofoam cups but the baked goods were all home made. I tried a piece of maple gingerbread, Les got rhubarb pie and Daisy sampled the apple pandowdy. Les insisted on paying for everything.

When we finished, Les and Daisy went back to their posts. I left through a side door blinking against the sunlight, and almost stumbled over a man tending a ground fire in a ring of stones. The back of the man's shirt held rows of colorful ribbons, his hair was in a braid and when he looked up, I saw a face that was brown and creased. A younger man, carrying a large drum, came and sat near the fire on a wooden stump. They told me they were from the Traverse Bay Tribe of Ottawa Indians.

The scene felt something like a movie set. Behind us loomed a large conical tent with an entranceway about four feet high. They must have noticed my wistful gaze.

"You can go inside if you want to," said the man with the ribbon shirt.

I thanked him, ducked my head and slipped inside the teepee. Inside, I stood quietly, fascinated by the sensation of being indoors but still surrounded by shadowless white light. I sat on a low wooden stool, reached down to touch a bearskin rug and noticed the skulls of several small creatures lying nearby. I picked one up and ran my fingers over the dry bone. In spite of the dead animals, the place gave me a feeling of serenity.

But the peaceful feeling didn't last long. On my way out, I almost knocked heads with a dark-haired woman carrying a camera who was on her way in. When she stepped back, I recognized Ivy Martin. I hadn't seen Ivy since our strange episode in the tea room.

"Tracy," she said, "what are you doing here?"

"Same as you, taking pictures."

"We need to talk."

I took this as a good sign. No doubt she wanted to apologize, or at least explain why she had stormed out of our lunch date. We both glanced around and wordlessly agreed to seek the privacy of the tent.

Once inside, Ivy turned on me, elbows jutting. "Damnit Tracy, you've got me in trouble, big time."

So much for the apology. "Ivy, what are we talking about?"

"About me and Greg, that's what."

"You and Greg?"

"You told the detective that Greg and I were—an item. Don't deny it."

Apparently Frank hadn't wasted any time. "I guess I did. He asked me if I knew Greg Wetherell, and I said yes. Then he asked how, and I said it was through you."

"Great. That's just great. So now he's got me on his short list."

"Short list? He thinks *you* killed Madeline?"

"Right. Like I was so jealous of her little—fling with Greg that I bumped her off."

"But you didn't even know they were—involved, did you?"

"Not until your buddy clued me in. And then had the nerve to ask where I was the night of May nineteenth."

"So tell him. You had a date didn't you?"

Ivy's face collapsed. "No. I mean yes, but he, no it was me, I canceled. I was feeling awful so I just stayed home." Her shoulders slumped. "Tracy, I've got no one to vouch for me."

"Even so, I don't see how anyone could suspect you. He must be grasping at straws."

"Well, I'm in hot water now, thanks to your big mouth."

"Ivy, I had no idea this was going to happen. I am so sorry —." I reached out to her.

"Don't touch me!" She swatted my hand away like it was a bug. "Do me a big favor, Tracy. Just stay away from me." She turned and ducked out of the tent.

I stood a few minutes and tried to gather my wits. I knew that Ivy had a temper because I had seen it unleashed before—but never in my direction. She had me rattled. I took some deep breaths, willed my pulse back to normal and walked outside. To my relief, Ivy was nowhere to be seen.

I said goodbye to the two men and decided it was time to go home. But then I was thinking so hard about Ivy that it took me a while to find my car.

Things weren't adding add up right. She didn't have an alibi for the night Madeline was killed. I thought back to the chamber breakfast and was almost certain that Ivy had never mentioned anything about being sick over the weekend. In fact I *thought* I remembered her saying that she had a "great time" Saturday night. Would murdering one's friend qualify as a great time?

Driving home, I fell into a serious funk. My life was at an all time low, at least where female friends were concerned. Madeline was dead. My attempts to help Jewell had only deepened the suspicions surrounding her husband. And now Ivy had just accused me of ruining her life. For once I was glad I didn't live alone. I pictured Brooke in the kitchen cooking up some gooey pasta dish for supper, and the prospect of comfort food and conversation was suddenly very appealing.

But no savory smells came wafting through the screen door. The house felt empty. I went to the kitchen to get a drink and that's when I heard sounds coming from upstairs. I stood at the foot of the stairway, listening, until I knew for sure that the sound I heard was crying.

My first impulse was to ignore Brooke and her problem. After all, I was dealing with some serious issues of my own and no one could expect me to take on any more. Could they? But the sobbing didn't stop, so I finally snailed into action. Making as much noise as possible, I climbed the stairs and approached Brooke's bedroom. The door was open and she was sitting on the edge of her unmade bed. She looked up at me with bloodshot eyes.

"Can I come in?"

"I guess so."

I went in, sat on the bed and put an arm around her. "Tell me what's wrong, " I said, trying to sound motherly. Or at least big sisterly.

She sniffled, shook her head and blew her nose.

"You can tell me."

"No I can't."

"Come on, Brooke."

"I can't talk about it."

Lord, how these kids dramatize. So maybe she'd had a fight with Derek. "Come on. It can't be that bad."

She blew her nose again, wiped her eyes. I gave her a reassuring hug.

"My – my period's late. I think I might be —."

CHAPTER TWELVE

"Pregnant?" I said the word that Brooke seemed to be choking on.

She nodded silently. Then, through tears, she took a deep breath and explained how it happened. She had *been* on the pill, but then she got busy with exams and missed her clinic appointment and then she never rescheduled because she wasn't seeing anyone anyway, and then she met Derek and well, it just happened.

I struggled to stay in the role of capable adult, but my insides felt like screaming. Then she said, "Oh, Tracy, what am I gonna do?" and the scream almost came out. How did I know what she should do? And why was she asking me? And why had I let this kid move in with me anyway?

But somewhere in my head I heard Jewell's voice. The Jewell voice said that Brooke was asking me for advice because I was an older woman and because I was her friend. The voice told me to stay calm, listen, and not rush to judgment or even into giving advice. So I heard Brooke out and then said, quietly, "How long overdue are you?"

"About four days."

"But you went off the pill. Doesn't that make your periods irregular?"

"I don't know. Maybe. I'm just so worried." She twisted a corner of the sheet.

"We should call your mother. I promised to let her know if we had any problems."

"Oh, please—no." She gave me a look I can only describe as terrified. "My mom will have a fit—and then she'll tell that husband of hers. I mean, we don't even know for sure yet."

She was right—so I agreed to leave her mother out of this, for now. I suggested getting a pregnancy test kit. Brooke said she had already looked in town but Anderson Drugs did not stock the item.

"There's two drug stores in Stanwood. I guess I could look for one tomorrow."

"People will think it's for you." She giggled through her tears.

That's exactly what I was thinking. If the clerk knew me, the news that Tracy Quinn was having a sex life would make it to the courthouse in a matter of hours. Before I could reply, we heard someone at the front door.

Brooke turned white. "I hope it's not Derek," she whispered. "I'm just not ready to —."

"I'll see who it is," I said, grateful for the diversion. "Come on in," I yelled, heading down the stairs. As I reached the bottom step, the screen door opened and my guardian angel appeared, this time wearing blue jeans and a denim jacket. Jewell was back.

"I just got in from Ann Arbor," she said. "Thought I'd stop by."

"Welcome back. How was the trip?"

"Just what I needed—being with Sarah was good medicine."

"It must have been. You look refreshed."

"Plus she gave me this jacket." Jewel did a turn, modeling the item, but stopped mid-turn and frowned. "Tracy, what's the matter?"

"Oh me? Just tired." I bit my lip, debating whether to reveal the drama unfolding upstairs. I didn't want to embarrass Brooke, but on the other hand, this *was* Derek's mother. So I gave up. "Jewell, I can never fool you. The fact is, we have a new problem."

Her look turned quizzical. "Problem? What kind?"

"It's Brooke. She thinks she may be—ahhh —." Now I was having trouble saying the word.

"Fired?"

"No. Slightly worse."

"Pregnant?"

"You are so perceptive."

Jewell absorbed this news in a matter of seconds, along with the fact that I wasn't handling it very well. "Is Brooke here?"

I nodded. "Upstairs."

"Let me talk with her."

I had the feeling of an enormous burden being shared as Jewell followed me up the stairs. Brooke was still sitting on her bed and started to cry again when she saw us.

"Hey, we don't need that," said Jewell. Acting as though this were an every day occurrence, she sat beside Brooke, put an arm around her shoulders and smoothed back the tangled hair. I sat on the other side of Brooke, causing the bed to sag.

"I'm so sorry," sniffed Brooke.

"Hey, listen," said Jewell. "You're not the first person this ever happened to. I don't think anyone gets through college without a pregnancy scare. Usually it takes one of these to make you cautious."

"But what'll I do if —?"

"If we find that you are, then we'll talk about options. But there's no need to do that yet." She quickly resolved the problem of the test kit. "I'll get one tomorrow after work and I'll come straight here."

"Would you really?" said Brooke.

"Sure, no problem. I have to pick up a prescription anyway." Jewell planted a kiss on Brooke's forehead. "By this time tomorrow, we'll have an answer. And we'll take it from there. Does that sound like a plan?" She handed Brooke a tissue.

"Yeah, thanks." Brooke blew her nose. "I'm so sorry, you guys. I mean—I just wish —."

"Don't beat yourself up," said Jewell. "This whole thing is Derek's fault as much as yours. Does he even know about it?"

Brooke shook her head.

"Well, he's in for a mother-son talk," Jewell said, and then deftly changed the subject. "So what have my men been up to while I was gone? Did Derek mow the lawn like he promised? If I find a sink full of dirty dishes, those guys are in a heap of trouble." Jewell kept talking until she had coaxed a smile from Brooke.

"Guess I'm okay now," said Brooke. She stood and peeked in the mirror. "Oh yikes, my hair's a mess. Guess I'd better take a shower."

"Good plan," said Jewell. "I'll be downstairs with Tracy for a while."

"Once again you have rescued me," I said to Jewell when we were in the kitchen.

"Glad I could help. You two looked pretty tense."

"Worse than tense. I didn't know whether to scream or throw up. But you take it all in stride. How do you manage?"

"I worked in family planning for two years. And I raised a daughter."

"Thank goodness for that."

We poured two glasses of iced tea and took them out to our favorite chairs on the front porch. The scent of lilacs and freshly cut grass hovered in the air. Jewell sipped her tea and said, "Any new developments?"

"Developments?" I was still so involved in Brooke's drama that I wasn't sure what she was talking about.

"Murder investigation, remember? Any news there?"

"Oh, how could I forget? Wait'll you hear this—I just found out that Madeline had an affair with Greg Wetherell."

Jewell stopped mid swallow. "Greg and Madeline? That's hard to believe."

"Believe it. Frank Kolowsky told me yesterday. He tracked Greg down from calls on Madeline's phone bill. Greg denied it at first, but after a few drinks, admitted to the affair."

Jewel pursed her lips. "Okay, I believe it. When did this happen?"

"Sometime this spring."

"Were they still seeing each other when—when she got killed?"

"I'm not exactly clear on that."

"Does Ivy know about this?" Jewell almost smirked. "I bet she's furious."

"She's definitely furious. But there's more to it than her being mad at Greg."

"How so?"

"This makes her third party to a triangle. And that makes her a suspect in Madeline's death. Frank sees jealousy as a motive."

"Jealousy. Oh, I see." Jewell's expression grew thoughtful. "Well, you know, we've both heard Ivy say things like, 'I could just kill that bitch'."

"Right. And she was usually talking about Greg's latest bimbo."

"True. But I always thought it was just high drama."

"Me too," I said, "until now. But here's the really strange part. She doesn't have an alibi for the night of May nineteenth." I told Jewell about Ivy's tale of the canceled date. "It sounds pretty weird, doesn't it?"

"It sounds downright suspicious."

"I know. But I just can't picture Ivy killing Madeline."

"Well, me neither. But at this point, it's her or Paul."

"Guess you're right. So for Paul's sake, let's try to picture it. Let's say Ivy and Madeline are out together Saturday evening. They go to the Sailors Rest and have a few drinks."

Jewell joined the scenario. "Things are quiet at the bar. They drive to the beach and walk out on the pier."

"Madeline has had way too many Margaritas." I was feeling like a scriptwriter. "She lets it slip that she's been examining Greg's briefs."

Jewell giggled. "And liked what she found."

"So then Ivy hits her over the head?"

"And pushes her in?"

"I guess that's how Frank sees it," I said, "but it's a little hard to imagine. I don't remember any rocks lying around on the pier. Where would Ivy get the weapon?"

"Maybe she carried it in her purse."

"If she did, that would mean she planned it ahead of time. I don't think so."

"Maybe we don't know Ivy as well as we think." Jewell drained her glass.

"You may be right. This afternoon I saw a side of her that gave me the creeps." I recounted Ivy's strange behavior in the teepee. "When she turned on me, it was downright scary."

"Wait a minute. Why does Ivy blame you for her predicament?"

"Because I'm the one who told Frank that Greg was her boyfriend."

"So now she's on your case—because you told the truth?"

"Looks that way."

"Seems like Ivy always blames someone else for her problems," Jewell said as she rose to leave.

"If Ivy is capable of murder," I said, "then I might be next on her hit parade." It was supposed to be a joke, but it didn't sound very funny.

Jewell didn't think so either. "Be careful," she said. "I wouldn't want anything to happen to you."

Jewell returned as promised the next afternoon and the three of us assembled in my living room. "Well, that was fun," she said, placing a white box on the coffee table. "The clerk all but asked me who it was for."

Jewell opened the box and handed Brooke a plastic container to take into the bathroom. Minutes later Brooke emerged and Jewell put drops of urine on a white wafer. Within seconds, a horizontal line appeared. We watched and counted out loud, waiting for a second line to appear. Nothing happened.

"It's negative," said Jewell. "Looks like a false alarm."

The relief in the room was tangible. Brooke cheered. Jewell and I took turns hugging her. Then the three of us joined hands in a sort of non-fertility dance until we collapsed on the couch in laughter. Brooke was relieved not to be facing an unplanned pregnancy. Jewell and I were delighted not to be facing grandmother status.

When the silliness abated, Jewell took a business card from her purse and handed it to Brooke. "This is the phone number of the family planning clinic. Call them and make an appointment. Now."

Brooke squinted at the card. "But this is in Stanwood. How will I get there?"

"Derek will take you. I had a talk with him last night."

Brooke found the telephone and began to dial. Jewell headed for the door.

"Thanks for everything," I said as I walked with her to her car. "You really didn't need another problem."

"Actually, it was a welcome distraction. I was happy to deal with a crisis that actually had a resolution."

"Unlike the one at home?" We paused by the row of tall purple lilacs.

"Unlike the one at home." She smiled grimly. "What a sad homecoming. Paul didn't even pretend he was glad to see me."

I hurt for Jewell. What had become of her husband, that lovable teddy bear of a man? I broke off a spray of purple blossoms. "Did you tell him about Greg and Madeline?"

"Never had the chance."

I handed her the lilacs. "Remember, my guest room is available."

"Thanks Tracy. But I really love my home."

On Thursday Ivy showed up at the county board meeting looking like she hadn't slept for days. Pouches of flesh sagged under bloodshot eyes and her attempts at eye makeup had just made everything worse. When I said good morning, she gave me a stony stare and scooted as far away from me as possible. All morning, Ivy never acknowledged my presence and never said a word to anyone. Her silence was disconcerting. I missed the old Ivy and was a little bit afraid of the new one. Did she have a hammer hidden in the bottom of that monogrammed handbag?

The meeting droned on. Shortly after eleven, Sheriff Benny Dupree showed up, red faced and puffing a little. The sheriff presented a letter from a group called the Women's Festival Committee. "The women want an overnight patrol out at their campground for three nights," he said. "They'll pay wages, gas and overtime. I need the board's approval."

"Have you done this before?" asked one of the commissioners.

"This will be the third year," said Dupree, "and there's never been any problem—except for the guys staying awake. The women pay in advance and the check is always good. It makes a nice bonus for a couple of the guys."

The board approved the extra patrol, and the sheriff was about to leave when Lathan Dirkse said, "Benny, are you making any progress at all on this murder investigation?"

Dupree's neck darkened. "We're working on it—full time."

124

"I know you are," said Dirkse. "But the tourism board is afraid an unsolved murder like this will be bad for business. We'd like to see this cleared up before the season gets under way."

"So would I," said Dupree. "We've got a couple new leads that we're working on. That's about all I can say right now."

And one of those leads was reporter Ivy Martin, sitting next to me and looking like death itself. To Dupree's credit, he avoided looking in her direction. As for Ivy, she made a quick exit while the board was still approving payment of bills. Too bad. I was just getting up my nerve up to ask her what this Women's Festival was all about. The meeting adjourned and I decided to ask Ann Doyle instead.

"Ann," I said, "what can you tell me about this—Women's Festival?"

"It's a big camp-out in the woods," she said, "with no men allowed. I've never been there so that's about all I know."

After Ann left I tried to remember if I had plans for lunch. Not with Ivy, that was for sure. The commissioners were gone, all except Lathan Dirkse who was talking with Ron Langlois. I was on my way out when Dirkse motioned me over.

"Tracy," he said, "did you cover that wind turbine meeting the other night?"

"Sure did. The place was packed."

"Sorry I couldn't make it. What happened?"

"The Greenenergy guys gave their spiel, and the group seemed fairly receptive. But all that changed when Tom Halladay opened his mouth."

Dirkse chuckled. "I hear he made quite a speech."

"He did, and it pretty much turned the tide. For some reason Halladay is dead set against having those turbines come in."

Dirkse gave me an appraising look. "I can tell you what's really going on out there—but it's strictly off the record."

"Fine." I fell into a chair beside him. "Off the record."

"Tom Halladay is making a big noise about the wind generators. But that's all a ruse. He really doesn't care one way or the other."

"Could have fooled me."

"What he really wants," said Dirkse, "is a liquor license for the Diamond D. And I mean he *really* wants it."

"People seem to connect golf and alcohol," said Langlois. "Whenever I play out there, people are always asking for the bar."

"So here's the scuttlebutt." Dirkse steepled his fingers. "Halladay has told certain people that he'll change his stand on the wind generators, publicly, if he gets approval for his liquor license."

"He's setting up a trade?"

"Exactly."

"Is that legal?"

Dirkse shrugged. "It's just small town politics."

"This Halladay character seems to show up everywhere," said Langlois.

"That's for sure." I nodded at Dirkse. "I heard that he might run for your seat."

"I've heard that too." Dirkse smiled. "County clerk says he hasn't filed yet."

"But there's still plenty of time," said Langlois. "And his chances are probably

as good as anyone else's."

Neither of them mentioned Paul Lavallen, but I knew what they were thinking. With a murder rap hanging over his head, Paul's political chances were getting slimmer by the day.

On my way out of the courthouse I remembered that it was my day to relieve Phoebe, the front desk clerk, for lunch. So I raced back to Shagoni River and arrived at the office about twelve-thirty five. I found Phoebe taking an order for wedding invitations from a young woman with fluffy blonde hair wearing tight jeans and a skimpy tank top. The prospective bride walked out with a dreamy look in her eyes.

Phoebe snorted. "Give her a couple of years and she won't be so starry eyed. These kids just don't know what they're getting into, and no, nobody can tell 'em." She collected her purse. "Guess I'll try that Blue Bird Tea Room."

"I think you'll like it," I said. "They've got it fixed up pretty nice. And Phoebe, what's this Women's Festival I keep hearing about?"

"I'm sure I wouldn't know." She gave me a blank stare and walked out.

Marge showed up ten minutes later so I asked her. "Marge, what *is* this Women's Festival?"

"Interesting you should ask." She dropped the mail on Phoebe's desk. "You may get a chance to find out."

"How so?"

"I could send you to cover it." She sat down in Phoebe's chair. "The first year I sent a college intern, but since then I haven't had anybody. Lorna refuses to go and I'm busy that weekend. Can't send the boys, obviously, so we've missed it for a while now."

"Why does Lorna refuse?

"Because these women are—*lesbians*." Marge lowered her voice as she said the word, even though there was no one else in the office.

"Oh. That's a problem?"

"It is for Lorna. Her church is on the, ah, conservative side. How about you?"

"Me? I've got no problem with women who like women."

"Well neither do I. Whatever floats their boat is what I say."

I was a little surprised to hear this from Marge. Just because she wore teased hair and plastic earrings, I had assumed that all of her views would be to the right of mainstream. I seemed to be wrong. "So what happens at this festival?"

"Thousands of women show up." Marge started sorting the mail. "They spend a long weekend on some land over by Salmon Creek. The camping is strictly primitive but they get some big name musicians – people like Holly Near and Ani di Franco."

"An all-female rock party." I tried to picture it—thousands of campers without a man around to change a tire or pitch an awning. "How does the community respond?"

"So far, nobody's picketing. Women like Lorna and Phoebe pretend it doesn't exist. The businesses out there don't mind because that's a whole lot of people buying gas and groceries."

"From what I hear, a couple of deputies get overtime just for hanging around in patrol cars."

She smiled. "I suppose there have been some attempts at gate crashing. So what do you think? Want to check it out?"

"Might as well. Can't be any worse than the biker bash."

"Good. I'll set you up with a press pass. But leave your camera home, Tracy. These ladies like their privacy."

"Trust me," said Brooke. "It'll look great."

"I don't want anything extreme."

"It won't be all that different. I'll just layer it a little and shape it to your head."

After several offers on her part and much hesitation on my part, I had finally agreed to let Brooke cut my hair—I think "style" was the word she used. She claimed extensive experience on her friends in college. So one night after supper she sat me down on a kitchen chair and wrapped a towel around my neck. Then she started doing something with a comb that felt like little critters walking around on my scalp.

"My period started today," she said.

"That's great. When's your clinic appointment?"

"Tomorrow." She started snipping. "Derek's going to take me. His mother really read him the riot act."

I smiled at the thought of Jewell lecturing her almost-grown son on the facts of male responsibility. "I'll be happy when I see that little package of pills in the medicine chest."

"That's funny. At home I had to hide them from my mom."

"It's easier for me, Brooke. After all I'm not your mother. How are things at work?"

"I meant to tell you. We have to go in early tomorrow—to practice for a show."

"What kind of show?"

"Oh, it's really stupid. I have to wear a skirt and we all do this square dance thing—sort of like 'Oklahoma'. One girl sings and Travis plays guitar." Brooke stood back and surveyed me. Started snipping again.

"Do you get paid extra for this?"

"Nope, it's just part of the job."

"How do you like it out there?"

"Mostly it's all right. The tips are good. But we have a lot of bosses and they all tell us something different—there's Brandi the hostess and Brian the headwaiter and the grouchy cook. Roxanne does our time cards and she gets spastic if they're a minute late. And then Boss Halladay comes in and yells at everybody."

"Sounds like one big dysfunctional family."

"Well, it's not forever, just the summer." She stood back for another survey, which apparently satisfied her, because she removed the towel. "Look in the mirror," she directed.

I peered into the mirror on the dining room wall and found that Brooke had done wonders. I still had rather thick, unruly hair, but the sides were tapered and lay close to my head. I felt rather glamorous. "Thanks so much. It looks great."

"Yes it does. Mr. Detective will swoon when he sees you."

"You're so smart. Actually, he did ask me to go out to dinner."

"A date with the detective! Tracy, that's so cool."

"Sure, but he's probably after clues. He thinks I'm hiding valuable information that will slip out when I'm off guard."

What dinner date? By Friday evening I still hadn't heard from Frank. I thought about going to the Belly Up, but the possibility of encountering Ivy scared me off. So I took a bath, crawled into pajamas, and channel surfed until I found a movie about two women running a hotel on a Caribbean island. I must have fallen asleep, because the telephone interrupted a dream in which I was naked and diving into a very large pina colada.

I picked up and mumbled hello. The caller was male and there was a lot of background noise.

"Is this Tracy Quinn?"

"Yes, who's this?" I heard music, laughter.

"It's Elliot Walters. Down at the Belly Up."

That explained the noise. Elliot was the bartender. "Elliot, what's up?"

"I'm sorry to bother you. It's about your friend Ivy."

"Is she okay?"

"Yes and no. I mean she's here, but she's had way too much to drink. She wants to drive home. I took her keys. Could have called the cops but I thought I'd try you first."

"I'll be right there."

Cursing, I dressed and drove to the Belly Up. The place was crowded and Ivy was at the end of the bar, nursing what looked like a Seven Up. Her mascara was smeared, raccoon style, and her blouse was hanging out of her jeans.

She looked at me, bleary-eyed. "Oh, if it isn't little Miss Fix it. Come to save me."

I took the stool next to her. "Sorry Ivy. It was me or the cops."

Elliot appeared, wearing a green striped shirt and a weary look that said he'd seen it all before.

"Elliot here thinks I'm a lush. Don't you Elliot? You're the one who called her, aren't you?"

"Yes Ivy, it was me." Elliot talked in a soothing tone while he moved a rag in circles on the bar. "It's no big deal. Everyone drinks too much once in a while."

"So you call my worst enemy. Very smart."

"Come on, Ivy," I said. "I'll take you home."

Ivy swore a few times but stood up. She took a long time putting on her leather jacket, then grabbed her purse. I put an arm through hers, maneuvered us out to my car and slid her into the passenger seat. She looked at me sidelong through that dark curtain of hair and said, "My place or yours, sweetie?"

Good question. Ivy's house was ten miles out of town, so it made sense to take her to my place and get her car in the morning. But then I wondered if I wanted to spend the night with a possible killer sleeping on my couch—a possible killer who didn't like me very much. I closed her door, walked around and got in. The creature sitting next to me looked too sloppy drunk to be dangerous. "Let's go to my place."

"Whatever you say," she mumbled. "Whatever you say. I have no choice in this matter. Elliot thinks I'm a lush."

At my house, Ivy shook me off and stumbled up the steps in her high-heeled boots. Once inside, I tried to direct her to the couch but she went straight into the bathroom and made vomiting up noises.

"Feel better?" I asked when she emerged.

"A little." She sat on the couch, took off her boots. "But I look like crap."

"Yes, you do. Want some coffee?"

"Yes, I mean no. Tracy, you think I killed her, don't you?"

I sat down across from her. "I don't know who killed Madeline. Nobody seems to know."

"That detective thinks I did it."

"You're just one possibility. It's his job to check out every lead. It doesn't mean —."

"He thinks I killed her."

"So, did you?" I was losing patience.

"See? Now you're at me too." She fumbled in her purse. "Damn, I forgot I quit smoking."

"Ivy, that was two years ago."

"Yeah, sure. Look, I need to tell you something. I need to tell you something, and you have to swear not to repeat it."

"Okay. It won't go any farther than me."

"Promise?"

"Cross my heart, scout's honor, whatever you want." All I wanted was to get this over with so I could go to bed.

"I didn't kill Madeline and—damnit, don't you have anything to drink?"

"Club soda, lemonade, root beer." I didn't mention the bottle of wine.

"Okay, give me a root beer—please." I brought her a can of root beer and popped the top. She took a swallow and looked up at me. "I didn't kill Madeline."

"Okay, that's good."

"And neither did Paul Lavallen."

"How do you know that?"

"Okay. Here it is. Paul didn't do it because he was with me." Another swallow. "And I didn't do it because I was with him."

My mouth went dry. "What are you saying?"

"I was with him that night on his boat. Oh, you don't have to look at me like that."

"So you and Paul—you and Paul were —."

"Yes, Paul and I were—together. Please, don't tell Jewell." Ivy started to cry. "Whatever you do," she sobbed, "don't tell Jewell."

CHAPTER THIRTEEN

"You can't tell anyone," said Ivy. "You promised."

"That's before I knew what this was about."

"But you promised."

"Maybe I did. But if you and Paul were together the night of the murder, it changes everything. You need to talk to the sheriff."

"I know, but I think Paul should be the one to do it."

"Well somebody should. You're both murder suspects because of this."

"You think I don't know that?"

We were in my kitchen the morning after Ivy's inebriated confession, arguing in whispers so as not to awaken Brooke. The precaution was probably unnecessary since Brooke usually slept like she was in a coma after her shift at the Diamond D.

"Ivy, I can't keep quiet forever. It's obstructing something." I stood and refilled my coffee cup.

"It's Paul's place to tell Jewell, don't you think?" The morning sun was streaming in through the window and the light did not flatter Ivy. Her skin looked dry, her face bony.

"Sure. But he's probably afraid to."

"So am I."

I was beginning to lose patience. "If you don't do something, then I will. Your fling with Paul has created a tangled mess for all of us."

Her mouth twisted into a pout. "I thought you were my friend. That's why I confided in you."

"You confided in me because you were drunk. It was me or Elliot."

"I wasn't that drunk." She swallowed her coffee, made a big show of looking at her watch. "I'd better get going. I have a noon assignment."

The assignment may have been a fabrication, but that was okay with me. My hospitality was strained. Ivy went into the bathroom and emerged a few minutes later looking marginally better, with lip-gloss applied and her hair in a bun.

I drove her to the parking lot of the Belly Up and handed over her keys. "Ivy, this is a mess. You've got to clear it up."

"I know," she said. "It's just that, well, neither Paul nor I expected anything like this to happen. Why did Madeline have to go and get herself killed that night?"

"I'm sure it wasn't just to inconvenience you."

Ivy got in her car and started the engine, then leaned out the window and yelled, "Remember, you promised."

I waved but didn't give her the reassurance she wanted. As I watched her drive away, more questions arose. Had the ill-timed cruise been her first rendezvous with Paul? If not, how long had this been going on?

I sat there and debated. Should I tell Jewell that her husband had committed adultery instead of murder—or should I keep quiet and wait for Ivy to crack? On the other hand, why didn't Paul come clean and straighten out the whole mess? For once I had a problem I couldn't take to Jewell. I started home but then did a U-turn and headed for the Treasure Chest to find Gavin. Gay people are good with secrets.

"Hi Tracy, how are you?" Rhonda, a short, buxom redhead was behind the counter.

"Hi Rhonda, I was hoping to catch Gavin."

"You just missed him. He's off to an estate sale and won't be back 'til late Sunday."

"Oh darn." Disappointed, I turned to leave.

"Well, don't run off. Come look at all the neat stuff we got in this week. There's a whole lot of china and some of that old Depression glass."

I was not interested in the glass, figuring I was depressed enough. But I knew that Rhonda, the mother of two-year-old twins, worked on weekends just to have some adult conversation. And I had nowhere to go except an empty house—correction, a house with a sleeping teenager. So I stayed and talked with Rhonda while she showed me the new inventory—green glass plates, gold rimmed teacups and oddly shaped blue bottles.

We were now in the back of the store.

Rhonda stood fiddling with the knobs on a credenza while she said, "You were Madeline's friend, weren't you?"

"Sure, we were friends."

"I was wondering—was there any sort of charity she was involved in?"

"Nothing comes to mind, why?"

"Maybe it doesn't matter. But you see, I borrowed money from her. I never got it paid back and then, bam, she was dead. It was only a hundred dollars but

I feel like maybe I should donate it to something." Her voice trailed off. She looked at me expectantly.

"That's not a whole lot of money. When did you borrow it?"

"It was sometime in March," she said. "I had cabin fever so Roger stayed with the twins while Madeline and I went to the casino. We saw a show—some country singer in sequins—and afterward we gambled. I was flat broke by ten thirty so Madeline lent me a hundred dollars, and I lost that too. So far I was never able to pay her back."

With two little kids and a part time job, this did not seem surprising. "If you feel like you have to do something, why not make a donation to the library? Madeline always said we had a great library for such a small town."

"The library. Oh, that's a good idea." Her face mirrored relief, like I had solved a huge puzzling equation. We walked to the front of the store where I finally managed to make my exit. "Thanks so much for your help," she said. "My conscience is clear now." I drove home, wishing I could say the same.

Brooke was in the kitchen eating a sandwich and the tuna salad smelled good so I made one for myself.

"Jewell called," she said. "Wants you to call her back."

I poured a glass of milk. "Okay. I'll do it later."

"Said she was going out pretty soon."

"Don't worry," I said, a little sharply. "I'll take care of it."

Brooke looked at me, puzzled. But I couldn't tell her why I didn't want to call my best friend. The fact was, no matter how hard I tried to sound normal, Jewell would know that something was wrong – but I couldn't tell her what it was so what would I say? I considered sharing my dilemma with Brooke – but I couldn't expect her not to tell Derek. And how would Derek feel when he heard this kind of news about his father? I stood and stared out the window. Brooke was talking about something until she realized I wasn't listening.

"Tracy, what's the matter? Is it the haircut?"

"Oh no," I said. "I love the haircut." I decided to go with part of the truth. "I'm a little stressed because—Ivy spent the night here and—she sort of dumped on me."

"I thought I heard you talking to someone."

"She made me promise not to tell anyone."

"Okay—that's cool."

An unmistakable clamor in the driveway announced the arrival of Brooke's transportation. She said goodbye and flew out the door. Left alone, I turned my frustration onto the house, scrubbed the bathroom and mopped the kitchen floor. Then, figuring Jewell would be gone, I called and left a message saying I was sorry to miss her call. Lies. I was beginning to hate myself.

I got in my car and drove to Lake Michigan.

This time I left my shoes in the car and walked directly to the beach where I threaded my way around kids who were digging holes in the sand and screaming while they splashed each other. The sun was hot enough to make me think it was time to dig out my bathing suit. Maybe even buy a new one. I walked out on the pier, all the way down to the end where I was pretty much alone with the water and sky. I sat down on the rough cement with my back against the channel light fixture and tried to focus on the moment—waves breaking against rocks, boats motoring in and out of the channel, seagulls screeching and soaring.

But pretty soon the whole mess resurfaced. How could Paul, the perfect husband, be having an affair? Why did Ivy have to tell me about it? If I told Jewell, would she thank me or hate me? My thoughts tumbled around like clothes in a dryer until I heard my stomach growl and decided that finding food would be welcome diversion. Knees creaking, I got up and made my way to the boardwalk in search of a juicy hot dog from the concession stand. But along the way I encountered a curious knot of people, all of them talking and gesturing as they looked out over the lake.

"What's that crazy thing out there?" said a woman wearing a purple tube top. She was pointing to a spot above the horizon.

I joined the group, looked westward and saw a pink and green parachute moving slowly across the sky, with a metal frame hanging below. It took me a few seconds to realize that we were looking at a powered parachute. From this perspective, the craft looked so flimsy that I was appalled to remember how willingly I had gone aloft in one.

"It's called a powered parachute," I said, and shared some details from my interview with Marvin Crouch.

Another couple joined the group. The man, tall and gray-haired, said he had flown helicopters in Vietnam. "Those things don't have much range," he said. "Is there an airport nearby?"

"It's probably from the Diamond D Ranch," I said. "They've got three of them out there and they give rides." Oh great. Here I was doing publicity for the Halladays.

"I guess they're not very hard to fly," he said.

"You must be right. The pilot wanted to teach me."

"That doesn't look safe," said his wife, a short woman in a red straw hat. "I wouldn't be caught dead in one of those contraptions."

"Supposedly," I said, "they're the safest recreational vehicle in existence." She didn't look convinced.

I left the group and walked to the concession stand where I bought two hot dogs and piled them up with onions and mustard. Then I got a drink and took my supper to the picnic area, where I chose a table that promised a panoramic view. Off to my left was the pier with the harbor light tower. To my right was a ridge of low dunes that conveniently hid the state park campground, a small city of recreational vehicles. And straight ahead of me was the Lake Michigan beach where a bunch of people stood watching a strange aircraft make its way across the cloudless sky.

I wondered if the pilot was Marvin Crouch and I wondered if it was the same aircraft I had gone up in. Then, as I started on the second hot dog, something peculiar happened. The parachute dropped sharply, but then recovered. While I watched and ate, the strange behavior continued. The craft would plunge and then level off, losing altitude each time. I hastily finished my food and rejoined the cluster of people who were watching the bizarre air show.

"Is he doing stunts?" said purple tube top.

"Maybe he's running low on gas," said the veteran.

After two more stalls, the craft was getting near the water and it was pretty clear that the pilot was not doing stunts. I wondered if Marvin Crouch knew how to swim. At this point the gray haired vet disappeared and returned minutes later with a pair of binoculars. He trained them on the scene over the lake.

"Looks like a boat heading that way," he said.

He pointed to a fishing boat with a flying bridge that had been heading toward the channel but was now changing course. The boat moved toward the struggling aircraft, which was now dangerously low to the water.

"There it goes," he said.

The propeller must have hit first. The impact created a massive rainbow spray, a flash of bright and delicate color that was breathtaking even at a distance. The arc of fabric came down next, folding in on itself and spreading out on top of the water. I leaned closer to the veteran, wanting very much to grab his binoculars. But I could only wait for his report as the fishing boat closed in on the floating blob of color.

"Can you see anything?" I said.

"Looks like they threw out a life ring."

"Did he get it?"

"Can't tell—wait, they've got a ladder down. Someone is going in." After what seemed an interminable period of time, he said, "Okay, one guy's on the ladder now—and there's another. They must be okay."

There was a collective sigh of relief from the group, which now included the park ranger. After a few minutes, the rescue boat turned and headed back toward the channel. The crowd began to disperse. Smelling a story, I shifted into reporter mode. I asked the veteran how far out he thought the incident had occurred. His estimate was half a mile. We did a time check. I thanked him, sprinted to my car and headed for the village marina.

The first person I saw was marina manager Parnell Weeks, decked out in a yellow shirt undulating with hula girls. Then, just as I was getting out of my Honda, a Shagoni River police car pulled up next to me and police chief Owen Bridges emerged. Bridges was about my height, with big ears and a ruddy face.

Bridges greeted me with a curt nod. Maybe I was tagged as the Woman with the Bad Lawn. Parnell, holding a quart thermos bottle, was more friendly. He said the rescue boat was the *Lorelei* and he had been in radio contact with the skipper, Chet Henderson. We talked for a few minutes and I told them what I had seen from the beach. When the *Lorelei* hove into view, the three of us walked down to the dock and waited at the empty slip. Day sailors, some tying down canvas and others relaxing with drinks, watched us from their boats with mild curiousity.

When the *Lorelei* approached the dock, a lanky kid in bathing trunks and sweatshirt appeared on the bow. The kid tossed a line ashore and Parnell caught it. As the boat drew closer I could see Henderson, a solidly built man in his fifties, at the wheel. In one continuous motion, he tossed another line, dropped the rubber bumpers, spun the wheel and cut the engine. Within minutes the boat was moored.

Henderson addressed us from the cockpit. "The guy's okay," he said. "Just a little chilled. You folks want to talk to him, come on aboard. He's in the cabin."

I followed Bridges and Parnell onto the boat and down narrow steps into the cabin. It was dark inside. Small horizontal windows admitted the only light and it spilled like honey over polished wood surfaces. The cabin was small, lined with drawers and cabinets, and there was a table with two seats like a breakfast nook.

As my eyes adjusted I saw a figure seated at the table. In a sweatshirt that was several sizes too big and with a crocheted afghan around his shoulders, Marvin Crouch looked like a yardsale refugee. His lips were gray and his sparse hair was plastered to his head. Parnell slid into the seat across from him, poured a cup of coffee from the thermos and pushed it across the table. Crouch nodded his thanks and grabbed the cup with both hands.

Bridges and I remained standing. The cabin was cramped, not designed for press conferences. When Henderson joined us, Bridges moved closer, the boat rocked and I fell against the wall, or bulkhead, or whatever it was.

Bridges put a hand on the table to steady himself. "So what the hell happened out there?"

Crouch smoothed his nonexistent hair. "Damned if I know." He sucked at the coffee. "I know the motor was okay. Hell, the prop was still turning when it hit the water." He coughed. "It was the parachute. Big rip opened up and then another and maybe a third one—by that time I wasn't looking. Lucky these guys showed up."

The kid joined us in the cabin and everybody shifted again. The place was awash in testosterone. Henderson introduced the kid as his nephew Skeeter.

"Skeeter did all the work," said Henderson. "Went down and fished him out from under that parachute."

"He wasn't hard to find," said Skeeter, "but he was sort of tangled up in all those cords."

"I can't figure it out," said Crouch. "That thing is practically new. And those seams are stitched with thread like fish line. I'd like to see that chute."

"I tried to snag it with my gaff," said Henderson, "but it went down. I got a GPS bearing so we can look for it later."

I wanted to ask what GPS stood for but the guys were pretty much ignoring me as they argued about which authorities should be notified. Chief Bridges said he would report the incident to the county marine officer. Henderson said someone should inform the coast guard. Crouch said it was a matter for the state aeronautics commission and Bridges was starting to look confused.

It was hot in the cabin and everybody (including me) was low on deodorant, so it was a relief when the meeting wound down. Single file, we climbed up the steps and onto the deck. I asked Henderson if I could take some photos. When he agreed, I jumped from the boat and ran down the dock, causing that structure to sway perilously under my weight. I returned with my Nikon and assembled Henderson, Skeeter and Crouch on the stern of the boat. I took several shots and asked Henderson if he wanted copies.

"Sure," he said. "It'll be good publicity for my charter business."

"Yeah," said Skeeter, "he can claim Mr. Crouch as his biggest catch."

"Skeeter," I said. "You're a hero. Your praises will be sung this winter at the Belly Up."

Skeeter just grinned. By this time, Parnell and Bridges had both left so I offered Marvin Crouch a ride out to the Diamond D. He accepted. Henderson handed Crouch a plastic bag full of wet clothes and Crouch put on his shoes, which were oozing. Once in the car, I turned up the heater and let him relax. Except for an occasional sneeze, he was quiet until we were about half way to the ranch.

"Tom's going to be furious about this," he said.

"There must be insurance, isn't there?"

"Yeah, but this is bad publicity."

"I'll try to keep it on the back page," I said, but it was a lame joke. Marge would put the story wherever she wanted.

Crouch was silent for another mile. Then he said, "Somebody must have messed with that parachute."

"Do you keep that hangar locked?"

"Only at night."

"You think someone sneaked in and slashed a parachute?"

"Must have."

"Why would anybody do that?"

"Maybe someone has it in for me."

"More likely someone has it in for the Diamond D," I said, "and you were just unlucky." I was trying to reassure him but actually, it seemed like a good theory. I thought about folks who had quarrels with the Diamond D—the nearby church, certain neighbors and now the wind turbine guys. But would any of them stoop to sabotage?

Crouch changed the subject. "That woman who was killed," he said. "When did that happen?"

"It was the weekend before Memorial Day. Saturday night they figure."

"So what was the date?"

"May nineteenth. Why?"

"Oh nothing. I was just wondering."

At the ranch, Crouch thanked me for the ride and got out. He seemed to hesitate for a moment, bracing himself. Then he grabbed his bag and was gone, his wet shoes squishing on the walkway.

When I got home the message light was blinking. I pushed the button and my heart did a little dance at the sound of Frank Kolowsky's gravelly voice. "Hi Tracy. Sorry I missed you. Call me if you get a chance. I'll be at this number for about an hour. Otherwise, I'll see you when I get back."

I quickly dialed the number, but there was no answer. I was disappointed, but another part of me was relieved. As much as I wanted to see Frank, I didn't think I could be with him and not spill the latest development about Paul and Ivy. This damned secret was messing up the love life I didn't even have yet.

"We didn't have to do our show last night," said Derek.

"You've got some on your chin," said Brooke.

The three of us were at the kitchen table eating a slurry of fresh strawberries over shortcake still warm from the oven. The shortcake was Brooke's handiwork. I wasn't sure if this was their breakfast or lunch.

"What happened?" I said.

"Marvin Crouch was supposed to set up the sound system," said Derek, "but he had that accident and wound up in Lake Michigan."

"And no one else knew how to do it," said Brooke.

"Mr. Halladay was really mad."

I pictured Tom Halladay stomping on his ten-gallon hat.

"Yeah. First he was mad 'cause no one could find Mr. Crouch," said Brooke. "Then Crouch showed up and told him the parathingy was in the lake."

"Then Roxanne was fussing over Crouch almost getting drowned," said Derek,

"And Tom was acting, well, weird."

"Jealous, it looked like."

"So then there was a disaster in the kitchen—I think the stove ran out of gas."

"By the time they got that fixed," said Brooke, "it was too late for the show."

"But we might have to do it tonight."

"Have some more shortcake," I said. "Sounds like you two had better fortify yourselves."

With Brooke gone, I had a late supper and left the dishes in the sink. Then I stretched out in my recliner and started reading an old mystery novel I had picked up in Gavin's shop. I was well into the story—the hero had just stumbled over the second bloody corpse—when the phone rang.

I was avoiding Jewell. But I was dying to hear from Frank, so I picked up. It was Jewell, of course. I started to say something about trying to reach her, but she cut me off.

"Tracy, just listen to me."

"Okay."

"Paul told me where he was—the night Madeline was killed." My breath caught in my throat. "He was on the boat—with Ivy. Can you believe it? I don't think I've ever been so—so devastated—so hurt and angry in my entire life."

I struggled for words. "Jewell, you have every right to be furious. I'm—well, I'm just relieved that he finally told you."

"You knew?" She sounded incredulous, betrayed.

"Let's say I suspected—but only since Friday night," I added quickly. "Oh Jewell, it's been killing me."

She sounded very close to meltdown. "What in hell are we going to do?"

"I guess someone will have to explain all this to Sheriff Dupree."

"I know, but who—and how? I feel so humiliated."

Jewell was asking for help and I had absolutely no idea what to do. I've never been good in a crisis—usually I just hide and wait for things to resolve. But I owed Jewell, big time, and a voice in my head was telling me to do *something—anything.*

Finally the answer came to me, like a vision.

"We'll go together," I said.

"We will?"

"You bet we will. All four of us are going to see Benny Dupree."

CHAPTER FOURTEEN

The four of us probably looked like high school kids in detention, sitting together in the hallway outside the sheriff's office Monday morning. Paul, stony faced, was on one end, with Jewell on his right, then me, and then Ivy. I'm sure Jewell was closer to Ivy than she cared to be, but any other arrangement would have put Ivy closer to Paul, also not acceptable. This left me between Ivy and Jewell, presumably to offer moral support to both.

I felt completely out of my depth. How does one offer counsel to both the perpetrator and the victim of such a monstrous breach of etiquette? The best I could do was to carry a giant-sized box of tissues, which I held in my lap, available to either party.

Ivy leaned over and whispered. "I didn't know *they* would be here."

"Yes you did," I whispered back. "I told you —."

At that moment Sheriff Benny Dupree came down the hall, glanced at the grim lineup and said, "Okay, who wants to go first?"

Without a word, Paul rose and followed Dupree into his office. Paul was dressed for work in a white shirt and pleated trousers but the shirt was wrinkled and the socks didn't quite match.

"I'll be glad when this is over," I said to no one in particular.

"Me too," Jewell said softly. I reached out and patted her hand.

The three of us sat in awkward silence until Paul emerged about ten minutes later. He cleared his throat, looked in Ivy's general direction and said, "I guess he wants you next."

Ivy sighed theatrically, stood and marched into the sheriff's office without so much as a glance in our direction. She was wearing black slacks and a short gray jacket accented by a red silk scarf. Her nose was red too.

When Ivy was gone Jewell said, "I wonder how much of this will get in the papers."

Paul, who was pacing in front of us, stopped abruptly. "Dupree said he would issue a statement that I'm no longer a suspect."

"Thank goodness for that." Jewell looked up at him. "Can we go now, or does he want to talk to me?"

"Let's wait and see," he said. "The idea was to get this over with—for everybody." Paul sat down and cautiously rested his arm on the back of Jewell's chair, but she didn't seem to notice.

Ivy's interview took a little longer. When she emerged, escorted by the sheriff, Paul asked him, "Do you need these other two?"

Dupree looked at Jewell and me. "Might as well," he said.

"You go first," I said to Jewell. "You've got a long drive to work." She gave my hand a squeeze before she rose and followed Dupree into his office.

"Well, I'm out of here," said Ivy, clearly anxious to leave the sad scene behind. She was well down the hall before she turned and said over her shoulder, "See you guys later."

I waved and Paul nodded.

Before long Jewell emerged and said to Paul, "I guess we can go now." I stood and gave her a hug. "Thanks so much," she said, "for seeing us through this."

"I'm just glad it's over."

"Me too."

Paul grunted something and they left together. I stood staring at their backs until I realized that Benny Dupree was waiting for me. "Your turn," he said.

I followed the sheriff into his office, a Spartan looking room furnished with a desk, a bookcase only half full and a filing cabinet. Dupree sat behind his desk and waved me into a plastic chair facing him. In a businesslike manner he asked for my name, address, social security number and date of birth, and wrote it all down. He asked where I worked, (though he already knew) and what was my relationship to Paul and Jewell and Ivy. Finally he said, "Okay, what do you know about this business?"

I briefly recounted Ivy's drunken confession on Friday night and Jewell's tearful phone call on Sunday. He wrote as I talked, asked for specific times and made no further comment. When we were finished he looked over his notes, which apparently satisfied him, because he told me I could go.

"Can you find your way out?" he said.

"I found my way in," I said. And that's about all there was to it.

I drove straight to work and arrived at a quarter past nine. Rather than trying to slink past Marge, I walked straight into her office and said, "Did you hear about the powered parachute that went down in Lake Michigan Saturday?"

"I did hear a rumor to that effect. Do you want to follow up on it?"

"Got it," I said smugly. "I was out at the State Park when it happened and then I drove to the marina to meet the rescue boat. It was Chet Henderson on the *Lorelie*. Marvin Crouch from the Diamond D was the guy who got fished out of the lake." I pulled a film canister out of my purse. "Pictures too."

Marge nodded her grudging approval. "Sounds like it might be front page," she said as she reached for the film. "Write it up and we'll see what these proofs look like."

I smiled and headed for my desk, satisfied with the strategy. Marge had forgotten to ask why I was late for work.

"Tracy, you really ought to wear a skirt, don't you think?"

"But I don't have any pantyhose."

"I can lend you a pair. "

"Brooke, look at my skirts. Everything is either too long or too short."

"Yeah," she giggled. "Mother Hubbard or cheerleader."

Frank Kolowsky was back in town and Brooke was helping me get ready for the long anticipated dinner date. While I appreciated her input, the whole process was only increasing my anxiety.

"Do you realize," I said, "that the only date I've had since I moved here was a guy who took me ice fishing in the middle of January?"

"Well, this is bound to be better," she said as she nixed the black stretch pants. "At least you get something to eat."

"Yes, but now I have to worry about spilling food on my clothes."

After much discussion and a flurry of modeling, we came up with an outfit that suited us both—Brooke's pale green sweater and my cream colored slacks.

"I've got just the earrings for that," Brooke said and disappeared upstairs. She returned with a pair of dark green earrings and watched while I put them on. Then she took me into the bathroom where she combed and sprayed my hair and proceeded to apply eye shadow and lip liner.

"Let's not overdo this." I said, coughing from the hairspray. "He might not recognize me."

Frank's arrival put an end to Brooke's makeover efforts. When I saw that he was wearing dress pants and a sport coat, I immediately wished I had chosen a skirt, but it was too late to change without looking like a doofus. I introduced him to Brooke and they chatted for a minute. He escorted me out to his Blazer and opened the door for me to climb in. When I slid across the torn seat covers, I decided the slacks had been a good call.

"You look nice," he said as he backed out of the driveway.

"Ah, thanks," I said, suddenly at a loss for words.

"I hope you're hungry."

"Starved," I said, hoping it didn't sound crass to admit to an appetite. "How was your trip?"

"It was pretty much a fishing trip. But I did find out a couple of things. I'll tell you while we eat."

The Captain's Table was Shagoni River's high-end restaurant and it boasted an aggressively nautical decor. Knotted ropes and pictures of sailing ships covered the walls, red and green lights flashed from the bar, and our table was surfaced with a navigation chart of Lake Superior under a thick layer of varnish. As a final indignity, the bathrooms were labeled 'Gulls' and 'Buoys'.

Frank ordered some wine called White Zinfandel, which turned out to be pink instead of white but tasted pretty good. The waitress handed us menus the size of billboards. I was still reading the menu when Frank ordered a steak, medium rare, so I went ahead and ordered the whitefish just to keep things moving. Then came the part where we sipped our wine and looked at each other across the table. Frank must have gotten a haircut for the occasion because his receding hairline was a little more noticeable. No toothpick. I wondered if there was a stain on my slacks and if the borrowed sweater was too tight. Once again I was at a loss for words.

"So how was your weekend?" he said.

That sort of opened the dam. "Actually it was pretty eventful." I shot a glance around the room. The rest of the clientele was well out of earshot, so I told him everything. I started with the powered parachute going down in Lake Michigan and the rescue of Marvin Crouch. I told him about hauling Ivy out of the bar and hearing her drunken confession. And finally I told him about the four of us converging on Sheriff Benny Dupree Monday morning to set the record straight.

Frank smiled. "I talked to Benny—and read the report. That was a pretty gutsy move on your part."

"Gutsy?"

"Bringing them all together like that."

"Oh Frank, I don't know about gutsy. It just seemed like the best way to make sure that everything got taken care of. Partly it was to make sure no one backed out. I didn't want to go through that more than once."

Somewhere in the midst of this conversation my salad arrived, but I was talking so much that it disappeared before I was finished. Apparently the

145

Zinfandel had loosened my tongue. When my whitefish and baked potato showed up I decided to concentrate on eating and let Frank do the talking.

"Tell me about your trip," I said, "the fishing trip."

"I finally caught up with Burt Plaxton." He splashed some dark looking sauce on his steak.

"The guy who had the appointment with Madeline?"

"Right. I found him at his apartment."

"So what was his story? Did he see Madeline the day she was killed?"

"No. According to him, he left for St. Louis that day." Frank attacked his steak. He didn't seem to have any trouble talking and eating at the same time. "Plaxton told me his father was in a car accident, spent a week in critical care and then died. Said he was gone almost three weeks, getting things squared away."

"Do you believe him?"

"He showed me newspaper clippings, plus the obituary." Frank shrugged. "It looked pretty real."

"So we cross him off the list, right?"

"For the time being." He refilled our wineglasses.

"What about Madeline's family—did you find them?"

He nodded. "The brother had gone back to California. But I found her mother and stepfather."

"What were they like? Madeline never said much about her family."

"They were polite enough but well—up tight—and definitely religious. There was a bible on the table, prayer tracts lying around."

"No wonder Madeline didn't like going home." I pictured my irreverent friend sharing space with her parents on strained holiday visits. "Were they helpful?"

"Not at first. They didn't like talking to me because they didn't want to believe that Madeline had been murdered."

"I understand that. I felt that way myself."

"But the mother finally relented. I convinced her that providing information was the best way she could help us find the killer."

"So what did you find out?" Had Madeline been married?

"Briefly. His name was Nathan Maxwell. They met in college when he was a senior and she was a sophomore. He graduated, they got married, and Madeline dropped out." Frank slathered sour cream on his potato. "They lived in Kalamazoo and he worked in the lab at Bronson Hospital. After about three years, they divorced, and no one has seen him since."

"I guess he's not a very likely suspect."

"Not unless there's something about him that we don't know."

"What about siblings? I heard Madeline mention a sister."

"Just one sister – about four year younger. I forget her name."

"Louise, I'm pretty sure. So she would be about thirty now."

"That sounds right. According to them, Louise did a stint in the Peace Corps and now she's bumming around Europe." He reached for a roll. "The mother said Louise is completely out of touch with the family. She doesn't even know that her sister is dead."

"That explains why she wasn't at the funeral. But doesn't that strike you as strange?"

"Being out of touch? Well, it happens."

"Sure, but there's usually a reason."

"Probably there is. But they didn't want to tell me about it."

"What about money? Did Maddie have a trust fund?"

"No trust fund. Family is squarely middle class, with no rich uncles."

Quite a date. Once again our main topic of conversation was Madeline and the investigation into her death. I took a sip of wine and leaned back in my chair.

"Well, at least Ivy and Paul are in the clear," I said. "That's a load off my mind."

"Maybe, maybe not."

I sat up straight. "What do you mean by that?"

"There's a possibility to be considered."

"What kind of possibility?"

"Maybe the four of you got together and made up the story." He cut a bite of steak. "To protect someone."

"I can't believe you said that!" I slammed my glass down so hard that the wine splashed. Now I really did have a spot on my slacks.

He looked at me, shrugged.

"Frank, you just accused me of lying."

"Well, maybe not you then." He buttered a roll. "It could have been the three of them. And you were just the dupe."

"That is absurd! And not even remotely possible." The whole miserable weekend replayed in my mind. "Frank, I *saw* what everybody went through, and they were in genuine agony. All of them."

"Well, you were there, I guess." He sounded unconvinced.

"No one would make up anything so hurtful." I felt the tightness in my throat that means I'm close to tears. "And I resent your talking that way about my friends."

He finally realized how angry I was and laid down his fork. "I'm sorry, I guess that was out of line." He turned back to his steak. "It's my job you know, to treat everyone as a suspect."

"Does that include me? Is that what this date is all about?"

"Of course not. Oh, come on. I'm sorry. Look, I told you the city made me suspicious of everybody. I could tell you stories —."

"I don't want to hear your stories."

I pushed away the food, my appetite gone. Frank tried to cajole me into having dessert but I refused, so he didn't get any either. We left the restaurant in awkward silence and walked to the marina where we strolled the docks, looking at boats. Frank offered more apologies and I accepted them, but my mood never recovered.

"I'd better get home," I said. "Tomorrow is a work day."

Neither of us said a word as he drove us home and walked with me onto the porch.

"Good night, Frank." I stood with my arms crossed. "Thanks for dinner."

"I'm really sorry I offended you." He was blocking the door so I couldn't get in.

"That's okay. I guess it just hit me wrong."

"Well okay. But couldn't we —?"

"Look, I'm really tired. I just want to —."

"Oh sure. Okay." He gave me a two-second hug and headed for the Blazer. Turned around and waved as he climbed in.

I walked inside, slammed the door, and heaved a sigh of relief when I heard the Blazer drive away. For the umpteenth time I reviewed our conversation. How could Frank have dared to suggest that *all four* of us were lying? The whole thing was ludicrous and at the same time left me enraged. What had ever possessed me to go on a date with Detective Frank Kolowsky? The man must have caught me in a very weak moment. Well, it wouldn't happen again, I was sure of that.

I wandered into the kitchen and found Brooke drinking tea while she explored my collection of cookbooks.

"Gee, you're home kind of early. How did it go?"

"Don't ask." I opened the freezer, searching for ice cream.

"Really—that bad?"

"Total disaster."

"Oh Tracy, what happened?"

I located a carton of Cherry Garcia. "It was okay at first. In fact it was sort of nice. But then we—got into an argument."

"Argument? What about?"

"About this murder business." I slammed the freezer door. "He's a detective and all my friends are suspects. Probably I'm on his list too." I found a bowl and spoon. "I just can't deal with someone who thinks the way he does."

"That's too bad. He seemed like a nice guy."

"There are no nice guys in this town."

"Well, Derek's okay."

"Oh, I didn't mean Derek," I said quickly. "I mean no guys my age." I started digging at the ice cream. "Sometimes I think I should get out of this town."

"You mean you'd sell the house?"

"In a minute."

"But I was hoping—you know—next summer."

"With any luck, I won't be here next summer."

Brooke looked close to tears. Now I had managed to make her depressed too – but her blues didn't last very long. The telephone rang and she was soon on the phone with Derek making plans for a late night date.

Thoroughly disgruntled, I poured chocolate sauce on the ice cream and carried it into the living room. Wallowing in self-pity, I ate my calorie laden treat while I listened to Ruth Brown sing that perennial complaint, "Unlucky Woman." That irrational jealousy of Brooke threatened to reappear. But did I want to be nineteen again? Not really. All I wanted was to be someone else entirely – somebody who was rich, famous, happy and loved. Was that too much to ask?

CHAPTER FIFTEEN

I was ready to leave work Friday when Marge came by my cubicle and said, "Stop by my office before you leave."

When I hear these words from Marge, it usually means she has extra work she wants to dump on me. This time was no exception. She wanted me to spend my evening covering something called the Start of Summer Celebration.

"Lorna was going to do it, but her youngest has a temp of a hundred and three. So could you?"

I groaned. It wasn't as though I had plans for the evening, but I was tired of covering Lorna's family emergencies. I waffled. "So what is this—celebration thing?"

"Didn't you see the barricades going up on Hancock Street?"

"I thought it was street work."

"No, it's like a block party—happens every year. There's a potluck dinner and live music and the mayor makes a speech. They have a beer tent and dance contests."

I was beginning to weaken. Maybe village manager Jim Mcneely would be there.

"Lorna left her lime Jell-O mold in the refrigerator," said Marge. "Take that and you can eat supper there."

The prospect of a free dinner clinched the deal. And the live music. Well, okay maybe the beer tent played into the decision too. "All right," I said, "I'll do it."

"Okay, good. And take your camera." Marge looked relieved. I had probably saved her from doing the job herself, since Kyle and Jake had already absconded.

Armed with my camera and the lime Jell-O, I ventured out into a warm June evening in Shagoni River. As promised, a section of Hancock Street was blocked off and beginning to fill up with people. A clown, big-nosed and green-haired, juggled multicolored balls before an audience of open-mouthed toddlers. Older kids held balloons. The retired snowbirds were back from winter migrations and most of them were dressed in shorts, the better to show off suntanned, knobby knees. I found the buffet table and plunked down the lime Jell-O, then got a plate and went through the food line.

When my plate was full I sat down and, within minutes, my prayers were answered. Village manager Jim Mcneely of the soulful eyes arrived and sat beside me.

"Hi Tracy. Found any more bodies lately?"

"Nope, and I'm not looking for any. Once was enough for me."

"Me too. But at least we got to sit together on the beach."

"During work hours too."

It was the first time Jim and I had talked since our afternoon on the dune when we had kept watch over Madeline's body. Sitting beside him now I had a perfect view of the sweep of his eyelashes. We talked about the upcoming election, the problem of skateboards downtown and the new dog-waste ordinance—which he referred to as the "pooper-scooper" law. But then, just as we got to dessert, Jim's cell phone rang and he excused himself to see about a problem at the wastewater plant.

Darn. Well, there was always the beer tent. I finished eating and wandered into the tent where I was pleased to find Elliot presiding over the bar. I bought a Samuel Adams and talked to Elliot as the place began to fill up. Some bald guys with accordions arrived and started setting up sound equipment on a makeshift stage at the far end of the tent. So this was the live music.

"Marge didn't tell me it was accordions," I said to Elliot.

"So who were you expecting, kid? Maybe Bon Jovi?"

"I was thinking more along the lines of Carlos Santana."

"Have another beer. You won't be able to tell the difference."

"You don't have that much beer, Elliot."

The bar was getting crowded so I moseyed over to the stage. A hand-lettered sign announced the Polka Contest at seven o'clock and the Chicken Dance Contest at eight. This was vital information. Marge wanted me to get photos of these events, preferably of the winning couples. My Nikon was at the ready. Just then I spotted mayor Clancy Fredericks in the crowd so I buttonholed him and asked about the history of the celebration.

"First one was five years ago," he said, "to celebrate the end of a street repair project. Everybody liked it so we've been doing it ever since. It's a chance for the locals to get together before the tourist invasion."

This was a tidbit I could remember without resorting to my notebook. So I was just standing there chatting with the mayor, drinking my beer and leaning on a tent pole, when this big guy in a plaid shirt appeared on the other side of the tent. Due to a temporary lapse of memory, I smiled in his direction. Then I remembered that I was finished with Frank Kolowsky. I had absolutely no interest in the man. None.

So I kept on talking to the mayor and ignored the guy in the flannel shirt who was inching in my direction. After a while Clancy drifted away and that's when I realized that Frank was on the other side of *my* pole, doing a little leaning himself. He peeked around the pole.

"Hi Tracy."

"Hi."

"Nice evening."

"Yeah."

"How you doing?"

"I'm okay."

He gestured toward the sign. "So what's a Chicken Dance?"

"Haven't a clue. But I guess I'm going to find out."

"You working tonight?"

"On assignment. Chicken dance and polka contest."

A blast of accordion music precluded further conversation so I walked away and sat in the section reserved for judges and dignitaries. The polka contest was loud, with much whooping and hollering and stomping of feet. Plump ladies in big skirts were rotated in endless circles, held fast by puffing, red-faced men. I got some action shots and afterward, did a mini-interview with the winning couple.

When the band took a break, the mayor stepped up to the microphone and I thought seriously about visiting the bar again. That's when Frank appeared beside me with a frosty looking Samuel Adams in his hand.

"You looked thirsty," he said.

"Guess I am, a little."

"Could we talk?"

The sight of the beer weakened me. His thoughtfulness, I mean. "Okay," I said, and he handed it over. "Where's yours?"

"I've had enough," was all he said. Maybe he was working too.

Together, we left the tent and walked north to the spot where Fourth Street meets the lake. We stood on the dinghy dock and watched a family of ducks—mom, dad, and four little quackers—swim by in single file. Frank threw his toothpick in the water.

"Guess I really messed up the other night."

"Well, yeah." I took a swallow of beer.

"I was never any good with stuff like that—formal dates, I mean."

I watched the ducks. Finally I said, "Guess I'm out of practice too."

"I was thinking maybe —." He stuffed his hands in his pockets, looked down at his feet.

"You were thinking —?" This man was pathetic.

"—that maybe we could try something different."

"Something different?"

"—if you wanted to, I mean."

"Okay, like what?" I didn't have all night. The band was starting up again.

"I have two kayaks. Ever been in one?"

"Once. When I was a camp counselor."

"Would you like to go down the river Sunday?"

So there it was. An invitation. But hadn't I made a resolution to avoid this guy? Why was I leading him on? I choked.

"Nothing strenuous. My cabin's on the river. From there to Sawmill Point is about five hours."

Five hours? Five hours in a tapered coffin sounded pretty strenuous to me. "Oh I don't know. I was planning to clean out the garage Sunday." That sounded lame, even to me.

"I'll pack the lunch. You won't have to do anything."

"Well, okay, I guess so." Did I really say that?

Frank looked relieved, like someone had just let him out of jail. "Great. I'll come by your place about ten. We'll have to spot the cars." He told me what to wear, what to bring.

"Just curious," I said as we turned to head back, "but why do you have two kayaks?"

"My part of the divorce settlement." His smile made wrinkles around his eyes. "She hated the water. Lucky me."

Shagoni River sang softly as it meandered through dense growths of jackpine, white birch and cedar. Overhead, the sun ascended into a cloudless sky, pushing the temperature toward eighty degrees. The two humans in kayaks moved so silently that a turtle sunning on a log barely opened one eye as they glided by. After basic instructions from Frank and a few awkward minutes of splashing and spinning, I had discovered that paddling a kayak was more an issue of offering guidance than making any major effort. The river flowed and the craft and I moved with it, at one with the universe. Sort of.

Frank slowed beside me and pointed out a red-winged blackbird. I named the cattails and he showed me Joe Pye weed which he said was named after an Indian.

"What's that pretty purple one?"

"Purple Loosestrife. It's pretty but it's not good. It's an alien species and it's choking out the natural vegetation."

"Where did it come from?"

"Boats on the Great Lakes." He back-paddled to stay beside me. "Ever since the St. Lawrence Seaway opened, boats have been bringing in all kinds of stuff from all over the world. First it was lamprey eels that killed most of the fish in Lake Michigan. And now we have zebra mussels that grow on everything from boats to drain pipes."

After the biology lesson, I fell behind and we were too far apart for conversation. There was little sound except the dip of our paddles, the babble of water over stone, and sometimes a yelp from me as I maneuvered around a rock or a jutting log. The sun moved across the sky and my breakfast became a dim memory.

"When do we eat?" I yelled.

"Pretty soon," was all he said. But a few minutes later Frank beached his kayak on a small island and hopped out to pull me ashore. That's when I discovered that climbing out of a kayak is probably the most ungraceful maneuver in the world—especially on jelly legs. Frank kept a straight face as he hauled me up and out. Then he pulled the kayaks onto the grass and secured the paddles inside them.

I walked around our tiny island until my legs felt better. Frank grabbed the lunch bag and found a hollow log for us to sit on. I sat beside him gingerly, hoping that no snakes or fuzzy things were sleeping inside. To my relief, nothing crawled out. Frank handed me a sandwich wrapped in waxed paper. "Hope you like liver sausage."

"Anything would taste good right now. And guess what." I produced a bag of my own. "A thermos of coffee."

"Real coffee?"

I nodded and his face lit up. This man was easily pleased.

Sugared coffee from a plastic cup was nectar of the gods. Liver sausage on rye was a banquet. I felt comfortable sharing a log with Frank and our conversation flowed as easily as the river. Of course there was something about this guy that I didn't like, but I couldn't remember exactly what it was. Surely it would occur to me later. After lunch we bagged our trash and he picked up some stuff that other people had left behind. Another point for detective Kolowsky.

Under way again, the heat turned up a notch. I stripped down to my tank top and slathered sunblock on my arms, but they turned pink anyway. Frank had his shirt off too, but he was already tan so he just got a little darker. Ahead of us, a long-legged heron took flight and flew silently downstream where it landed in a tree and waited until we came closer. Then it headed downstream again.

Time stretched out. Mosquitoes and black flies appeared, seemingly attracted by my insect repellent. My shoulders were sore and my knees were stiff. I tried to relax by leaning back and stretching my legs but nothing helped very much. All the trees and cliffs looked exactly the same and I was no longer enchanted by the great outdoors. Frank was always way ahead of me except when he stopped and waited. Then he'd paddle up close and say something meant to be encouraging, but I was wilting like a daisy in a sauna bath.

When I heard the sounded of traffic, my heart leapt. "Are we getting near civilization?" I yelled.

"That's Arrowhead Drive up ahead," he called back. "After the bridge it'll be another 20 minutes."

I almost cried with relief as my mind raced with visions of a cold drink and a hot shower. When I passed under the bridge it registered as a moment of shade accompanied by truck noise and the scent of diesel. After that, sunshine again. Then, to my surprise, Frank spun his kayak around and started paddling furiously up stream.

"What are you doing?" I said as he closed in on me.

"Thought I saw something." He kept on paddling.

I managed a clumsy U-turn and tried to follow him. Upstream paddling, I discovered, is much harder than the other way. Frank glanced back at me just before he rammed his kayak into the marshy bank and hopped out into the water. He waited until I got close, then grabbed my bow and pulled until I dragged bottom.

"Hold onto our stuff," was all he said before he turned and started walking upstream. I clambered out into knee deep water and lost my paddle in the process. Struggling against the current, I retrieved my paddle and then had to fight with the two kayaks as they tried to head downstream. They bumped and nudged against me like dolphins wanting to swim away. My shoes were full of water and slipping on the rocks and my jeans were soaked well above my knees.

Frank was still wading upstream. He came to a fallen tree, climbed over it and stopped. He bent down, with one hand on the log and the other hand groping in the water. I was puzzled, but he seemed to know exactly what he was doing. Finally he stood and lifted something out of the water. All I could see was a dripping, shapeless mass.

"What is it?"

"Looks like a purse."

"Really? Let me look."

Hastily, I shoved the kayaks as far as they would go into a stand of cattails and waded toward Frank. It felt like one of those slow motion dreams where you can't get your legs to work right. Finally I got a hand on the log where he was standing. Frank was on the other side, holding a water-soaked leather purse with a shoulder strap.

My throat tightened with recognition. "It could be Madeline's."

"Let's look. But don't touch anything."

He laid the dripping purse on the log, opened it and began to pull out the contents. He treated the stuff like artifacts, spreading the items carefully on the tree trunk. Most of them could have belonged to anyone of the female gender. There was a lipstick, small hairbrush, handkerchief, pack of gum, breathmints, ballpoint pen, soggy notebook and a leather wallet. Frank opened the wallet. The papers and photos were soaked beyond recognition. But then he extracted a plastic credit card that cleared up any doubts we might have had. The card was imprinted with the name of Madeline Maxwell.

River sounds drifted up from behind a thick stand of cedar trees as Frank and I relaxed on the deck of his A-frame cabin, eating bowls of spicy venison chili. Our adventure on the river had given me a healthy appetite and I was almost through my second generous sized bowl.

"What do you make of the purse business?" I said. "Does it tell us anything?"

"Not a whole lot. It means at some point the killer drove down Arrowhead Drive and tossed her purse off the bridge."

"Right. But think about this. If she had been on the hypothetical boat, the killer would have tossed the purse into Lake Michigan."

"Unless he found her purse on the boat, later, and tossed it."

"But I just think a guy with a boat would dispose of the purse in the lake—either Lake Michigan or Arrowhead Lake."

"Probably. But maybe she went out on the boat without her purse."

"Not likely," I said. "Women always want their make-up and stuff."

"Unless she didn't go willingly."

"Or maybe she was killed somewhere else."

"And loaded on the boat for disposal."

I shivered. "Can you get any fingerprints from the purse?"

"Not likely after all that time in the water. But we'll try."

"Frank, it's been a month and it doesn't look like we're any closer to finding her killer. Are we? Are you?"

He gave me a look, then stood and collected our dishes. Finally he said, "I thought we agreed not to talk about the case. That's what ruined our last date."

"You're right—we did agree." I sighed. "And we were doing fine until we found that damned purse."

"She has a way of intruding on us, doesn't she?"

We agreed not to talk about Madeline any more, ate some donuts for dessert and then walked to the river along a narrow path that wound through sweet smelling pine and cedar. Sitting together on his rickety dock, we watched the trout come leaping out of the water to feed on dragonflies. When the sun dipped behind the tree line, Frank put his arm around me and I snuggled against him. And when he finally kissed me, I was in no hurry to come up for air, as we used to say at Shagoni River High. He gave me his jacket to wear on the walk back and it was almost dark when we reached his cabin. All of a sudden I felt awkward.

"Guess I'd better be going," I said.

He wrapped his arms around me. "You're welcome to stay the night."

Well there it was, the invitation. And I was sorely tempted. But since I had only recently overcome my misgivings about dating an officer of the law, it seemed a bit premature to be hopping into bed with same officer. What if I talked in my sleep? What if I confessed to past transgressions, ranging from illegal U-turns to pot smoking? This definitely needed some thought.

So I thanked him for a wonderful day and drove home, where I lost no time falling into bed. I slept soundly and had a wonderful dream. I was Cleopatra, floating down the Nile on a golden barge, entertained by harp players and dancing boys.

Frank called me the very next day and made a date for lunch at Schooners on Thursday. But the lunch date turned out to be an anticlimax. As soon as we had ordered, he told me he was going out of town again, for the weekend and part of the coming week.

"Well darn. Just when I thought I might have a Saturday night date." As soon as the words were out of my mouth, I regretted them. I didn't want to sound needy.

"It's kind of special," he said apologetically. "My daughter's having a birthday party for Timmy. He'll be three years old."

"Oh, Frank that's great." I really meant it.

"And while I'm down that way, I'll try to find some of the people Madeline used to work with. Sometimes friends can tell you more than family."

We finished eating and walked to his Blazer where he gave me a kiss on the forehead. Very demonstrative guy. "I'll try to call you Sunday," he said. And then he was gone.

Well that's how it is when you date a detective, I thought as I watched him drive away. They're always going somewhere.

Friday after work I stopped by the Treasure Chest. Gavin was there. He closed up the store and we went to the back and sat on some old velveteen furniture that no one ever wanted to buy. We talked about Paul and Jewell and the fiasco with Ivy.

"I just hope this doesn't kill their marriage," he said.

"Me too. I'm angry with Ivy, but of course Paul is equally at fault."

"Ivy is a bit of a flirt."

"Even with you."

"Even with me." He laughed. "She just can't help herself."

"Paul and Jewell were my ideal couple," I said. "Now I'm completely disillusioned."

"Well what about you? I hear you've got a thing going with that detective."

"News travels fast, doesn't it?"

"Sorry."

"Oh, I don't mind. But at this point, I'm not sure what we've got going. Frank will probably run the other way when he finds out he's a better cook that I am."

"Give him some credit. Cooking is not the only thing that men are interested in."

"Gavin, I know what men are interested in. And he didn't get that either."

He chuckled. "Nothing wrong with being cautious."

"Anyway, he just took off for the weekend. Again." I sighed. "For all I know he's got a woman downstate somewhere."

"Tracy love, don't sit home tonight and brood. Come on down to the Belly Up. I've got company in town and I'm showing them the sights."

"I'll think about it—but don't count on me. Sometimes I like to sit home and brood."

Gavin's invitation won out in the end. I arrived at the Belly Up about nine-thirty, and the place was full of people I didn't know. Finally I spotted Gavin at a table in the back with Rhonda and her husband and another couple that he introduced as his sister and brother-in-law. They were both drop-dead gorgeous, of course. I joined the table and hung my jacket on a chair next to Gavin.

"I'll be right back," I said and headed off to the ladies' room.

When I came out of the bathroom I saw something that stopped me in my tracks. There was a man in a light brown windbreaker sitting at the far end of the bar. I knew I had seen him before but, for the life of me, I couldn't remember where. I stood in the darkened hallway, staring at him until I figured it out. It was the guy that Madeline had been hiding from, in this same bar, just a few weeks before she was killed. My brain went into high gear as I formulated a plan. Then I walked back to the table where Gavin and the others were talking and joking as they debated what kind of pizza to order.

"Watch my back," I whispered to Gavin as I nodded toward the stranger at the bar. "I need to find out who that guy is."

He followed my glance. "Is this about Madeline?"

I nodded.

"You be careful."

"Don't worry, I will." I practiced a seductive smile, fluffed my new hairdo and headed for the bar.

CHAPTER SIXTEEN

I wiggled into a spot at the bar about two seats down from the mystery man and tried to pretend he was not my reason for being there. In his tan jacket and khaki pants, he didn't look like a killer. But then, what was a killer supposed to look like, anyway? The guy was drinking a Heinekin and using the mirror behind the bar to check out the action in the room, which now included me. I drummed my fingers on the bar in a show of impatience until Elliot appeared.

"So what kind of beer do you have?" I said, before Elliot could offer me my usual.

Elliot rattled off the list of beer labels as though he had never seen me before. He may not have known what I was up to, but Elliot had seen enough of bar games not to blow my cover. I made of show of struggling with my decision and finally said, "Okay I'll have a Heineken." I cast a heavy lidded glance toward the stranger.

When Elliot delivered my Heineken, the stranger glanced back. "I see someone else knows good beer," he said.

"There's just not much choice around here." I affected a dramatic sigh.

Now the guy swung around to get a closer look at me. This worked both ways of course. He was attractive, in a Hollywood director sort of way—dark wavy hair, wire-rimmed glasses, sideburns with a touch of gray. His jacket was open just far enough to reveal a rectangular bulge in his shirt pocket. *Great.* I slid onto the stool next to his.

"Don't suppose I could bum a cigarette?"

"Sure." He extracted a hard pack of Menthol Lights, tapped out a cigarette and held it out to me. I took it from him, our fingers briefly touching. *Ah, this is fun.* He produced a lighter; I put the cigarette in my mouth and leaned toward him. The flame leapt and my cigarette caught—my bangs almost caught, too. *Tracy, you are so cool.* I pulled back, inhaling like an addict long deprived.

"Thanks a lot." My words came out in a puff of smoke. He smiled and lit a cigarette for himself. "My friends are trying to get me to quit," I said with a nod toward Gavin's table. "Everyone is smoke free these days. It's such a pain."

My smoking buddy nodded sympathetically. I turned away to blow out the smoke I had accidentally inhaled. Dizzy from the nicotine, I couldn't figure out what to do next. *Throw up, maybe?* I coughed, took a pull on the Heinekin.

"I think I've seen you here before," he said.

"Hey, that was my line."

"Then it must be true. I mean we've both been in here. Can I buy you a drink?"

"I just bought my own."

"Oh right. Heinekin." He pushed an ashtray toward me. "So where are you from?"

"Chicago mostly. Living right here for now." I tipped off the ash. "And you?"

"Pellmont, but I work in Manistee."

"That's a bit of a drive. What brings you down here?"

He tipped his head back, blew a smoke ring. "I like to get out once in a while."

So the guy was probably married. I drank some beer and tried to figure out what do to next. If I mentioned Madeline's name, he might head straight for the door. But if I could just find out who he was, Frank could take over when he got back. Looking around I saw a couple dancing by the jukebox and two guys in torn blue jeans playing a noisy game of pool. A pizza arrived at Gavin's table and I wondered if there would be any left for me. When the pool players concluded their game and headed out the door, trading obscenities, I saw my opening.

"Do you play?" I said with a nod toward the table.

"Sure, but I'll beat your ass."

"We'll see about that."

We stubbed out our cigarettes and moved back to claim the pool table. Blue dust fell to the floor as we chalked our cues. Together we racked the balls into a neat triangle and then he blasted them apart, rolling the seven straight into a side pocket.

"Hey, good start," I said cheerily.

"Told you I was good."

"Humble too."

He missed his next shot so it was my turn. I leaned over the table and put the twelve in the corner pocket. But then my next shot went wild and rearranged everything on the table. "So what do you do in Manistee?" I said

"I sell real estate." He walked around the table, eyeing different shots, then dropped the five in a side pocket.

"What a coincidence. I'm in the market for a place up that way—something really nice—on a few acres."

"I'm sure I can help you." He rolled the three right to the edge of a corner pocket, cursed softly and then flashed me a salesman smile. "We just got some new listings that might be in your price range."

So what did he know about my price range? I'd show him. "This will be as soon as my inheritance comes through." I moved around, checking the layout. "Some time in the next month, I expect."

His eyes reflected renewed interest. "We've got anything you want—city, country, waterfront."

"Near enough to town so I can work." I hit the cue ball and it rolled straight into a side pocket. "Can't retire yet."

"And what do you do?" He finally dropped the three.

"I'm a writer."

"Hey, don't put me in your book."

"Oh, not that kind of writing—just newspaper stuff. But I've got a place here I'll have to sell first." I figured this would get his attention. New listings are like candy to real estate people.

I was right. "I'd be glad to list it for you." He pulled out his wallet, extracted a business card and handed it to me.

Bingo. The card said Ford Mathews, Greenwood Real Estate, Manistee. I felt like cheering but I just smiled instead and slipped the card into my back pocket. He bought me another beer and I played just hard enough to make things interesting. After two games, I said I'd had enough and we put up the cues. Then, just to see what would happen, I went for it.

"I had a friend in real estate," I said. "Madeline Maxwell. Ever hear of her?"

His eyes narrowed slightly. "No, can't say as I ever did." A muscle in his jaw twitched.

"Just wondered. She used to go to Manistee some times."

Beads of sweat appeared on his forehead. His eyes darted around the room. "Guess I'd better be going." He chugged the beer, grabbed his jacket and headed for the door. "Nice meeting you," he said just before he disappeared.

I reclaimed my spot with Gavin and his group and found that they had saved me one skinny slice of pizza.

"What happened?" said Gavin, pushing the remnant toward me. "We thought you had a live one there."

"Guess I scared him off. I do that sometimes." I looked around the table. "Anyone up for another pizza?"

Jewell invited me to go on a trip with her to Traverse City. Although I rate shopping as slightly less fun than having a root canal, I was willing to do anything that might improve her mental health. It all turned out okay. The day was fine and she took me to lunch at a restaurant where we sat on a deck that had real trees growing through it, surrounded by tropical plants and serenaded by the sounds of a waterfall. Our food arrived with little orange flowers that we were encouraged to eat.

"How are things going with you and Paul?"

"Oh he's all repentant, remorseful, the whole works. But I'm having trouble forgiving. I feel betrayed, by both him and Ivy."

"Because you were."

"Ivy I can walk away from. But Paul, well—I've got an investment there."

"Of course you do. I can only imagine how it feels after—how long?"

"Twenty-three years."

"I still have trouble grasping this. Paul always felt like such a family man."

"He swears it was the only time. That it only happened because Ivy came over while I was away—taking care of my mom."

"How convenient for them." I sampled my chocolate mousse. "I think somebody should make chastity belts for men."

"What a great idea. We should take out a patent on that."

"Seriously though, I can't understand why he didn't tell you sooner."

"Paul said he was hoping the murder would be solved and he wouldn't have to confess. Said he didn't want to hurt me—or the kids."

"I'm really sorry about the story that ran in our paper."

"Don't feel guilty. Yours wasn't the only one."

"But when he was exonerated, that was buried on the bottom of page five."

"Guess that's the newspaper business. But enough of this. What's happening with you and Frank?"

"I wish I knew." I sipped my coffee. "Our dinner date was a disaster – but then we had a great day on the river. I told you about that."

"The day you found Madeline's purse."

"Right. See it always comes back to something about Madeline. That's really the only thing we have in common."

"Oh come on. You have lots of things in common."

"You think so?"

"Sure. You're both city folks trying to make a new life in the country. Both divorced. You both work in public positions."

"He's probably dating me because he can't find anyone else."

"He's dating you because you're attractive and fun to be with."

"Thanks for the vote of confidence. Anyway I wish he'd get back from his trip."

"See, you're missing him already."

"No, there's another reason. I found someone I want him to check out."

"Another suspect?" I nodded "Who is it?"

So I told her about meeting Ford Mathews, our pool game at the Belly Up and his hasty retreat when I mentioned Madeline's name.

"The guy sounds weird. And you say he works for Greenwood Realty?"

"Right. And that's the company where Madeline made so many late night phone calls."

"I think he's a liar. He must have known Madeline."

"I think you're right. People in that business know each other."

"Are you going to tell Sheriff Dupree about him?"

"I probably should, but I don't feel like seeing Benny Dupree again right now."

"He's probably tired of us too. But when will Frank be back?"

"In a couple of days, supposedly."

"Let's hope Ford Mathews doesn't disappear before Frank catches up with him."

Monday afternoon at work I got a call from Irma Babcock, the bookkeeper at Flagstone Real Estate, and she sounded distraught.

"Tracy, could you possibly come over? There's somebody here. I mean Phil's gone and I'm alone and —."

"I'll be right there." I was out the door in seconds, wondering who had Irma so upset. Of course she had been jumpy ever since Madeline's death. Was this somehow connected?

"She's in the back," Irma said as I flew through the door. "And thanks for coming." She moved closer and whispered, "I just couldn't send her away after giving her the news."

"Who—what are we talking about?"

"This woman," Irma said with a nod toward the back. "She came by looking for Madeline—said she was an old friend and just happened to be in town. So I had to tell her that Madeline was dead, and well—I just think she needs to talk to someone."

Irma led me into the kitchen where I saw a woman with short, dark hair sitting and staring into a cup of coffee. When the visitor looked up, Irma said, "This is Tracy Quinn. She knew Madeline." Irma poured me some coffee and left us alone.

The woman stood and shook my hand. "Hi. I'm Darla French."

Darla looked to be in her thirties and I liked her right away. She had a generous nose, bushy eyebrows and freckles scattered across her cheeks. She wore a faded purple tee shirt and a pair of worn Levi's that strained across her thighs when she stood to greet me.

"This must have been a terrible shock." I sat down and tried the coffee which tasted like rubber boots. She nodded gravely. I stirred in lots of sugar. "When's the last time you saw Madeline?"

Darla looked at me, dark eyes brimming. "Just before she moved here." She ran a hand through her cropped hair. "That was about two and a half years ago. But we talked last summer. I was living in Wisconsin and we made plans for me to come for a visit, but things didn't work out. I had a rather crazy job that I have since gotten rid of. Excuse me a minute." She reached into a cloth bag and pulled out a bottle of aspirin, took two of them, waved the bottle at me.

I shook my head.

"So now I'm on this extended vacation, to chill out, rediscover myself, whatever. I was on my way to the Women's Festival when I saw how close it was to Shagoni River, so I drove into town. I knew Madeline worked for a real estate office so I stopped at the first one I saw."

"You came to the right place—unfortunately a few weeks too late."

"Irma told me Madeline was in an accident. What happened exactly?"

So it was my job to break the news to her about the murder. Darla frowned and bit her lower lip while I gave her a rough sketch of Madeline's disappearance ending with my discovery of her body on the beach.

"Holy shit," she said. "I had no idea. And they still don't know who did it?"

I shook my head. "Whoever it is, he's still running around."

"That sucks." She blew her nose. "Did you go to the funeral?"

So I told her about the service. And she told me about the last time she had seen Madeline, on a quick trip through Lansing. The door opened and Irma peeked in but didn't say anything.

"Looks like Irma wants to close up," I said.

"Oh sure. Well, I guess I'd better —."

"How about coming to my house for supper?" I wasn't about to let Darla get away.

"Well sure, but—how do you feel about a dog?"

"Depends on the size."

"Medium sized and very friendly. Her name is Fargo."

"Bring her along. She can go after the moles in my lawn."

Fargo was indeed very friendly, black and white with a short stubby tail. On her release from Darla's van she exploded into my back yard, digging holes and darting from one intoxicating smell to another. Darla and I watched her through the kitchen window.

"I don't normally eat meat," she said. "I hope that's not a problem."

"I guess we'll just have to get creative."

We did a quick survey of my refrigerator and decided to make stir fry vegetables. While we chopped and cooked, Darla told me about the series of jobs she had tried and quit, the most recent one as a paralegal for a law firm. Her life resembled mine in that she had seen a lot of job changes. Unlike me, she had never married. Apparently she had lived with a series of men and found them all wanting. I recounted some of my adventures and misadventures with Madeline. We laughed and shed a few tears.

"How did you meet Madeline?" I said as we sat down to eat.

"We lived in the same dorm at college but weren't especially close. After her divorce she moved in with me and stayed for a few months while she got on her feet."

"How about the divorce? Was it amicable?"

"Pretty much. She was the one who wanted out. There were no kids and very little property. She got a beater car and he got the computer and that was about it."

I slid into detective mode. "Darla," I said, "can you think of anyone who had a grudge against Madeline? Anyone who would want her dead?"

She frowned, shook her head. "No. Nothing like that."

"Did you meet her parents?"

"Just once. Her mother's name is Sylvia and she struck me as being awfully uptight. I think she and Madeline probably didn't get along."

"What about Madeline's sister, Louise? I don't think she was at the funeral."

"Oh that. Well, Sylvia disowned Louise when she found out that she was a lesbian."

"Aha. No wonder mom was upset. When did this happen?"

"Maybe four years ago. Sylvia told Louise not to come back unless she could be 'normal'— whatever that means."

"That seems terribly harsh."

"It was. Of course, Sylvia might have dealt with it better if Louise had been more tactful. But she wasn't. She just showed up with her girlfriend and said, 'This is me—get used to it.'"

"Is Louise still out of the country?" I pulled a carton of ice cream out of the freezer and dished up two bowls.

"She's back. I had an e-mail from Zoe, that's Louise's partner, a couple of weeks ago. They were spending a few weeks at a farm in Vermont."

"I wonder if Louise knows that her sister is dead."

"Seems like she would by now."

"I sort of hope so."

"Zoe said the two of them were heading for the Women's Festival. I'm hoping to connect with them while I'm there."

"Really?" I couldn't help thinking that Louise might be a missing link. "I'd love to meet Madeline's sister. If I come to the festival, will you help me find her?"

Darla hesitated briefly, then smiled her broad smile. "I think she would want to meet you. So yeah, I'll do it."

"Great. Just tell me when and where."

"Things get pretty hectic out there. But we'll work something out."

"What's your schedule?"

"I'm heading for Salmon Creek tomorrow. Stage should be up. I'm working on sound and lights."

"Might as well spend the night here."

"Sounds good to me." She slipped her ice cream dish under the table to Fargo. "It'll probably be my last night for a while in a real bed."

Brooke came home and the three of us took Fargo for a long walk, first to the top of Old Baldy and then downtown. The dog made friends wherever she went. Brooke peppered Darla with questions until I was afraid she was making our guest uncomfortable, but Darla didn't seem to mind. She had lots of funny stories to tell and we all stayed up until one o'clock, talking and eating popcorn.

In the morning Darla was up in time to have coffee with me. Brooke came downstairs just as Darla was getting into her van, so she walked barefoot out to the driveway. She told Darla goodbye and hugged Fargo, who was already leaning out of his window in anticipation of the breeze.

Brooke stood with me and waved as the van pulled away. "After I graduate," she said, "I think I'll get a van and a dog."

The next day Broke invited Derek to have supper with us – again. I didn't mind, because he was good with odd jobs and I felt like I was helping Jewell a little by having him there. The kids were laughing in the kitchen and I was getting ready to take out the garbage when I saw a black Blazer pull into the driveway. I dashed to the porch and met Frank who swept me into a bear hug.

"I tried to call you Sunday," he said, "but the line was always busy."

"Blame the kids. When they're not together, they're talking to each other."

"What's that smell?" He tried to peer through the screen door

"Beef stroganoff. Want to eat with us?"

"Is the pope Catholic?"

We laughed. I took Frank inside and introduced him to Derek, who set another plate while I located a fourth chair. The two guys tucked into the food and simultaneously launched a discussion about possible causes of the latest problem with Derek's truck. Brooke looked at me and rolled her eyes. I smiled. This was the first time I had assembled four people at my table, and it felt good to share the house. Brooke was a darling and pretended that I had done the cooking.

After supper Frank showed us pictures of the birthday party featuring himself and two grandsons, all in party hats. Brooke and Derek cleared the table and left, so Frank moved up to the sink like a truly liberated man. While he washed and I dried, I told him about meeting Darla and what she had told me about Madeline's sister.

"That's pretty impressive," he said. "And you got all this without even leaving town."

"There's more," I said, trying not to sound too smug. I told him about Ford Mathews and our pool game at the Belly Up.

He passed me a plate and a stern look along with it. "You were taking a chance there. What if Mathews is the killer?"

"I wasn't stupid. We were in a public place and I had friends to keep an eye on me." I found Mathews' business card and handed it over.

Frank examined the card, holding it carefully in his wet hands. "I need to talk to this guy," he said. "The sooner the better."

"Good. He's all yours. But how about you? Did you find anyone who remembered Madeline?"

"I found the title company where she worked. Three of the people, including her boss, were still there and they were all willing to talk. Problem was, they didn't have a whole lot of information. General consensus was, she liked to go out and party, but she didn't let that interfere with her work. She had a semi-steady boyfriend that none of them had met, and she only gave two weeks notice when she decided to move up north."

"What reason did she give for leaving?"

"She told her boss she just wanted a change of scenery. But one of the gals, Julie something, said it was because the boyfriend had dumped her."

"Did any of them know Louise?"

"Julie did. She said Madeline and her sister were pretty close. I'd like to find that sister and ask her some questions."

"Louise is supposed to be at the Women's Festival this weekend."

"Great. Maybe I could catch up with her there."

"Sorry, there's no men allowed."

"Oh that's the thing Benny was talking about. Maybe we could send a female deputy."

"I'm going to be there. I'm covering for the paper."

"Think you could find Madeline's sister? Ask her a few questions?"

"Sure. I already set it up with Darla."

"You already —?" He started to say something but stopped. "Okay, it's your job then. When do you plan on going?"

"I'm thinking Thursday would be good. It's the Fourth of July and the town will be crawling with tourists. I'd just as soon get out of Dodge."

"Then I'll go visit Ford Mathews. I'd like to catch him away from the office."

After coffee, we walked to the park and hiked up Old Baldy where we had the lookout platform all to ourselves. We made small talk for a while, watching the pre-holiday activity in town as the clouds began to take on color. Workers were assembling a revue stand on Hancock Street and the marina bustled with boats motoring in and out of their slips, some of them already decorated with red, white and blue streamers.

"Looks like the Fourth will be a working holiday for both of us," I said.

"Unfortunately." He put an arm around me. "So let's get together Saturday and compare notes."

"Oh sure. And we'll spend the whole evening talking about this murder business."

He let me go and leaned against the railing. "Well, it wouldn't happen if you weren't such an ace detective."

"Frank, I didn't go looking for any of this. It just fell into my lap."

He shrugged. "You don't have to find Louise if you don't want to."

"No, I really want to meet her." I wondered why I was being so petulant. "And I really want to know who killed Madeline."

"Okay, how about this? On Friday we'll meet and compare notes. On Saturday we'll go out and have some fun. Assuming you're free both nights, that is."

"I'll check my calendar."

Back at the house we found Brooke and Derek sprawled on the living room floor, watching a movie about space aliens. They invited us to join them but Frank begged off, pleading exhaustion from his trip. That was fine with me because I wasn't eager to see humanoid spiders from another galaxy wreak havoc on earthlings.

Outside, Frank and I indulged in a rather steamy good night kiss. "Maybe one of these nights," he said, "you can come out and try my waterbed."

"That sounds like quite a luxury item. Was it part of the divorce settlement?"

"Yep. That and the kayaks. I told you she hated water."

"Lucky me."

CHAPTER SEVENTEEN

The sky was filled with ominous clouds by the time I made it through the main gate at the Women's Festival grounds. I left my car in the day-parking lot and followed a footpath through scrubby woods until I emerged in a clearing in front of the information booth. I stood there for a few minutes thoroughly stupefied, staring at the alternate world I had wandered into.

I was surrounded by a sea of women, a gently moving ocean that demonstrated the infinite variety of female bodies on this planet. Skin colors ranged from ebony, coffee or chocolate to bronzed, freckled or pale; hair was in dreadlocks, braids or ringlets and sometimes not there at all. Bodies were tall and gangly, short and plump, clothed or unclothed. In my jeans and tee shirt I felt way overdressed.

At the information booth, a woman wearing overall shorts and a row of silver earrings handed me a paper with a map on one side and a list of Women's Festival rules on the other.

"I'm looking for a gal named Darla," I said. "She's part of the stage crew."

"If she's part of the stage crew," came the reply, "then she's working her butt off right now to get ready for rain. Forecast says scattered showers." She pointed to a piece of plywood leaning against a tree. "That's a bulletin board over there. You can leave her a note."

I had brought along Brooke's backpack stuffed with all the things Darla told me would be essential. Now I dug through it until I located my note pad and pencil. I wrote, "Darla I'm here. Tracy," on a piece of paper and ripped it off. The board was three deep in messages and I didn't have a thumbtack, so I stole one and wiggled my note into a corner. A gust of wind sent all the messages fluttering and I felt that my chances of finding Darla any time soon were pretty remote.

The lady in overalls pointed me in the general direction of mainstage and I set off to find the music. It wasn't difficult. I just followed the strains of a mean guitar riff echoing through the trees and soon fell in with a stream of women hauling blankets, chairs, coolers and umbrellas. Along the way I chatted with Fran and Harriet, two gray hairs I had met on my way in from the parking lot. Fran told me they were from Colorado and they had been coming to the festival for years, it was their annual summer vacation. Minutes later the stage came into view, perched on a hillside and surrounded by several acres of female bodies.

We found a spot and settled down to listen. Fran and Harriet had cute little folding stools but I had to make do with the blanket in my pack. I could barely see the musicians but their music carried nicely across the valley as they belted out harmonies about horses and whiskey and wild, wild women. The instruments were guitar, fiddle, banjo and the dreaded accordion, but even that sounded pretty good.

I hauled out my note pad and asked Fran the name of the group. She said it was 'Sagebrush Suzy' so I wrote that down along with some comments about the music. Just then a fat raindrop spattered on the paper, so I stuffed my writing gear back into the pack and pulled out a rain poncho. I slipped the thing over my head and spread it out around me to keep my ground cover dry. Well, mostly dry.

It was a squall. The rain got heavy and beat down with an intensity that matched the music, then it was over and clouds went scudding away. When the sky brightened into a rainbow, the musicians led us in a cheer and then ended their set with a rousing Cajun waltz. Fran said the music was over until evening and invited me to join them for supper but I declined their invitation, figuring this was my chance to look for Darla.

Bucking the stream of women that poured out of the concert area, I slogged through wet grass and mud. The backstage area was roped off and swarming with figures who were winding up cords, dismantling microphones and stowing electrical looking stuff in a van. I spotted someone in a hooded sweatshirt that looked like Darla and yelled out her name. The figure turned and waved back.

"Tracy!" Darla came and hugged me across the rope. "You made it. How'd you like that rain? We ordered it just for you."

"So the mud and grime are all part of the festival experience?"

"Absolutely. We wanted you to have it all. I'll be done here in a few minutes. Just wait for me, okay?"

So I stood and waited while various hooded and blue jeaned women moved speakers, cords and light boxes under cover or wrapped them with plastic tarps. When Darla finally joined me she said, "Things are a little crazy right now. Normally we'd be setting up for the evening show, but with this weather we're keeping things under wraps. Come on, let's get some food. I haven't eaten all day."

The food was free. But first we had to hike to Darla's tent for dishes and then we stood in a long line at the food tent. All around us women were laughing and joking, and nobody seemed to mind the wait. Finally a gal with spiked hair filled my plate with curried rice, steaming beans, cabbage slaw and a large hunk of whole grain bread. As we sat down to eat I felt a sudden longing for a juicy burger from the Brown Bear.

"Darla," I said, "is everyone here a vegetarian?"

"Probably not. But think about it. With no refrigeration, why mess with meat? Grains keep forever."

Despite my reservations, I ate everything. Then we washed our dishes at a makeshift sink and walked back to Darla's tent where one of her neighbors, a plump brown woman named Juniper, offered to share a thermos of coffee. We scrambled to find cups. Juniper's tent mate appeared with a huge bar of dark chocolate that she broke up and passed around. We sat on coolers and campstools, spinning yarns and telling jokes, until I remembered that I was on assignment.

"What about Louise?" I said to Darla. "Is she here?"

"I saw her this morning. She's over at Buttercup campground."

"Can we go see her?"

"We can look."

Darla led me through the RV camp where women sat under awnings attached to their vans, campers and motor homes. Buttercup was in a stand of piney woods. A woman with a turkey feather in her hair pointed to an orange mountain tent and said it belonged to Louise and Zoe. Clearly no one was home. Turkeyfeather's partner, who had several fascinating rings in her nose, said she would tell Louise and Zoe that folks were looking for them.

Darla had to get back to mainstage so I stayed a while talking with Turkeyfeather and her friend. They gave me a beer and shared their bug repellent in preparation for the evening show. Then we walked to the concert area and listened to a duo called 'Soul Sisters' who played Chicago-style blues on guitar and harmonica. At least it didn't rain. Again I waited for Darla. By the time she was finished and led me through the piney woods again, I was stumbling behind her in the dark.

We reached Buttercup campground but Louise and Zoe were still nowhere to be found. "I think they went into town," said an Asian woman in a long red dress. "You know that little bar on the corner? They're having kerioke tonight—just for us."

I heaved a sigh.

Darla turned to me. "We're not going to find them tonight," she said. "Why don't you stay over? We'll catch them first thing in the morning."

"You have room?"

"Sure. My tent's a three man Patagonia. I mean three person."

Spend the night? Here? To my way of thinking, a campground was supposed to have flush toilets, hot showers, blow dryers, bottled water and candy machines. This place had *nothing*—nothing except acres of tents and rows of orange portapotties. I had no toothbrush, no washcloth, no —.

"I've got an extra sleeping bag," said Darla. "It's brand new."

Yes. No. Maybe. I wanted a shower – I wanted my own bed. But damnit, I had promised Frank I would find Madeline's sister. I pictured myself facing him with nothing to report, and that settled it. "Okay," I said. "I'll stay over."

Later, when I was snuggled into my sleeping bag with Brooke's backpack for a pillow, I said to Darla, "Thanks for taking care of me."

"No problem. You took care of me. And in case you're wondering, I'm not a lesbian."

"Well, your history sounded pretty hetero."

"Sometimes I wish I was though."

"Really?"

"Sure. I know so many cool women who would make great partners. But the chemistry just isn't there. Believe me I've tried."

That got me to thinking. "What about Madeline? Did she ever —? Was she —?"

"Bisexual? I don't think so. But then, who knows? After Louise came out, we used to joke about how much easier life would be. You know, the toilet seat business and all."

"I guess it would, in a way."

"But girls don't do it for me," she said. "So I'm stuck trying to find a man I can relate to. Believe me, it's not easy."

"I've not done too well in that area either. Maybe I should get a dog." I tried to adjust my lumpy pillow. "Hey, where's Fargo?"

"Had to put her in a kennel. Can't have doggie doo around here."

"You could have left her with me."

"Yeah right. Like you feed me and let me stay over and then I give you my dog?"

"Next year I'll keep her."

"Next year you'll be here, right?"

It's a rare occasion when a not-yet-senile woman stops even wondering what she looks like. Morning at Women's Festival was that occasion for me. I crawled out of the tent and stood shivering in the damp air, even though I was already wearing all the clothes I had with me. Darla handed me a quilted vest and I put it on. We made a trip to the portapotties, which smelled like the third level of Hades. Back at the tent we shared a can of warm Pepsi and I used the last of it for mouthwash. So much for morning ablutions.

The caffeine in the Pepsi woke up a couple of my brain cells. "Oh shit," I said. "Nobody knows where I am."

"You need to call home?" said Darla.

"Right. Can we do it?"

"Sure, come with me."

Darla led me to an area of medium sized tents where we found a woman in a caftan doing her partner's hair in cornrows. Darla introduced me to Lonnie who left off braiding long enough to produce a cell phone. I called home, got the machine and left a message for Brooke explaining that I had spent the night at the festival. When I tried to give Lonnie some money, she waved me away. "Just pass it on," she said. Then Darla and I headed for Buttercup campground.

We stood outside the orange tent and Darla sang an off key rendition of "Wake up, Little Susy." Someone inside the tent yelled at us to go away. Darla yelled back that we weren't going to leave.

Finally two bodies emerged from the dome shaped tent. The first was short, dressed in army fatigues and sporting green hair. She looked around, revealing a pixie like face, and yawned at us. Next came a taller woman in sweats who bore a striking resemblance to Madeline once I got past the fact that her head was shaved. The two of them stood and stretched, surveying the world with little interest. They recognized Darla and greeted her halfheartedly. Then Darla introduced me, explaining that I had been a friend of Madeline's. This sparked a bit of interest in Louise.

"I never even knew my sister was dead," she said, "until I got back to Vermont. Can you beat that?"

"I'm sorry," I said. "It must have been a shock."

"My mother could have reached me. She's just a vindictive bitch."

"Well —." I struggled for a tactful reply.

"Let's go get breakfast," said Darla, observing that the pair was in critical need of caffeine. "I think they have coffee."

We found the food tent and filled our cups with coffee that was hot and strong. The oatmeal had lumps which proved to be raisins and nuts and it all tasted pretty good, especially with maple syrup poured on top. After we washed our dishes, Darla asked Zoe to come and help her on mainstage. Zoe quickly agreed and the two of them headed off together, which left me alone with Louise.

What now?

Now that I had found the missing sister, I couldn't figure out where to start. Should I tell her I was helping with Madeline's murder investigation—or would that just make her clam up? My back hurt, my socks were wet and my mouth tasted like old coffee grounds. *What on earth had possessed me to go on this stupid camping trip anyway?*

"Come on," said Louise with a jerk of her head. "Might as well start the day out right."

I followed her to a grassy slope where we sat on a log to catch the morning sun. Her face was square, like Madeline's, with the same deep-set eyes and strong cheekbones. When she pulled off her sweatshirt, I saw the parrot tattoo on her left shoulder and a blue tinged crystal around her neck. Carefully, she untied a leather pouch from her belt. From the pouch she extracted a triangular stone, a silver lighter and a small plastic bag. She dumped some green stuff from the bag into a hollow in the stone.

"In memory of Madeline," she said, and flicked the lighter. The green stuff glowed as she inhaled deeply from the business end of the stone pipe. Lips compressed, she held it out to me. I hesitated for a split second while I decided it was all in the interests of science, then took the pipe and inhaled. I handed it back; she inhaled again and handed it to me. I took a second toke, handed it over and let her finish the bowl.

It was pretty good stuff—certainly better than the cigarette I had smoked at the Belly Up. The heat of the sun soaked through my shirt, the birds began to sing and suddenly there was no place on earth I wanted to be except right there at the Women's Festival, sitting on that particular hillside, talking to Madeline's sister. Louise laughed and opened a can of root beer. We passed it back and forth while we talked about life and death, love and hate, men and dogs, relationships and Madeline. The sun was climbing into the sky by the time I recovered my investigative mode.

"About Madeline," I said. "Who was her boyfriend when she lived in Lansing? Did you ever meet him?"

"Troy? Sure, I saw him a lot. See, after my mom disowned me, I used to go and stay with Madeline instead of going home."

"What was he like? What kind of work did he do?"

"Something to do with finance. Number cruncher in some kind of investment firm." We watched a golden butterfly land on my knee. "Something about Troy seemed a little off," she said. "I never felt like I could trust him. But Maddie was crazy about him so I kept my mouth shut."

"How long were they together?"

"Couple of years, maybe longer."

"How did it end?"

"Now that's the strange part. He told her he was going on a ski trip, and then he never came back. She went to his apartment and found it empty. Nobody knew where he was. Maddie waited. She was sure he would contact her eventually, but he never did."

"That *is* strange. Any theories?"

"I think he was in some kind of trouble at work."

"What was his last name?"

"Damned if I can remember."

"When I knew Madeline, she never let herself get attached to any guy."

"Well, she did with this one. She was blown away when he left."

"How much later did she move to Shagoni River?"

"Nine or ten months – almost a year. That's how long it took her to give up waiting for him."

"Did she get involved with anyone else—afterward?"

Louise shook her head. "She hardly even dated after Troy left."

"Well, she had men friends in Shagoni River, but nothing serious."

"I just hope they find the bastard that killed her."

"Me too."

Louise stood and stretched. "The vendors should be open by now. I need to get some CD's and stuff. Come with me and look around."

The vendors area was in a grove and we walked on a carpet of needles through dappled sunlight that fell through the branches of tall pine trees. It felt magical. Women talked and laughed and badgered us to buy their wares— chunky jewelry, silver buckles, velvet bags, baskets shaped like mythical animals. A tall black lady carved on a piece of wood that seemed to change color while I watched. The busiest spot was the body piercing booth, where the proprietress advertised her work with rings in her nose, eyebrows, tongue and other places too tender to mention.

Louise spent a long time deciding on a couple of CD's while I just stood around and gawked. Then she said, "The afternoon concert is going to be a gas. You're going to stay, aren't you?"

Why not? After all, it was a beautiful day and Marge wasn't expecting me at the office—or was she? Was it Friday or Saturday? I wasn't sure and somehow it didn't seem to matter. Being with Louise felt good – it was a little bit like having Madeline back. I spent my only cash on a pair of silver earrings for Brooke

Zoe and Darla were at the orange tent when we returned. We ate some trail mix and cookies for lunch and washed it all down with Gatorade. The afternoon concert was possibly the best of them all—a piano player named Diamond Lil beat out syncopated rhythms behind a singer called Ruby Tuesday. They did ballads, blues and ragtime, punctuated with raucous stories. The four of us laughed and hooted like wild women.

After the concert seemed like a good time for me to leave. But Louise somehow convinced me to stay and eat with them again, and back at the tent Darla brought out a bottle of wine which we shared with a dark skinned woman in a red turban. The woman, who called herself Rhianon, did a tarot card reading for each of us. Louise's cards promised travel; Darla got romance; Zoe got money, and I got friendship. Lucky me. Darla needed to go back to work and I needed to get going, so I told everybody goodbye and packed up.

Dark clouds were rolling in again so I hiked double time to the parking lot, intent on getting out before the rain. It took me a while to find my Honda, and then I couldn't find my keys. Cursing, I conducted a thorough search of all my pockets and dumped out the backpack, all to no avail. I hiked back to Darla's tent and searched. Still no keys. Then I vaguely remembered Darla picking my keys up off the ground and putting them in her fanny pack so I wouldn't lose them again. Of course she was wearing that pack.

By this time the evening show was well under way and I knew I wouldn't get any where near Darla until it was over, so I found a spot and sat down to wait out the show. I was impatient, hardly listening to the music. The rain hit suddenly and hard. The musicians kept playing until it was clear that the audience was scattering for shelter, and then they wound it up. I went back to the tent, crawled inside and waited in the darkness for Darla to return. When she finally showed up she located my keys and handed them over. But that wasn't the end of it.

"I'm really sorry," she said, "but you can't leave tonight."

"You're kidding—right?" I was in no mood for jokes.

"You'd never make it out. We've got three vehicles up to their hubcaps in mud. Ground crew says nobody leaves until morning."

And that's how I came to spend a second night at the Women's Festival.

When I crawled out in the morning, the sun was shining on grass and rocks that were steaming like a sauna. This time I was determined to escape. I sat on a stump to put on my shoes, grabbed my pack and said goodbye to Darla who was still in her sleeping bag. My exit route took me past Louise and Zoe's camp, where I found them rigging a line to hang out their wet clothes. I told them goodbye and invited them to visit me in Shagoni River.

"I will," said Louise. And you know what? I thought of that guy's name, Madeline's boyfriend. It was Hilman, Troy Hilman."

"Tracy where have you been?" Brooke's face registered dismay as I walked through the door—dirty, wet and thoroughly disheveled. "You're tracking mud on the floor," she added, in a maternal tone.

"I was at the festival. Didn't you get my message?"

"I got a message. But that was about Thursday night, wasn't it? Today's Saturday."

"Oh. Well, yeah." Who the hell knew what day it was, anyway?

"You'd better call Frank. He was here last night, looking for you. Did you guys have a date or something?"

"Oh dear." I dropped her backpack on the floor. "I guess we did. What did you tell him?"

"I told him about your message on the answering machine. He came in and replayed it." She giggled. "Like maybe he thought you were kidnapped."

"Not quite." I headed for the kitchen and the smell of coffee. I poured a cup, brought it back to the living room and dialed Frank's number. He answered on the second ring.

"Hi, it's me."

"Hey, I thought maybe you had been abducted."

"I was camping with lesbians, not aliens."

"Everything okay?"

"Sure, I'm fine. Just tired. It took me a while but I found Madeline's sister. Had a long talk with her. She told me—"

"That's great. Look, I'm in a meeting right now but you can fill me in tonight. I think we have plans for supper."

"Maybe. To tell the truth, Frank, I'm not sure what day it is."

"Trust me, we have a date. Let's eat at your place. I'll pick up some Chinese."

Frank arrived about six thirty looking very sweet in his yellow polo shirt—maybe because he was the first man I'd seen in three days. We took the food to the picnic table in my back yard.

"Did you find real estate mogul Ford Mathews? What did he have to say? And this is good, by the way."

"I found Mathews at home." Frank abandoned his chopsticks for a fork. "He's got a pretty nice place—swimming pool in the back. We had a couple of beers on his patio."

"Oh, hard work."

"Hey, it was a holiday."

"I figured he was married. Was I right?"

"He claims a wife and two boys, but they weren't around. He said they were in Oregon visiting her parents."

"So why was he not with them?"

"Said he didn't get along with his in-laws. But then, we know he's not exactly a family man."

"Right. Family men don't drive fifty miles to hang out in bars. Did he acknowledge knowing Madeline?"

"Sure. Said all the real estate people knew each other."

"Ha! Anything else?"

"When I showed him the phone records, he admitted that he and Madeline had carried on some private business—after hours."

"Monkey business, I'll bet."

"He claims it wasn't sexual."

"Then what was it?"

"A little scam they were pulling on their employers. They passed referrals to one another under the table and shared the commissions. It minimized their bosses' share and somehow helped with their taxes. It wasn't a whole lot of money but in the course of a year, it added up. That's how he explained the late night phone calls."

"So when did he see Madeline last—according to him?"

"About two months before she was killed. He denied ever stalking her. Said their relationship was friendly."

I pointed my chopsticks at him. "Frank, I know she was hiding from him that night at the Belly Up."

"You're probably right." He rubbed his chin. "So why do you think she was she avoiding him?"

"Maybe she wanted out of their arrangement."

"Or maybe she was scamming the scam."

"I think this is the guy who killed Madeline," I said emphatically. "I just have a gut feeling."

"Maybe, but feelings aren't evidence. And Mathews has an alibi. Said he was with friends the night of the murder."

"Have you questioned them?"

"One guy—his story meshed."

"People lie," I said stubbornly.

"Don't you think I know that? Let's not jump to conclusions. Tell me about Madeline's sister."

So I filled him in on Louise and what she had told me about Madeline's boyfriend, Troy Hilman. "Louise said Troy dropped out of sight almost a year before Madeline moved up here."

"He's the next person I need to talk with."

"How would you find him?"

"There are ways. We know his name and where he lived. Do you know who he worked for?"

"Sorry. Forgot to ask that."

"That's okay. You did a good job."

Brooke and Derek were both working so we had the living room and VCR all to ourselves. We started to watch a video but must have fallen asleep on the couch because I was thoroughly disoriented when the jangling of the telephone awakened me. The TV was flashing and I was pinned under a hairy arm. I wiggled and stretched, trying to read the hall clock and reach the receiver without disturbing Frank. He was just beginning to stir as I got a grip on the receiver and mumbled hello.

"Tracy, this is Brooke."

"Are you kids broke down?"

"No. The truck's okay."

"Where are you? What's going on?"

"Just checking in. We were almost home when I remembered I left my purse at work, so we came back to get it. That's where we are now." Her voice volume rose and fell. "The employee entrance is locked so we're going to try the back. I wanted to tell you why we're late. We couldn't get an answer at Lavallens."

"Okay, good. I'll tell Jewell if she calls."

Brooke's next words came in faintly because they were not directed at me. I heard her yell, "Be careful!" and then, "No! Derek, look out —!" before the connection went dead.

Frank was awake now, sitting up and looking at me.

"The kids are out at the Diamond D," I said. "It sounds like they're in trouble."

"What kind of trouble?"

"I don't know."

He reached for his boots. "Let's go find out."

CHAPTER EIGHTEEN

We were in Frank's Blazer about two miles from the Diamond D when the wail of a siren overtook us. A flashing red light came up behind us and Frank pulled over to let the Cedar County ambulance go past. Then he said "Hang on," as he turned on his own flasher, pulled back onto the road and hit the accelerator.

"Do you think it's one of the kids?" I said. "Do you think there was a prowler on the grounds?"

"I don't think anything yet—except that ambulance is going the same place we are."

His words conjured up images I didn't want to deal with so I just kept quiet and hung on. Within minutes we were bouncing up the driveway of the Diamond D Ranch and the two-story lodge loomed over us in the darkness. There was no activity in front of the building but when we drove around to the back I saw that Frank had been right. The ambulance was there and so was a car from the Cedar County Sheriff's Department.

Frank parked and we both jumped out. The place was lit by overhead fluorescent lights that flanked the Olympic sized swimming pool. Two EMT's, one male and one female, were working over a body on a stretcher. The male technician held a rubber mask to the victim's face while he squeezed an attached rubber bag. From my hospital days, I knew that the "bagging" action was forcing air into the victim's non-functioning lungs. The body on the stretcher was covered with a blanket and looked about the size of—Brooke?

"Who is it?" I said, talking past the lump in my throat.

The technician didn't look up. "Don't know."

"A girl?"

"No, it's a man."

I breathed a sigh of relief and looked around to see a cluster of people gathered at one end of the swimming pool, talking and gesturing. Frank was there, along with two uniformed deputies, one short and one tall. The rest of the faces were in shadow but I recognized Tom Halladay by his cowboy boot stance and Roxanne by her hair, almost white in the artificial light. Next to Roxanne was a slender figure with long braids that had to be Brooke. On the other side of Brooke was a tall guy with an odd haircut, Derek. My family was safe.

Brooke saw me and hurried over. "Boy, you guys got here fast," she said, giving me a hug. Her shirt was damp and smelled faintly of chlorine.

"I'm just glad you're okay. Who's on the stretcher?"

"Marvin Crouch. We found him floating in the pool."

Brooke and I stood aside to let one of the EMT's get past us to the ambulance. "So what happened? What'd you guys do?"

"Derek jumped in and moved him down to the shallow end. Then he pushed and I pulled 'til we got him out. Boy, was he heavy. Derek climbed out and started doing CPR. I had the phone so I called nine-one-one." She twisted one of her braids and water ran from her hair. "After I made the call, Derek told me what to do and I helped him with the, you know, pushing on the chest."

"Coming through here." We stood aside as the taller deputy helped the EMT's load the patient into the ambulance. The man who was "bagging" hopped in with the stretcher and the deputy closed the ambulance doors.

The other attendant, a short woman with curly brown hair, was moving toward the cab of the ambulance. "Can you tell me his condition?" I said.

She kept moving. "Are you a relative?"

I followed her. "No. I write for the *News*."

"Can't tell you much except he's got a pulse now." She opened the door and climbed in. "But he's still not breathing," she said as she slammed the door. The ambulance moved out into the night.

I walked back to Brooke and put an arm around her. "I hope he'll be okay," she said. "He looked really awful."

The taller deputy, who was lean and dark skinned, got some yellow tape from the sheriff's car and started laying it out around the pool. He stopped when he came to a clear glass bottle lying between two lounge chairs. Carefully, he pulled a plastic bag from his pocket, and slid the bottle inside.

"He must have been loaded," I heard Tom Halladay saying to the other deputy, who was taking notes. I gave Brooke's hand a squeeze and moved closer to the group. "He's been acting strange lately, sort of depressed, drinking too much."

"I didn't notice anything," said Roxanne, "and I spend as much time with him as—"

184

"He hides it well," Halladay interrupted, "but I've been finding empties down at the hangar." He sighed. "Fact is, I've been worried about Marvin."

"You never mentioned it to me," she said.

"Well, we talked about it." Halladay looked at his wife. "Marvin admitted that he had a problem, but said he was handling it. I didn't think I should —."

"You should have told me," Roxanne cut in.

"He asked me not to." Halladay looked down and kicked some imaginary pebble at his feet. "He was afraid you'd fire him."

A half moon peeked through the oak trees and an owl hooted in the distance, lending the scene a Gothic air. Derek came over and joined Brooke and me. He was dressed in his Diamond D outfit, but the black jeans and red shirt were completely soaked. He was shivering.

You need some dry clothes," I said. "Have you got any in your truck?"

Derek shrugged. I went to the Blazer and rummaged through Frank's stuff until I found a sweatshirt which I appropriated for Derek. He stripped off his wet shirt, used the sweatshirt for a towel and then put it on. Brooke picked up the soggy shirt and squeezed it out. The group by the pool was still talking, but things seemed to be winding down. Frank pointed to the yellow police tape that now encircled the pool.

"This area is off limits until we clear it," he said. "No one is to go inside the line."

"That's stupid," said Halladay. "How long do we have to put up with this nonsense?"

"We'll clear it sometime tomorrow," said Frank.

"Get real," said Halladay. "We're trying to run a business here."

"Couldn't you finish tonight?" Roxanne directed a rare smile at Frank. "We've got families here and they expect to use the pool."

"Sorry," said Frank, "but we need to look around in the daylight. And get photos. I'll try to be finished by noon."

"This is ridiculous." Halladay's voice grew louder. "The guy got drunk and fell in. Now you folks are trying to make a federal case out of it. Don't you people have enough to do?" Halladay threw in a couple of obscenities, clearly spoiling for a fight. I held my breath, wondering if Frank would take the bait.

But apparently Frank had dealt with a lot worse than Tom Halladay. "If you want it done early," he said, "I'll come back and do it myself. How about eight o'clock?"

"Make it seven," said Halladay.

"Fine, no problem." I had to admire Frank's cool.

185

"We'll tell them it's being treated," Roxanne said to her husband.

"Tell them whatever you want," said Frank. "Just don't you or anyone else come inside that line."

The matter of the yellow tape settled, Roxanne took Brooke inside to get her purse. When they emerged, Brooke joined Derek who was talking to the deputy with the notebook. The officer apparently dismissed them because they turned and headed for Derek's truck.

"Tracy, do you want to ride home with us?" said Brooke.

"No thanks, you guys go ahead." I wasn't eager to ride in Derek's truck. And besides, I wanted to be around in case there was any more action.

But there wasn't. Frank and I left the ranch about ten minutes later. When we got to my house, Brooke was making coffee and Derek had traded his soggy jeans for a pair of sweat pants that ended at about the middle of his calves. It was getting on toward five o'clock but we were all too wired up to think about sleep, so we decided to make French toast for an early breakfast. I started breaking eggs, Brooke went to the cellar for maple syrup and Frank located the skillet. Derek hauled plates out of the cupboard.

"Derek," I said, "shouldn't you call you parents?"

"They're not home," he said. "I finally remembered. They went up north to spend the night at a motel—to sort of, you know —."

"Work things out?"

"Yeah, right."

"Well, that's good," I said. "Let's hope the stay is helpful."

"I wonder if Mr. Crouch is going to be okay," Brooke said as we sat down to a stack of golden slices.

"How did he look?" said Frank.

"I really couldn't tell much about his color," said Derek. "The lights out there are so weird." He pushed a chunk of butter around on his toast.

"Did you get a pulse on him?"

"A faint one, maybe. It was really hard to tell. I know for sure he wasn't breathing."

"What's the official theory on this?" I asked Frank.

"Halladay figures he fell in and was too drunk to get out."

"Do you buy that?" I refilled his coffee.

"I'm not sure. I wonder why he was out by the pool at almost three in the morning."

"Well, it was his job to check the filters and stuff," said Derek.

"Yes, but those jobs are normally done in the daylight," Frank said, stifling a yawn.

"Doesn't it seem strange," I said, "that Marvin Crouch has almost drowned twice in just about two weeks?"

"Maybe someone doesn't like him." Derek stabbed the last slice.

"He seems like a nice guy," Brooke said with an unstifled yawn. "A lot nicer than the rest of the people out there."

By the time we finished breakfast, birds were chattering and daylight was giving shape to the trees in the backyard. Derek left for home and Brooke went up to bed. But Frank had an early morning appointment that precluded sleep. I sat with him while he drank the last of the coffee in preparation for his return to the Diamond D.

"Thanks for breakfast," he said as he stood and stretched. "And sorry I fell asleep on you last night."

"Good thing you did, the way the night turned out."

I walked with him down the hallway and he gave me a peck on the cheek as he headed out the door. "They wanted me early," he said. "They've got early."

I slept until almost noon, took a shower and tried to remember what day it was. After two nights at the Women's Festival and one at the ranch, my interior clock and calendar were both profoundly confused. I made a peanut butter sandwich and took it along with a glass of milk to the picnic table in the back yard. The weather was not conducive to any serious thought so I sat in the sun and watched butterflies flit around my grandma's yellow roses. That's where I was, pulling weeds and getting scratched for my troubles, when Jewell showed up.

"Jewell." I stood and gave her a hug. "How was your getaway?"

"Not bad. But get this. An hour after we got home, Paul went out on his boat and I went running." She laughed. "So much for togetherness."

"Have you seen Derek? Did he tell you what happened?"

"You bet. He woke up when we got home and told us the whole story. I'm glad you and Frank were around to—oh, leave that one with the shiny leaves, I think it's a day lily."

"Thanks. Let's get out of the sun."

Jewell and I went inside and got some iced tea. Just as we were clearing space on the coffee table for our drinks, the hallway clock chimed three.

"Yikes. Are the kids supposed to work today?"

"Almost forgot," she said. "I'm supposed to tell Brooke that Derek called in and finagled the day off—for both of them."

"That's good—since Brooke is still in bed." I took a swallow of tea. "Is Derek all right? I mean, what a bizarre experience. Did it upset him?"

"Are you kidding? He slept like a log. And now he wants to be a paramedic."

"Ah, the resilience of youth."

"What happened out there anyway? Has anyone figured out how the guy ended up in the pool?"

"It looks like he got drunk and fell in. There was an empty bottle by the pool. It looked like gin or vodka to me." We both looked up at the sound of a vehicle in the driveway.

"Sounds like you have company," she said.

"It must be Frank," I said, heading for the front door. "Maybe he can tell us something."

Frank was on the porch, looking a little bleary eyed. I led him into the living room and said, "You remember my friend Jewell, I guess." There was no doubt that she remembered him.

Frank said hello to Jewell and collapsed into the recliner. "This feels good," he said as he leaned back and closed his eyes.

I brought him a glass of iced tea. "Did you get any sleep?"

"A few hours." He gulped down half the tea. "I just came from Wexford Hospital." He looked at Jewell. "Is that where you work?"

"Yes. I'm afraid so."

"The intensive care staff is not very friendly."

"They do tend to be overprotective." She smiled to show that she wasn't offended. "Did you get in to see him?"

"For about three minutes."

"It'll be better when he gets to a regular floor," she said. "What's his condition?"

"He's still unconscious, but starting to breathe on his own. The doctor said she expects to take him out of ICU tomorrow."

Brooke came down the stairs wearing a ragged tee shirt and sweat pants. Don't kids these days own pajamas? She listened to us for a few minutes and then said to Jewell, "Do you think Mr. Crouch will get well?"

Jewell pursed her lips. "We don't know how long he was in the water. But Derek thought he still had a pulse. So I'd say he's got about a fifty-fifty chance."

"Of living?" I said.

"Of recovering brain function."

"And if he doesn't recover brain function, then he'll be a —."

"A vegetable?" suggested Brooke.

"That's the usual terminology, yes," said Jewell.

"Maybe we shouldn't have rescued him," said Brooke.

"Don't even think that," Frank said quickly. "You kids did a great job. You did what was right."

"What was his blood alcohol?" Jewell said to Frank.

Frank shook his head in disgust. "For some reason, it didn't get drawn until this morning. The results were negative."

"Not very helpful."

'They're running more tests today," he said, "for narcotics or sedatives."

"Sedatives?" said Brooke. She came and sat between Jewell and me. "Like what?"

"Phenobarb, morphine, stuff like that," said Jewell.

"Why?" I said, and then answered my own question. "Are they thinking he tried to commit suicide?"

"It's one possibility," said Frank. "I found an unlabeled bottle by his bed—with about half a dozen little white pills."

"You searched his room?"

Frank nodded. "This morning when I was out there. He's got a little place on the grounds—used to be the caretaker's cabin."

"Did you need a search warrant?"

"No, the Halladays were cooperative. Surprisingly so."

"That's a change," I said. "Last night they wanted the police to go away and not come back."

He smiled, that gap toothed smile of his. "Maybe they were grateful that I got the pool cleared for them. I was done before anyone showed up for breakfast." He rubbed his jaw. "Guess maybe I need a shave."

"What do you think of the pills?" I said to Jewell.

"It sounds like Phenobarb to me." We all looked at her. "They're your basic sleeping pill," she said. "With an overdose, you just never wake up."

"They're not very hard to get," said Frank. "Unfortunately."

"Phenobarb and alcohol," said Jewell "have become the combo drug of choice for suicides."

I thought for a minute. "So let's say Marvin Crouch decided to kill himself. He must have really hated the Halladays to do it in their pool on a big holiday weekend."

"Good point," said Frank. "Nothing like a dead body in the swimming pool to scare away the tourists."

"Should we mention the empty gin bottle?" I said to Jake. It was Monday morning and we were collaborating on a front-page story about the near drowning and surprise rescue of Marvin Crouch. Although he was in charge of the piece, I had written most of it, including some great quotes from the young rescuers.

"No, let's leave that out for now."

"How about photos of the kids?"

"Kyle should be doing that right now."

"Marvin Crouch seems to be having a run of bad luck lately."

"Bad luck or something else." Jake took off his glasses, cleaned them with a wrinkled handkerchief. "Fact is, we don't know much about the man."

"No we don't—and he never seemed inclined to talk about himself. When I interviewed him, he just wanted to talk about airplanes."

"Maybe there's a reason," Jake replaced his spectacles. "Sheriff Dupree did some checking into Marvin's past. His second wife died in an auto accident and he got a pretty big insurance settlement."

"So what happened to the money?" I swiveled my chair and looked at Jake.

"Apparently he made some bad investments and lost it all in a couple of years. Then he went back to work for Midwest."

"Until Tom Halladay called and said he needed help at his dude ranch."

"Right. Halladay calls, so the guy comes running." Jake stood and arched his back.

"Well, they go back a long way. There's probably a whole lot we don't know about their relationship."

Jake blew his nose. Same handkerchief. "Did you get a condition report from the hospital?"

"Yes I did. Marvin Crouch is critical but stable." And we used that to end the story.

Tuesday afternoon was busy as usual. Jake was gone, but had left instructions for me to get an update on Marvin Crouch's condition before the paper went to press. I waited until a little past four, then called Wexford General. The operator who answered had a whiny voice and sounded like she had flunked high school English.

"This is Tracy Quinn with the *Shagoni River News*," I said in my best non-threatening tone. "I'm calling to find out the condition of one of your patients, Mister Marvin Crouch." I even gave her the room number to make her job easier.

There was a long silence. Finally she said, "Um, sorry, but I'll have to let you speak to the nursing supervisor."

She put me on hold and I was subjected to a country music station. Tammy Wynnete advised me to stand by my man; someone complained of achy breaky heart. Finally I heard a click and a woman's voice said, "This is Gillian Tupple, afternoon supervisor."

Again I explained who I was and what I wanted. All she said was, "Oh dear." I heard an intake of breath and then a whispered conversation with someone on her end. She came back on the line and said, "I'm sorry, but I can't give out any information about that patient. The situation is confidential. I've been instructed not to release any information."

I was getting annoyed. From my own experience working in a hospital I knew that she was required to tell the press *something*, even if it was a lie. "Instructed by who —?"

"The hospital administrator. I'm sorry."

"Okay," I said, just wanting to wrap up and go home. "Is Marvin Crouch still your patient?"

"Ah, yes he is."

"And is he still alive?"

"Ah yes, I can confirm that."

"And is his condition still critical but stable?"

"I'm sorry," she said, going into tape recorder mode again. "I'm not allowed to release any other information. The situation is confidential."

She sounded really nervous. Did someone have a gun to her head?

I hung up and finished the story with, "As of press time Tuesday, Crouch was still at Wexford General Hospital and his last status report was critical but stable. The hospital spokesperson declined to provide any further information."

Before I left, I reported the odd exchange to Marge and she nodded grimly. Probably she would make another call to see if she could do any better with Ms. Tupple. I was tired and hungry so I picked up my mail and went home, determined to put the whole thing out of my mind. But it didn't take long before curiosity got the better of me. I called Jewell at home.

"What's going on with Marvin Crouch?" I said. "The nursing supervisor acted like she was being held hostage or something."

"Oh Tracy, it's really weird. Crouch is on Two West in a private room. Something happened this afternoon—I'm not sure what—and by the time I left, the administrator was there and doctors and cops were swarming all over the place. There's a deputy posted at his door and no one is allowed in the room."

"A guard? Did Crouch try to leave?"

"Hardly. He's not even conscious."

"So what happened?"

"Tracy, please don't repeat this because it's just rumors."

"I won't tell anyone, not even Frank."

"He probably knows. I saw Frank at the hospital as I was leaving, but we didn't talk. The story is that someone went into Crouch's room and messed with his I V, opened it up to about ten times the rate it was ordered and—well, all that fluid can kill a person—it's just like drowning."

Drowning?

Again?

CHAPTER NINETEEN

"Could it have been a mistake?" I said after Jewell told me about Marvin Crouch nearly drowning in his I V fluid.

"It doesn't look that way."

"How did it happen? Aren't those things regulated by computers?"

"They are. But the tubing was ripped right out of the computer box."

"But there's an alarm that's supposed to go off."

"I know, Tracy, and here's the scary part. The machine was unplugged from the wall."

"So this had to be deliberate."

"I can't see any other explanation."

"But who could have done it?"

"Unfortunately, it could have been almost anyone. Two West has open visiting hours and doesn't require visitor passes, so anybody can walk in off the street. I suppose that's all going to change now. So much for trying to be visitor friendly."

After the phone call I sat and mulled over this latest strange turn of events. According to my count, Marvin Crouch had nearly drowned three times. Once, or even twice, I was willing to attribute to accidents or just bad luck. But three times? No way. The only possible conclusion was that some one was trying to kill him. But why? What could this quiet man have done to generate such ill will?

Did Crouch have another side, I wondered, completely at odds with the mild mannered person I had seen? Maybe he was in Cedar County to escape some shady past. Maybe his name wasn't really Marvin Crouch. Maybe somebody had a "contract" on him. Maybe —.

I picked up the phone and started to call Frank, but stopped half way through. Jewell had said the hospital was swarming with doctors and cops, so it was probably not a good time for the lead detective to take a call from his girl friend. My overwhelming curiosity didn't seem like adequate reason to interrupt whatever Frank was doing.

Culinary noises were issuing from the kitchen so I wandered in that direction. Brooke was in the midst of a baking project. The table was covered with flour and sugar sacks, measuring cups, bowls, an eggbeater, a flour sifter and two cookbooks. Her hair was tied up in a kerchief and she was pouring an oddly blue-tinged batter into a baking dish.

"Looks interesting," I said. "What is it?"

"It's called blueberry buckle." She looked up from her work. "This friend of Mrs. Fritzell brought in fresh blueberries and I bought two quarts."

"I can hardly wait. Should I make something for supper—meatloaf maybe?"

"Oh no," she said. "There's plenty of chicken left."

I got the feeling that Brooke was not fond of my meatloaf. "Guess I'll go out and bring in the clothes," I said, heading for the back door. But I stopped short when I saw a newspaper clipping lying on the table. "Brooke, what is this?"

"I dunno." She was cautiously balancing the baking dish as she slid it into the oven.

I picked up the clipping for a closer look. It was torn and a little discolored, with no date or dateline. There was a headline—"Executive Resigns under Accusations" – and there was a photo of a clean-shaven, middle aged white guy in a suit and tie. I waved the clipping at Brooke and said, "This wasn't here this morning." She shrugged.

I sat down and scanned the story. "Troy Hilman, employed for the past three years by Verotech Inc., was dismissed last week amid allegations he had diverted almost $100,000 of company funds to his private use." The name sounded familiar but I couldn't place it. The story went on with Hilman proclaiming his innocence, followed by some technical stuff about auditing procedures. The story ended with "A Verotech spokesperson said the board will meet this week to decide whether criminal charges should be filed."

"Help me out here," I said. "Where did this come from?"

"Isn't it from your paper?"

"No. It's old. And I don't clip my own paper."

"Maybe it fell out of a cookbook." She licked batter from a spoon. "Some of them had bookmark things."

It seemed a possibility. At this point it seemed the only possibility. I examined the book she had used for the blueberry recipe. It was a Betty Crocker that my mother gave me for my sixteenth birthday—and never once had I made blueberry buckle. The other cookbook was bright red with a curious title—"300 Aphrodisiac Desserts." Completely mystified, I thumbed through sections with headings like "Chocolate in Bed" and "Kama Sutra Cookies" until I remembered the afternoon that Ivy and I had ransacked Madeline's apartment. The cookbook had belonged to Madeline.

Then I got it.

Troy Hilman was Madeline's old boyfriend, the one who had left Lansing in such a hurry. The clipping proved that Louise had been right in her suspicions. Truly Hilman had been in "some kind of trouble at work." I stared at the paper, trying to figure out how this might tie in with Madeline's death.

Madeline had saved the article, so she definitely knew why her boyfriend left town in such a hurry. But apparently she hadn't told anyone, not even her sister. Maybe she had been seeing Hilman on the sly, protecting his secret location. But then, why had she saved this story about his fall from grace? And where was he now?

I stumbled into the living room and sat on the couch, trying to puzzle out the pieces. After several minutes I still didn't have an answer – but I did have a reason to call Frank. I dialed his cell phone and it rang several times before he answered.

"I found a newspaper story," I said. "It's about Troy Hilman, Madeline's old boyfriend. Apparently he embezzled money from his employer."

"Hang on," said Frank. "Things are starting to—just a minute —. " He was off the line, then came back on and said, "I'm tied up at the hospital, but I'd like to see that clipping. Would you be willing to drive up here?"

"No problem," I said, eager to be in on the action. "I'll be there in half an hour."

"Great. I'll buy you supper in the cafeteria."

"Oh, hospital food. I can hardly wait."

"I'll meet you in the lobby," he said. "If I'm not there, have me paged."

I told Brooke I wouldn't be home for supper and she promised to save me some blueberry buckle. Within minutes I was in my Honda navigating Arrowhead Drive, oblivious to the lake front scenery. Once on the freeway I covered fifteen miles in record time, then took the Wexford exit and had to slow down on the two-lane. Still, I was right on schedule when I reached the Wexford city limits.

To avoid stoplights, I took a side street that I knew would bring me right into the hospital parking lot. The street had a posted speed limit of twenty-five miles per hour, which never made any sense to me because it was lined with mostly warehouses and self storage units. So I was probably going about forty, I swear not a bit faster, when a black mini-van came through an intersection headed straight at me. I hit the brake, which was a mistake, because if I had kept going, I probably would have taken the hit on the rear bumper. As it was, the van hit me broadside. I careered through the empty intersection and slammed up against the curb.

I sat there stunned and cursing under my breath. Cautiously I turned my head, wiggled my fingers and toes, and was relieved to find that everything worked. I checked my face in the mirror, but found no blood. Then I saw a very pregnant woman emerge from the mini-van and look apprehensively in my direction. She stood outside my door and I rolled down the window.

"I'm so sorry," she said. "Are you all right?"

Probably I was. But I was angry at her for delivering what might well be the deathblow to my Honda. "I don't know," I said, irrationally wanting to prolong her anxiety. I turned my head again. "My neck hurts."

"I'm so sorry. I stopped at the sign, I know I did. I had just started up again when you —."

"Yeah sure —."

Just then a Wexford Police car pulled up and an officer emerged. He was tall, with dark wavy hair and chiseled features. His movie star good looks seemed to mellow out both the pregnant woman and me. By the time the officer had questioned both of us and filled out his reports, I was through being furious and felt mostly bewildered.

Another cop had arrived and was directing traffic. I walked and stretched enough to decide that I didn't need medical attention. My Honda, however, had not fared as well. The left front wheel was popped off the rim, and the passenger door had a dent the size of Arizona. The cop called a tow service. When wrecker guy arrived, he hooked on to my car and we conferred briefly about where he should take it. Then I stood by feeling totally bereft as my wheels were hauled away. The cop asked me if I needed a ride anywhere.

"Yes. To the hospital."

"Are you hurt?"

"No, I'm not hurt," I said, for about the tenth time. "I'm meeting someone at the hospital. That's why I drove up here."

"Oh, sure," he said. "Hop in."

It was my first ride in a police car. At least I got to ride up front. When I walked into the hospital lobby it was deserted except for a black woman behind the reception desk. I told her I was looking for Frank Kolowsky. She seemed to know where he was because she picked up the phone and made a call.

"He'll be here in five minutes," she said.

I walked over to the gift shop and stood there looking at teddy bears in tutus while I worried about my car. Was the damage fixable? Was my insurance paid up? I saw Frank emerge from a door beside the elevators and hurried over to him.

"Tracy," he said, giving me a restrained hug.

"Sorry I'm late. Some chick broadsided me."

"Oh no." He held me at arms' length and looked me over. "You okay?"

"I'm not hurt. Just angry and confused."

"How about hungry?"

"I think so."

"Tell me about it while we eat. Supper's over, but we can get sandwiches and coffee."

"That sounds good." I was starting to feel better just being around Frank.

We walked down a series of halls until we reached the cafeteria. The place was eerily quiet, with empty tables and lots of stainless steel gleaming under fluorescent light. Frank put money in a machine that coughed out sandwiches while I filled two cups with coffee from a large electric pot. We loaded our tray and took it to a table in the corner.

"Not much of a meal," said Frank. "Sorry about that."

"It's not your fault. I'm the one who's late." I unwrapped my sandwich and glanced around the room. The only other occupants were two guys in brown uniforms who seemed oblivious to our presence. "What happened with Marvin Crouch?" I said, keeping my voice low. "Jewell told me a little about the IV business."

"No one knows for sure," Frank said, also glancing around the room. "Crouch was moved to a private room this morning, still unconscious but breathing okay. Around two o'clock a nurse checked his IV and found it running wide open."

"Whoa. That's dangerous."

"I know. Anyway she stopped the IV, paged the doctor, and everyone went into high gear to counteract the effects of the fluid—whatever it is they do."

"Probably gave him Lasix." Frank raised an eyebrow at me. "I used to work in a hospital, remember?"

"Oh yeah. I guess the fluid fills the lungs."

"That's what happens. Jewell said it's just like drowning."

"Right. So when the administrator arrived on the scene, he called me."

"You personally?"

Frank nodded. "I had left him my number, with instructions to call if Crouch woke up." He glanced around again. "Everyone here is walking on eggs. Don't tell anybody you write for a newspaper."

"Hey, I didn't even bring my notebook."

"Good."

"Any idea who did it?"

He shook his head. "I just spent over two hours grilling everyone who was in the building—staff, visitors, patients. The only lead I've come up with is a short Hispanic looking woman in a lab coat who was in his room. This is from Tom Halladay. He said he was leaving Crouch's room a little after one-thirty and saw this woman going in. He assumed, of course, that she was hospital personnel. But the staff can't match that description to anyone who works here."

"Lab coats are easy to get. And I guess anyone can walk in here."

"Well, not any more. No one is getting into Crouch's room without hospital ID. I parked myself outside his door and stayed there until Dupree sent a deputy to stand guard."

"I've been wondering about Crouch," I said. "I mean, who is he anyway? Has anyone contacted his family?"

Frank shook his head. "Can't find any family and that's a problem. Hospital folks get very nervous when they treat someone who doesn't have a next of kin."

"I know. There's all kinds of legal issues. How about the Halladays? Do they know his family?"

"They're not much help. Tom said he knew the first wife but that was years ago. No kids."

"And the second wife died in a car accident, according to Jake. But don't you have access to stuff—computer data bases?"

Frank nodded. "I did some checking this morning, but I didn't find any family. What I did find was that Crouch had been fired from Midwest Airlines. The reason was listed as 'personal problems'."

"Interesting. Doesn't that usually mean alcohol?"

"Alcohol or drugs." Frank pulled a toothpick from his pocket. "That would fit with what Tom Halladay told us about Crouch's drinking and depression."

"It would also explain why Crouch was willing to be general handyman and gopher at the Diamond D."

Frank left to refill our coffee cups. When he returned he said, "Hey, didn't you have something to show me?"

"Oh, right. That's why I'm here, isn't it?" I reached for my purse but we were interrupted by a woman's voice over the PA system.

"Mister Frank Klowsky," she said, pronouncing it badly. "Mister Frank Klowksy to room two thirty two. Stat please."

"Stat means right now," I said.

Frank was already on his feet. "I know. Let's go."

We sprinted out of the cafeteria. Frank bypassed the elevator, found a stairwell and took the steps two at a time, with me right behind him. We emerged in a patient corridor and nearly collided with a cart full of supper trays. Some of the more alert patients looked up from their newspapers as we raced down the hall. We slowed to avoid collision with a black man on crutches, then detoured around a tiny stooped woman who was walking between a nurse's aide and a wheeled IV pole.

Voices, loud and angry, echoed down the hallway. Frank hung a left and I followed. As I rounded the corner I saw three people standing outside a room that no one had to tell me was the current residence of Marvin Crouch. The loudest voice came from Tom Halladay.

"This is total bullshit," he said to the deputy who stood blocking the doorway. "I want to see the supervisor." The guard looked about sixteen years old, despite his considerable bulk and the Cedar County Sheriff's Deputy uniform. His nametag said Lars Hanson.

Roxanne stood beside her husband. She tried a more conciliatory tone. "We're the only family he's got. Couldn't we go in for just a minute?"

Hanson stood with his arms folded, filling the doorway. Behind him was a short, plump nurse in a flowered scrub suit who was probably trying to get out. "It wouldn't make any difference if you were family," he said. "My orders are not to let anyone in unless they're a hospital employee with identification."

"Orders from who?" blustered Halladay. "This is a total violation of patients' rights."

"From the hospital administrator," said Hanson, "and the sheriff."

"And me." Frank stepped in beside the deputy, who looked enormously relieved.

Halladay seemed to shrink a couple of inches. "You again," he said, glaring at Frank.

Frank just nodded. Roxanne smiled at him. "Would it be okay," she said, "if just one of us went in?"

"Sorry," said Frank. "Nobody. That's final."

Tom Halladay's eyes flashed anger. Underneath it though, I thought I saw a trace of fear. "Let's get out of here," he said to his wife. "These bastards aren't going to let us in."

They turned and walked away, Halladay still talking loudly. "You can hang around if you want to," he said. "I'm not staying another minute." They were heading for the elevator, Halladay walking so fast that his wife fell behind.

The nurse, whose nametag said Crystal, rolled her eyes at the departing couple. "I hope they just go home," she said. "They've been here all day and they're driving us crazy."

"How's our man?" Frank said, with a nod toward room 232.

"Waking up," she said. "That's why we called you."

"Is he talking?"

She grinned, showing dimples. "He told me to 'get the hell outta here', but I didn't take it personal."

Frank smiled. "Let's see what he says to me. It might be worse."

Nurse Crystal headed for the desk. Deputy Hanson seemed to be following the movement of her behind. When Frank started to go in, Hanson shifted his attention to me.

"What about her?" he said to Frank.

Frank stepped back and looked me over as though I were a stranger. "Crouch might remember you," he said at last. "Maybe you can help. Come on in."

I followed Frank into room 232.

Marvin Crouch was in a pretty standard hospital room – gray tile floor, cream colored walls and beige curtains on a window that offered a view of the parking lot. The room was warm, despite air blowing noisily from a unit under the window. A door on the right presumably led into a bathroom. I opened that door and Frank shot me a curious look.

"Sometimes these bathrooms are shared," I said. "If there's a door to the next room, then someone could have got in that way."

"Interesting."

The bathroom offered a commode and sink, but no second door. "Scratch that theory," I said, and joined Frank at the bedside.

Lying in the hospital bed, Marvin Crouch looked years older than when I had last seen him. His face was ashen, the hair almost white. His eyes were closed and his breath came in ragged gasps. An IV ran into his left arm, oxygen tubing ran from his nose to the wall, and a bag under the bed was collecting his urine.

Frank leaned over the railing and spoke Crouch's name a couple of times. There was no response except a noisy snore. Frank stepped back and motioned for me to take his place.

"You go ahead," he said.

Go ahead and do what? I felt like I had wandered into one of those dopey hospital scenes in a soap opera. So I took my cue and played the part. I put a hand on Crouch's bony shoulder and said, as gently as I knew how, "Marvin, it's me, Tracy Quinn."

The eyelids flew up, revealing watery blue eyes that showed alarm but no comprehension.

"See if he remembers anything," Frank whispered.

"Marvin, what happened? Out there at the Diamond D. The kids found you in the pool."

"Pool," he repeated through cracked lips. His voice sounded like dust.

Frank nodded encouragement at me. "Do you remember anything," I said, "anything at all?"

The watery eyes rolled. Crouch made some incomprehensible sounds and then slurred, "— tried to kill me."

Frank moved closer, leaning over to catch the words. "Who tried to kill you, Marvin? Who was it?"

"Tried to kill me," Crouch mumbled, "twice."

Frank shot me a look. "Who—who was it?"

Crouch's eyelids fluttered. He looked like he wanted to return to some pleasant country of oblivion.

"Marvin," I said, "can you tell us who it was—please?"

"Twice." Crouch said, his voice fading. "The no good —." His head flopped and he started snoring.

Crystal was in the room, holding a tray with a syringe full of yellow fluid. Frank and I made a few more attempts to communicate, but Crouch had slipped away from us.

"Guess that's all we're going to get right now," Frank said, and then turned to Crystal. "Let me know if he gets talkative again."

She promised that she would. Out in the hall, Frank conferred briefly with Hanson. Finally Frank turned to me and said, "Do you think our coffee's still hot?"

"I doubt it—but I'll bet there's more in the pot."

This time the cafeteria was empty and we bought sweet rolls to go with our coffee. Frank jotted in his tiny notebook as we reviewed Marvin Crouch's mumbled statements.

"Okay," said Frank. "First he said, 'tried to kill me'. Is that what you heard?"

"That's what I heard. So he didn't wind up in the pool by accident."

"And it wasn't a suicide attempt either." Frank took a bite of cinnamon roll. "Then, didn't he say, 'tried to kill me *twice*'?"

"I'm sure he said 'twice'. So what was the other time?"

"Maybe he saw the person who messed with the IV. That could have been the second attempt."

"What about the powered parachute going down? Was that a murder attempt?"

"We don't know yet. Dupree and Henderson went out today to see if they could bring up any wreckage."

I was quiet for a moment, concentrating on my Danish. Then I said, "Frank, do you think all of this could somehow be connected with Madeline's death?"

"Maybe—but I can't see the connection. Did Madeline even know the guy?"

"I don't think so. She died about the time he came on the scene."

"That's worth thinking about."

"Like maybe he was the hit man? And now someone is trying to kill him?"

"Slow down, ace detective." Frank smiled. "Hey, let's see that clipping."

"Oh, right." I reached into my purse, found the clipping and handed it over. Frank read it through, his brows drawn in concentration. Then he slammed a fist on the table.

"Good lord, Tracy. Look at this." He laid the clipping on the table between us.

I looked at the clipping and then at Frank. For the life of me I couldn't fathom what he was talking about.

"The photo, I mean, the guy." He was getting excited. "Who do you see?"

I stared at the picture of Troy Hilman, trying to see what I was missing.

"Add a mustache. Then add about five or ten years. Who do you see?"

Finally I saw it. "I don't believe this."

"Believe it."

"It's him."

"Yes, it's him."

We were looking at a picture of Tom Halladay.

CHAPTER TWENTY

"So Troy Hilman is Tom Halladay?" I stared at Frank, then at the picture, struggling to absorb the implications of our discovery.

"There's no doubt in my mind."

I tried to reconcile this new information. "So this means—what? That he was Madeline's boyfriend until —"

"Until he got caught cooking the books."

"Then he went underground and—"

"And reinvented himself as Tom Halladay, who married into money."

"Okay now," I said, "it can't be coincidence that he and Madeline both ended up in Shagoni River. She must have followed him."

"You're right. So tell me, what was Madeline's relationship to Tom Halladay?"

I thought very hard and came up blank. "She never mentioned his name—had no dealings with him that I knew of. Wait a minute—does this mean Tom killed Madeline?"

"It means he had a good reason to. She knew about his past. If she wanted to, she could have blown his reputation, his chance for a liquor license and probably his marriage."

Thinking of Tom Halladay as a killer made my skin feel crawly—but everything Frank was saying made sense. "So—what do we do now?"

"We need to catch Tom Halladay." Frank stood, looking at his watch. "How long ago did they leave here?"

"About half an hour, I guess."

"Let's hope they're not on US 31 headed for Chicago already."

I swallowed the last of my coffee and followed Frank out of the cafeteria. Back on the unit, Frank told the clerk he wanted to see the nursing supervisor and within minutes a tall, gray-haired nurse appeared. Her name pin identified her as Gillian Tupple, obviously the same lady I had sparred with on the phone. But of course she didn't know that and I saw no reason to enlighten her.

203

"I need a secure line to make a phone call," said Frank.

She seemed to know who he was. "Come with me."

We followed Ms. Tupple through a maze of hallways to the executive wing where she unlocked an office door.

"Just dial nine to get out," she said. "This is hospital business, isn't it?"

"Yes ma'am," Frank said in his most deferential tone.

"Pull the door shut when you leave. It'll lock."

The small office was almost filled up by a desk, swivel chair and filing cabinet. Frank slumped into the chair and picked up the phone.

"Benny, this is Frank," he said when he got a connection. "We need to arrest Tom Halladay." He told the sheriff about Halladay's change of identity and the embezzling charge. "That's right, he definitely had a shared history with Madeline Maxwell. And now I'm wondering about the business here at the hospital. —— He's heading for the ranch as far as I know. —— Okay, the Shagoni River exit. Can you bring somebody? —— Good. About twenty minutes." He turned to me. "Let's try Crouch one more time."

Back in room 232, Marvin Crouch was asleep and looked peaceful. Frank didn't bother with being gentle this time. He reached over the bed rail and shook the man's thin shoulder.

"Marvin," he said, "who tried to kill you?"

The eyes didn't open.

"Can you tell us who it was, Marvin?" I said.

The eyelids fluttered but there was no other response. Frank looked at me and shook his head. I shrugged in agreement and we left the room. Out in the hall I stood aside while Frank spoke briefly to Hanson. "And keep a close eye on that nurse," Frank said. "Let me know if she gives you any trouble."

Hanson blushed crimson.

We left the unit and hurried downstairs. In the front lobby, Frank turned to me and said, "This might be a good time for you to go home."

"I've got no car, remember?"

"Oh right." He frowned. "Guess you'd better come with me then. But don't get hurt."

Frank's Blazer had been sitting in the sun long enough to feel like an oven when we got inside. There was no air conditioning, so we rolled down the windows and tried to catch some breeze. When we hit the freeway, Frank broke the speed limit.

"I'm beginning to think," he said, "that Halladay is the one who messed with the IV."

"But what about that Hispanic woman?"

"That story came from Tom Halladay, remember?"

"Oh right. And you know what? Tom looked really nervous when he got the idea that Crouch was starting to talk."

Frank pulled out a toothpick. "And he got very hostile when Hanson wouldn't let him in the room."

"Well, I'm beginning to think it was Tom Halladay who sliced Marvin's parachute."

"If you're right, that makes three tries. I wonder why he was so intent on killing his buddy?"

"It must have something to do with Madeline."

"Maybe." Frank chewed the toothpick. "But what?"

A Cedar County sheriff's car was waiting at the freeway exit. Sheriff Dupree and Sergeant Laman were standing nearby. When Frank got out and joined them for a powwow, I stood by the Blazer and listened.

"Halladay may not come quietly," said Dupree. "If he knows we're onto him, he could try to get away."

"But he doesn't know how much we know," said Frank. "If we say it's just for questioning, maybe he'll cooperate to avoid a scene."

"Especially if they have people staying at the ranch," said Laman.

There was a little more discussion about access roads to the ranch. Then Dupree said, "Let's get going." I started to get in the Blazer and the sheriff seemed to notice me for the first time. He looked at Frank. "She going too?"

"She's with me," said Frank. "Her car got creamed."

"Okay," said Dupree. "But keep her out of the way."

Frank was silent as we sped down Arrowhead Drive. We turned onto a gravel road and he mumbled a few curses about eating dust from the sheriff's car. Driving up the long Diamond D driveway we found nothing out of the ordinary. The parking lot held a half dozen cars, a red pick-up truck and now the sheriff's car which had pulled in just ahead of us. On the hill in front of us was the wide front porch of the main lodge, devoid of any sign of life. A patch of woods beside the lot hid the path that led to the hangar.

The three men walked up onto the porch, with me lagging behind. But just as Dupree approached the front door, it flew open and a woman burst out, nearly colliding with him. There was blood on her mouth, and her face was contorted with pain. Finally I realized we were looking at Roxanne Halladay in total disarray, her cheeks discolored and her hair hanging in limp strands. She stared at us. We all stared back.

"You're looking for Tom, aren't you?"

"That's right," said Frank. "We just want to ask him some questions."

"Don't bother being nice." Her voice was hoarse. "I saw it all. I saw him try to kill Marvin."

Dupree glanced at Laman, who fumbled for a notebook.

"Back at the hospital —." Her eyes darted about as the words tumbled out. "Tom thought I was gone, but I saw what he did with that IV line. At first I couldn't believe my eyes, so I kept quiet. But when we got home I confronted him—told him what I saw." She put a hand to her ruined face and started crying.

Oddly enough, I felt a strange surge of empathy for Roxanne Halladay. Despite all her money and face-lifts, she was just another battered woman right now – a woman who had trusted the wrong man. She regained her composure enough to continue. "He tried to tell me I was crazy, that I was losing my mind. For a minute I thought I was." She looked from Frank to the sheriff. "Then he started hitting me – and threatened to kill me if I told anyone what I saw."

"So where is he?" said Dupree, eyeing the building behind her.

She shook her head. "He wanted me to go with him but I said I wasn't going to live on the run—so he grabbed some money and ran to his truck."

We all turned and looked at the parking lot to see if the red pick-up truck had disappeared while our backs were turned.

"But then he saw the sheriff's car coming up the drive—so he got out of the truck and ran down to the hangar."

"The hangar's right down there," I said, almost tripping as I ran down the steps toward the hangar path.

But Frank grabbed me. "You stay here," he said as he pushed me aside. The three men ran past me toward the hangar. Dupree had his gun drawn.

Then I heard Roxanne yell, "He's getting away." She pointed to the sky where a pink and green parachute was already above the treetops, floating up and away.

"Well, I'll be damned," said Dupree.

The men stared in confusion as the strange craft continued to rise and then headed west across the sand dunes.

"How fast do those things go?" said Dupree.

"Forty miles an hour," I said, "top speed."

"So we tail him till he runs out of gas," said Laman.

"But he's flying across the dunes," said Frank. "We can't follow him there. We'd be stuck in a minute."

"We can't go on the dunes," said Dupree, "but I know someone who can."

He pulled out his cell phone, punched in a number and issued a request.

Denny Dragoo was waiting in a dune buggy with the engine running when we reached his staging area. "Is this search and rescue?" Denny said as the sheriff climbed in beside him.

"Not exactly," said Dupree. He pointed to the parachute. "Just follow that guy."

Before I was even buckled up, Denny gunned the engine and headed for the sand dunes. Denny was dead serious now, driving fast and actually watching the road. Frank and Laman were in the middle seat which left me alone in the back. Frank was talking to the sheriff but I couldn't hear what they were saying. We lost sight of the parachute as we pounded across Termite Bridge and up the trail through the scrub oak.

But as soon as we climbed the first hill, we had an unobstructed view of the multicolored parachute against the evening sky. Racing across the dunes, it was easy to track Tom Halladay. Well, relatively easy. The buggy had more speed than the flying parachute, but we had to travel up and down the hills which pretty much evened things out.

"Maybe we could shoot a hole in his parachute," said Laman.

"Not a good idea," said Frank. "Unless he shoots first, of course." They were yelling over the noise of the engine and the wind.

"Do you think he's carrying a gun?" said Laman.

"We should have asked Roxanne," said Frank.

"Yeah, like she would have told us."

"I think she would have," said Frank. "She seems pretty fed up with her husband right now."

We trailed the fleeing Tom Halladay for about half an hour until we reached a barrier the dune buggy couldn't surmount. Denny braked to a standstill on the shore of Lake Michigan – and we watched the parachute continue west. All five of us climbed out and stood at the water's edge, watching the fugitive parachute continue westward over the lake as the sky turned gold with sunset. A brisk wind came up off the lake and I hugged myself, wishing for a jacket.

"So what do you think?" said Denny. "Is someone going to meet him with a boat?"

Dupree shook his head. "He didn't have time to make any plans."

"Do you think he'll circle back and try to land somewhere?" said Laman.

"He'd kill himself landing in the dark," said Frank.

"How much gas do they carry?" said Dupree.

"Enough for three or four hours," I said.

He's working against the wind," said Laman. "He's never going to make it to Wisconsin."

Dupree rubbed his neck. "I think this is one for the coast guard."

No one else had a better idea, so Dupree made the call. He told a probably incredulous coast guard dispatcher that a man was heading west over Lake Michigan in a powered parachute that wasn't going to make it across.

"Beats me," he said in response to a question. He looked at the men. "Where are we, anyway?"

"About a mile north of the Point Sable light house," said Denny.

Dupree relayed our location to the coast guard dispatcher. "If you guys get him," he said, "lock him up somewhere. He's involved in a murder and attempted murder. ——Right. So be careful."

We stood and watched the aircraft until it looked like a large mosquito buzzing against the crimson sky. A wave came in and wet my shoes.

"Unless you're planning to camp here," said Denny, "we'd better head back. These dunes all look alike in the dark."

"Okay," said Dupree, "let's go back."

Frank sat beside me on the return trip and I was grateful for his warmth. He was clearly disappointed by Halladay's escape and didn't have much to say. I was quiet too, but my brain was in overdrive. Ever since we left the ranch I had been struggling to retrieve an intriguing slice of visual memory. The elusive image kept swimming through my consciousness like a slippery fish – and the fish kept going through my net.

It was nearly dark when we arrived back at the lodge and Roxanne met us on the porch again. She had fixed her hair but a purple bruise was rising under her left eye. "Where is he?" she said.

"He's still out there," said Dupree, "flying straight into the sunset."

"I hope he dies out there," she said bitterly. Then she blew her nose and reconsidered. "No, I don't want him to die. I want him to pay for what he did to Marvin—and I want to know why he did it."

"Looks like Tom really wanted him out of the way," said Frank.

"Poor Marvin," she said. "The guy never did anything to Tom but try to help him."

As we stood in the twilight, that elusive image in the back of my mind finally crystallized into a thought. The thought demanded action, but I hesitated—afraid I would make a fool of myself. But then, what did I have to lose—nothing except my credibility. I touched Frank's arm and motioned him aside. He looked at me with a trace of annoyance. I ignored it. We stood together on the edge of the porch.

"That morning when you searched out here," I said, "did you look in the hangar?" He shook his head. "The day I interviewed Marvin, I saw something in there – something that could be important. I think we should go look."

Frank was quiet, considering my request. "I guess it can't hurt to look," he said at last. He turned to Roxanne. "We'd like to search the hangar."

"Go ahead," she said. "It's probably wide open. Tom left in a hurry."

Dupree and Laman were already on their way to the parking lot. Frank caught up with them and told them what he wanted to do. The sheriff may have been skeptical but he didn't say anything as he went to his car and pulled out a flashlight. Frank got another flashlight from the Blazer and we walked single file down the footpath. I stumbled a couple of times in the darkness and kept wondering if I was going to come out of this looking like the idiot of the year.

One of the hangar's garage size doors was open so we walked right in. Frank flipped a switch and the place lit up under the glare of two hanging bulbs. I looked around. Everything was pretty much as I remembered it. There were the two powered parachutes, shiny and ready to go. There were the cracked Vinyl chairs, the cluttered table and rusty tin cupboard that probably still held instant coffee and speckled sugar cubes. In the far corner was that old sofa, still covered with newspapers and surrounded by piles of debris. I pointed to the sofa.

"Look over there," I said.

The three men approached the sofa and started pawing through the rags and trash. Frank looked at me, shook his head.

"Look underneath," I said, "please."

Frank and Laman grumbled as they got down on all fours and aimed flashlight beams into the morass of dirt and refuse under the sofa.

Then Frank said, "I'll be damned." He reached under the sofa and pulled something out. He stood up, turned toward the light and held his discovery out at arm's length.

It was a woman's shoe and it swung ever so gently as he held it by the ankle strap. "Is this what we're looking for?"

My heart pounded as I moved in for a closer look. The shoe was cream colored and it had a wedge sole. "That's it," I said.

We were looking at Madeline's missing shoe.

At the sheriff's office, there was little to do except wait for word about the fate of Tom Halladay. Benny Dupree assigned me the job of making coffee, a sign that he had accepted my presence on his task force. Either that or none of the guys knew how to use the percolator. Laman found some donuts in the break room refrigerator and we had just divided them up when the call came in.

Benny took the call and put it on the speakerphone for the rest of us to hear. It was Mason County Sheriff Jerry Lattimore telling us that the coast guard had plucked Tom Halladay out of Lake Michigan, nearly drowned and not putting up any fight.

"What shall I do with him?" said Lattimore.

"Keep him till morning," said Dupree. "I'll have a car there by seven to pick him up." He glanced at his watch. "Hell, I'll do it myself. It'll be a pleasure." Dupree hung up, leaned back and looked around with the satisfied air of a man who had just won the next election. Which he probably had, though it was still two years away.

By the time Frank took me home it was well after midnight, but lights were on all over the house. We walked in and found Brooke and Derek asleep on the couch with the television droning.

Brooke stirred. "Oh hi," she said. "We were sort of waiting up for you."

Derek moved. "Hi guys. Is everything okay?"

"Better than okay," I said.

"We found out how Marvin Crouch got in the pool," said Frank "You guys foiled a murder attempt out there."

"Cool," said Brooke.

"No shit," said Derek. "I figured there was something weird about all that."

"And Tom Halladay isn't really Tom Halladay," I said.

"And we found out who killed Madeline," said Frank.

"Jeez," said Derek, "and we've been sitting here watching the bad movie marathon."

"Hey, are you guys hungry?" said Brooke.

"Starved," said Frank.

"Let's have some blueberry buckle," she said, "and you can tell us everything."

So we did. While the four of us demolished Brooke's blueberry creation, Frank and I took turns relating events of the evening. Eventually everybody started yawning, so the guys went home and Brooke and I went to bed. I slept better than I had in weeks. The next morning I woke up about nine-thirty, called Marge and told her I wouldn't be in because I had to deal with my smashed car. She could learn the rest of the story later.

Ivy made an unannounced visit the next day and used the opportunity to explain, unburden, and I suppose ask forgiveness.

"It wasn't something I planned," said Ivy. "It just happened. I was so upset about Greg fooling around again that I stopped to see Jewell. Paul was there and, well, he was consoling me and one thing led to another. Then we decided to take a moonlight cruise."

"I guess I can understand how it happened," I said. "But remember, I'm not the one who's been wronged."

"Oh, I know. I guess I'm sort of practicing for Jewell. Do you think she'll ever forgive me?"

"I honestly don't know. I don't know what I would do if I were in her place."

Ivy's features took on a martyred expression. "It would be awful," she said, "if they stopped inviting me to their parties."

"Yes, they do give great parties."

"I'd better run," she said with a glance at her watch. "I need to use your bathroom."

"Sure, go ahead."

While Ivy was occupied I pulled a book with a bright red cover out of my kitchen cabinet. When she emerged I said, "I've got a present for you."

"A present? How exciting."

"This is something that belonged to Madeline," I said, handing it over. "I think she would want you to have it."

Ivy peered at the book, mystified. "What an interesting title. Why, I never heard of—Aphrodisiac Desserts."

"Well," I said, "you have now."

"Madeline was blackmailing Tom," said Frank. "If she couldn't have him, she was determined to have some of his wife's money."

"That explains the deposits to her account," I said. "But why did he kill her?"

"Hard to say. Maybe she upped the ante—or maybe Roxanne was getting suspicious. In any case, Madeline met Tom down at the hangar expecting a pay-off. But instead she got a hammer to the head."

"Where did Marvin Crouch come in?"

"I'm pretty sure he was duped. His story about the night of the murder is that Tom roused him after midnight and told him to drive the truck into town and pick him up. Tom said he was returning a friend's car—actually it was Madeline's Cutlass."

"So that's what Mrs. Fritzell saw the night of the murder—the guys and the truck."

"Right. But early the next morning, Marvin saw something else strange. Tom came flying into the landing strip with one of the parachutes. When Marvin asked him what he was doing, Tom said he just wanted to see the sun come up."

"Oh sure, a real nature lover."

"But actually he had just finished dumping Madeline's body in Lake Michigan."

"Didn't Marvin think all of this was strange?'"

"Strange but nothing more. He didn't read the newspapers so he didn't make the connections at first."

"I remember now he asked me what day she was killed."

"Right. He was finally beginning to make connections between Tom's weird behavior and the unsolved murder."

"So when Marvin got suspicious, Tom decided to get rid of him?"

"Right. It was Tom all three times. I saw the parachute and it was definitely cut."

It was late Sunday morning and the sound of birdsong was giving way to the put-put of lawnmowers. Frank and I were in my bed, wearing nothing except one of my grandma's flowered sheets. I cuddled against him, thinking how nice it was to have a warm body in my bed. But my brain wouldn't stop working.

"What happened at the swimming pool?"

"Marvin said he and Tom had a friendly drink after closing. That's all he remembers. But Marvin's drink was spiked with phenobarb, so when he started snoring, Tom dragged him into the pool—and planted the tablets by Marvin's bed."

"So if it hadn't been for Brooke forgetting her purse —?"

"Then Tom would have gotten away with murder number two."

"What about Roxanne?"

"I think she really didn't know anything. She was madder than hell when she found out about Tom's past—and believe me, he had some scrapes with the law before the embezzling charge. She's been cooperating."

"And what about —?"

There was a perfunctory knock on the door just before it swung open and Brooke walked in, holding a tray and singing, "Happy birthday to you, happy birth —." She gasped when she saw the second body in my bed. "Oh Tracy, you have—company."

"Brooke, how sweet of you." I clutched the sheet. "I forgot all about my —." Could it be true? Was I forty-five already?

Brooke deposited the tray, which held a cup of coffee and a single long-stemmed rose. "Guess you'll need another coffee," she said, assuming her waitress mode.

"Make it black," said Frank, who had just recovered his voice.

EPILOGUE

TOM HALLADAY is lodged in the Cedar County jail awaiting trial on charges of murder and attempted murder. ROXANNE HALLADAY refused to post bond for her husband and is suing to have the marriage annulled. MARVIN CROUCH has recovered from his mishaps and is helping Roxanne run the Diamond D.

BROOKE QUINN is back at Iowa State, where she is considering a major in environmental studies and also a nose ring. DEREK LAVALLEN is working as a carpenter for his uncle in Arizona. He and Brooke keep in touch by e-mail and plan to meet in Shagoni River next summer.

PAUL LAVALLEN gave up his bid to become county commissioner, but his name is still on the ballot, so anything could happen. He and Jewell are in marriage counseling. JEWELL LAVALLEN received an offer to become director of nursing at Wexford General but isn't sure she's ready for a career move.

IVY MARTIN is once again dating the playboy lawyer Greg Wetherell. Go figure.

FRANK KOLOWSKY is still around and we see a lot of each other. With Frank in my life, I feel a lot different and I'm not so sure I want to sell the house. We'll see what winter brings.

Printed in the United States
56726LVS00005B/358-399